A SAFE CONDUCT

Peter Vansittart

A SAFE CONDUCT

PETER OWEN
London & Chester Springs

PETER OWEN PUBLISHERS
73 Kenway Road London SW5 0RE
Peter Owen books are distributed in the USA by
Dufour Editions Inc. Chester Springs PA 19425–0007

First published in Great Britain 1995
© Peter Vansittart 1995

A catalogue record for this book is available from the British Library

ISBN 0–7206–0953–4
0–7206–0977–1 (*paper*)

Typeset by The Electronic Book Factory Fife
Printed and made in Great Britain by
Biddles of Guildford and King's Lynn

PREFACE

This novel began, very vaguely, almost fifty years ago, when, in a Bournemouth turret, I read in Lewis Mumford's *The Condition of Man* about

Hans Bohm, later called, 'The Little Piper' who used to pipe and drum at festivities. This Hans, 1476, had a vision in which the Mother of God told him to burn his pipe and drum, and preach: he performed his mission, urging people to lay aside ornaments, become brothers, share all things, withhold their taxes and dues, dethrone pope, emperor and prince. The German knights captured Hans and burnt him: but they did not quickly halt the movement he had started.

Bohm came from Niklashausen, near Würzburg. A few of his words survive: *Princes, ecclesiastical and secular alike, and counts and knights, should possess only as much as common folk. Then all would have sufficient.*

The Little Piper was an off-stage presence in my early novel *The Overseer*, and I had thought that this would exorcize him. But no: his story lingered, reinforced by half-memories of Jakob Wasserman's novel. *The Triumph of Youth*, read during the London blitz, and then, years afterwards, by events in Hungary in 1956.

My Hans is very different from Bohm and has no politics. All other personages are imaginary but the theme, alas, is relevant to all times.

P.V.

To
Kenneth Minogue
and Beverley Cohen –
Ken and Bev –
with much love

To
Kenneth Minogue
and Beverley Cohen –
– Ken and Bev –
with much love

1

That a man, even a rich man, should kill his wife, is seldom approved by God and not always by his neighbours, however 'noisy and impertinent' she might have been. His well-wishers may cease to wish him well.

2

Though frequently proscribed by the Castle, up there on its granite scarp, magic is so commonplace that few mention or even notice it. Sometimes a gate sways, or leaves rustle, at a windless noon. Certain simples, if plucked seven heartbeats before dawn, cure fits. Demons range darkened fields, disguised as hares and rats: your soul can leave your sleeping body and roam abroad as a bird, sometimes indeed a ferret. If it returns, you awake with jagged memories of distant towns, glimpses of the sea, abysses, gardens, even paradise. Occasionally it wanders, too far, is trapped or lost, and then . . . just so!

In the villages widely huddled beneath Castle and mountains, many deaths – Jakob the Swineherd, Mother Marthe – are very obviously due to cruel magic. Blessed Thomas Aquinas is invoked against thunder and sudden death, you can rout a demon by uttering his secret name, never easy to discover; a mistletoe twig, if carried into the underworld, assures your safe return, even if the priest maintains you have never departed. Midwinter yule fires have again revived the dying sun. To swallow dragon's blood is more effective than gulping Farmer Hegeber's over-priced beer, for it enables you to understand birds' speech; the difficulty is not in killing a dragon but finding one. Astrologers value cocks' eggs for cock-eyed tricks of changing mud to silver.

If you bend the sunlight you can overcome God himself, some

whispering that Knight Siegfried did this so strenuously that light has never wholly recovered, thus explaining the lengthening winters, regular murrain, Turkish victories, collapsing morals, devil-worship.

Smiths and miners, alien as Egyptians – gippies – and Jews, are adepts in magic; Klaus the Smith bartered his soul to the Devil and was promptly hanged by the fatherly Graf in the Castle. Gippies abduct children by enchanted zithers, diabolical potions, and strengthen their incantations with cards strewn with pentacles, certain numbers, crowned heads.

Women, no longer permitted to bear arms, must now rely on magic, often becoming witches. Remember, to shit on their thresholds weakens them. Foxes, who start harvest fires with their tails, haunt graveyards, are vigorously training ghosts, and may once have been witches.

Castle folk, despite the Graf's distaste, use their particular magic rite, chess, which induces withdrawal from the world, in a silent trance. There are also the new mirrors and eyeglasses by which great ones see creatures, countries, stars hitherto invisible, reinforcing their control of common folk.

The Archangel Ithuriel possesses a spear which detects the truth, usually unpleasant, hidden in every mortal body.

There are, however, increasing hordes of impostors. One scoundrel, claiming to be from the Lands of the Phoenix, a bird capable of speaking French though not yet known to have done so, offered to sell the Emperor the Virgin's wedding-ring, which ensures multiple births, though all know that it lies safely in Poitou.

Inescapable is the magic of boundaries, paths and, particularly, crossroads where presences notoriously hover. Certain boulders must be avoided. Up north, Prussian side-roads and woods are forbidden to pious strangers, for human sacrifices occur there. To whom? Best not imagine.

Here, in the Castle regions, one road, formerly important, has degenerated to holes and landslips, obstructing travellers but without obstructing plague, famine, protest, certain forebodings. Near it a grave, two pikes long, was found empty but for what some thought a crucifix but others maintained was a giant hammer. These hastily crossed themselves, after muttering a forbidden name.

Invisible lords rule. Emperor, Prince, Pope, Bishop, Graf are mere shadows of these, while the highest too are tinged with magic, barely comprehensible though this is. Mortal lords cherish clocks which, by controlling time, can prolong their lives. Henry, the Lion of Saxony, gave Brunswick ecclesiastics a phoenix feather blessed by Palestine suns. This cures blindness, if accompanied by the suppliant's faith.

John, Lord of Aquitaine, King of England, with a face empty as a cannon mouth and as menacing, descended from a supernatural world, by processes not always understood. More spectacular, when the infidel Turks overwhelmed Constantinople, very holy, very corrupt, the Christian Emperor was transformed by an angel to a statue which will restore the Empire.

When? Later.

Writing is another manifestation of magic. St Virgil, diabolical Ovid, create from nothing: from a movement of hand, they beguile, they enrapture, they swindle. By trickery of pen, flourish of a document, a home vanishes, a meadow is grabbed, a hanging is seen. The young Castle Clerk, taxmaster, sometimes called the Sexton, has parchments made from animals, which gradually thin villagers' blood while thickening that of the rich. By these parchments he demolished a windmill, confiscated two farms. An entire hamlet vanished into the hands of the Castle and indeed, massive, jagged, akin to the surrounding heights, the Castle does seem to secrete hands, the more grasping by being unseen.

In the last peasants' rebellion, much enlarged by rumour and fear, many such parchments were ravaged, salt dropped over their ashes to remove ghosts, yet the iniquitous spells persisted.

The nearest village had supported a scrivener, unpopular with the Castle authorities who lately chased him away. His powers were strange, none save Albrecht, a boy though by no means boyish, being certain of what these actually signified. A handful of words, nevertheless arranged in particular positions, could somehow unite the ends of the world in a brilliant growth of suggestion and discovery! *A threefold dome, an isle of reeds, the wings of the dawn.*

That such powers are profitable is undeniable: few had not borrowed from the scrivener, always receiving less than anticipated, explained by reference to incomprehensible scrawls. Jowled, one-eyed (having, people said, sold the other to a banker), with a beard like rats' tails, he is not much regretted, no bog-trotting woman has been tempted to make a home with him on a mountain, particularly after his boast that he had learnt letters from terror dreams lent by a mare-headed Babylonish hag.

Rumour now has it that a unicorn has been seen in the mountains, doubtless seeking a virgin to ram. A magic beast, for, though it may not exist, its appearance foretells death, so that, to appease it, a death should be provided and perhaps will be.

3

'Let's dig out Redhead.'

'Grub up stones. There's a sling in Great Barn.'

'The hunt. Hoy! I've brother's club.'

The village held some forty children, most of them with names, boys the most numerous, with cowpat faces and starved eyes, though more girls were born than was admitted. In the dead season, with its mists, weird lights and mountain shades, the children were difficult to count, not always to be identified. None, save Albrecht, had schooling. Local monasteries were depopulated and indifferent to anything but their moneybags and the Castle agreed with Blessed Jerome that monks should mourn, not teach.

Without hope of spring, the shivering children were sullen and almost famished. Christmas had been joyless, no bounty fell from the Castle. Ordered to pray to the Lord, they had mumbled requests to the unseen Graf, a veritable *Von und zu*, but vainly. Sky and mountain were thick and grim, stars crackling as they froze, infants lay blackened under the hedge and in the byre, cats rotted in the ditch. Only the capture of a pedlar's barrow had briefly redeemed the Lenten harshness. That God had fashioned mankind from a hunk of the Devil's flesh was readily believed in dank hovels and morose tyes.

In winter, children suffered customary blows, but their jobs were more random. A few were conscripted for the Castle, replacing those dead from coughs, ague, rheum, but the rest, with little to do, chafed by east winds, were listless, roused only by an impulse to bury a live cat in Break Back Field, drown a rat, piss at an old woman to drown her evils. 'Witch, witch,' they yelled, but with dulled ardour. The better-looking, very few, might assist the priest, in ways of which they gave small, bitten grins but kept silence.

In warmer days, of course, they must stone birds, tend orchards, help in forests, boat-huts, stables, always scheming to steal time and dodge the Bailiff's whip, fathers, the priest, even the terrible unseen Sexton behind the towering battlements. Occasionally they rebelled, at an unspoken word, a furtive sign, fleeing across the fields to Great Barn or Felon Stream, to stand suddenly diminished, spiritless, throwing a twig from hand to hand or repeating lewd rhymes –

> *I'm a devil, you're a runt*
> *Both from up a pigling's cunt.*

– yearning to gnaw a crust or herring while envisaging perpetual creamy feasts within the Castle, until driven back to labours. On holy days, from hunger or caprice, in animal bark-masks, careering, whooping, waving fiery tow, they chased the mad girl, the blind donkey. 'We're boars. Turks.' Much sickness derived from beasts angered by such unnatural pursuits. Or they stripped off their rags and capered naked round some hastily made effigy, crudely explicit, with threats, obscenities, genital mimes, before firing it. Once they swooped into another valley and threw infant twins into a deep, oozing swamp, purging the uncanny.

*

13

'We can stamp him dead . . . then let the sheep fuck him.'

'He came from mud. Stewpit. Can go back to it.'

'Redheads go to hell. Flames are their brothers.'

The boys clamoured beneath a dying elder, accursed though none knew why, until Albrecht, with his clever, dainty speech, suggested that it had failed to pay taxes. Today, he was not among them but all were aware of him. Tattered, mostly bare-footed, with starveling skins, they were far beneath tall Albrecht, chestnut-haired, graceful and clean in remnants of cast-off finery. He wore, not clogs but leather sandals kneaded with faint reds and greens; instead of some frayed, cowhide jerkin handed down from successive brothers, he had a woollen cape patched with fur. While others toiled, he would be somewhere else, curiously immune, his own authority undisputed. He could read and write too, thus, like priest and scrivener, possessing 'influences', unimaginable and best not imagined. Also, he was reputed to have a secret name, which he disclosed, or sold, to favourites, who would die if they betrayed it. His mother, Frau Bett, had been beautiful, like a princess, but was now only a disfigured hen-wife. His father? Ah!

Not quite a boy, not yet a man, with the disposition of something else, Albrecht did not live with Frau Bett, whom he seldom cared to visit, but with the Graf's steward in a stone keep under the Castle, where he was alternately caressed or neglected. To the villagers, he knew the extraordinary.

'Here's Heiner. . . . Kick the dog Heiner. . . .'

The pack was almost complete, a maze of chapped lips, chipped dirty fangs, expectant eyes. The lean, the crooked, the stumpy, the withered. Their nicknames were more important than those, usually inherited, stamped on them at the font. The Graf himself, exhalation of the Castle, was frequently 'He', sometimes 'It'. Amongst the children had been Lump Klaus, with a swollen foot which, urged by girls, the boys dared each other to touch, believing that they would thus live for ever. One day they touched too fiercely, his parents seeming unaware that he had vanished.

His ghost drifted awhile above the slime-pond, once joining a raid on the priest's orchard. Amongst this lot was Scarcely Seen, so called to avoid the Evil Eye; the Jackdaw, outbidding the rest in thievery, his mother having in his infancy too often scraped his hands clean, despite warnings that this would leave them incurably restless and that she would lament the consequences. This she did not, for her cupboards were continually replenished by this restlessness.

Also the Ant, a sallow girl with thick legs and breasts but little between; Broken-Tooth Heinrich, long abandoned, who lived alone in a hut which squeaked like a maltreated cub. The Stinger's soul was believed to have been lost, poisoned by a midsummer adder, this accounting for his constant twitchings and grimaces.

Albrecht being away, Heiner was leader, though this could be disputed by Johannes Ox-Face, who now joined him. In sacking tunic and torn breeches, Heiner was straw-headed, square-chinned, bristly, warty; he had been conceived under a lightning flash, so that his father was not, perhaps, Cowman Dorf, but a thunderclap, thus he too would have no soul, like a nixie. He was, however, unconcerned with souls and now scowled, tightened fists at his stamping, impatient followers, then winked, pointing to the fields, rough blue eyes glaring. 'He's out there. Stuffed for the roast. Prime. The sheep won't help him.'

'Now,' Johannes growled, and they swung away from the drab, smoky cottages and hovels, a few scrappy dogs darting around them as, cawing, hooting, they flapped outspread arms, flowing jerkily away over the frosty scrub, beyond which, looming at several levels beneath the obscure woods, ravines and the twin peaks of Broken Mountain, hung the Castle.

The boys moved stealthily, stooping beneath hedges, edging round skeleton trees, soundless but still flapping arms like wings, until reaching outer pasture almost in the shadow of the mountains, its growth unusually high because of the outsize testicles of a bull once buried there, so that, some way from a placid group of sheep, a red head, its hair not thick but spiky, appeared resting on tips of coarse grass.

The head, irregularly shaped, was motionless, as if deaf, sunk in thoughts probably crazed. All had seen its owner often enough, rolling on grass or dirt, babbling incoherently to a bush or tree, slobbering over his sheep, blowing his pipe to the fire-birds and flying horses of his tales, knocking fists against his soiled forehead as if striving to open it.

Life collects its mistakes. Hans's cramped, freckled face would split with agitation, his tongue get blocked as if with grit so that he stuttered helplessly, frantically, unless he was allowed to tell the stories that only so infernal a head could contain.

The gang crept forward, the Stinger plodding behind like a distorted, unkempt swimmer on dry land. A bird whistled from a bare copse, then was silent. Now the red head was fuller, more distinct, as if its bearer were squatting to shit or imitating Mother Holle, squalid and bloody Lady of Birth.

Now clutching stones, broken boughs, mud, still unseen, they encircled the shepherd, a boy of perhaps twelve – twelve centuries, some jested – whose stuttering rage at even a soft rebuke to any animal, even a toad, showed him witless, separate, inviting injury, mocked as a Jude, lover of impossibilities.

He still heard nothing, but the sheep were uneasily drifting away towards Dancers' Wood where the trees, stark but protective, must be holding their breath.

In silence rigid as ice, grinning malevolently, hunched and stocky, watched jealously by Heiner, Johannes Ox-Face lowered a hand, fondled his rock as he might pig-flesh, then slung it, hitting Hans's back. 'Jah . . . Jah . . . Jah!'

The cries scattered the last sheep. Hans fell, prone on the grass, the rest emerging, to yelp, shout, while pelting him as, motionless, soundless, perhaps stunned or dead, he lay outspread for wolf or kite, beloved creatures in his stories. Or he might be shrouded in the cunning with which the weak and crazed survive these tormented times.

But the attack ceased, halting in mid-motion. Burly Heiner was abruptly outfaced, like all of them reduced to a small blot under sky, mountains, Castle, because, without warning, slightly menacing, Albrecht was amongst them. Unseen in the wide, deserted landscape, he seemed to have newly risen from the earth.

16

Calm as flower or swan, slender, bare-headed, hair deep and glowing, in contrast to Hans's raw carroty jumble, in a frayed cloak silvery in winter lights, his silence a rebuke, he stepped through them to the shabby, still-breathing heap with its inert, askew limbs, the head ashine in a brief wisp of sunlight.

With pale, silken skin, features ridged and delicate under the longish, slightly curled hair, grey-blue eyes somewhat flat in their disregard of all but his own intentions, Albrecht was Prince Handsome, aloof from vicious mouths and ruffianly garb, from snouts and claws and hungry teeth, always moving direct, glancing neither to left nor right as though to a very precise plan, unknown to all others, which protected him from contradiction, from ambush. An Albrecht is never whipped or burnt, never seen in slime or herding pigs at the common trough. Were he to stand naked, you would look away, awkward or scared. Sometimes he is seen riding a Castle horse, neat against the blue. He speaks no peasant dialect, indeed he speaks seldom, never threatens or cajoles like the priest, who was always as if addressing multitudes; an Albrecht commands by a slight pressure of mouth, a quick chill in the eye, though he can produce high-flown Castle speech when he so desires (not often) quiet but very distinct, at times unpleasantly so, in an intimacy never sufficiently friendly. He attracts wonder like revenue and, from women, sidelong admiring glances which he cannot fail to sense.

The glances now were not sidelong but openly apprehensive. The urchins stood about him, debased courtiers, aware that Albrecht periodically showed, if not kindness then certainly for-bearance, to ugly, absurd Hans. His high demeanour, emphatic in its silence, was an order and already they were trudging away, limp as if after punishment, while Albrecht deigned to lower himself over the misshapen little shepherd, about to condemn his supineness, direct him to recover, or, thought a few, looking back, to knife him, though touch him he would not.

4

Villagers would say, musingly, glancing behind them, 'At one time. . . .'

At one time, when angels strode the land, there had flowered a Garden of earthly delights, where innocent people had lived naked in love. Any lustful, intrusive knight or clown was instantly forced to devour a poisoned apple. Watered by four rivers, the Garden was shaded by trees, had brilliant roses, many-tinted pools, and lovers were ravished not by immoderate desires but by music dropping from stars. Even today, old folk remembered, or claimed to, massive golden suns, burnished harvests, smiling priests, when a dazzling Graf feasted everyone; the Castle must have been made of sweetmeats and from slopes not gaunt but like gently flowing yellow wine.

The Garden has long vanished, folk brood over it as they might over a Gothic prince buried under a river or an elfin promise of an ice palace beyond mountains. Only great estates now prosper, small farmers are backward, often ignorant of the horse-collar or sullenly rejecting it.

Times, confessedly, are evil; while peasant and labourer sink, the rich rise so high that the eye aches in search of them. The usage of Jacques Coeur of Bruges, whose wealth would have dazed heaven itself, had long been copied by German merchants. He had trained pigeons to bear reports throughout his realm of documents, files and written pledges.

Throughout the German Empire you hear a ditty:

> *The wicked sit in Earth's high seat*
> *And trample the good beneath their feet.*

Recent years have seen knights' wars, peasant rebellions, the latter brutally suppressed but recurring like summer arson, often led by angry priests. Few now speak of Christendom.

Remember Reiser, Swabian heretic, follower of the long-burnt Bohemian, Hus, agitating against landlords and sinful ecclesiastics dispensing sacraments. Calling himself Bishop of True Men, Reiser demanded a German Bible, available to all. This would prise out the mysterious untruths by which bishops justified their riches. *To silence my truth*, Reiser shouted, *they must step over my corpse*. They did just that when, trapping him at Strassburg, they hustled him also on to the flames.

Emperor Frederick III rules, though lately fleeing Vienna from the savage Hungarians and at present drifts from one monastery to another, beseeching succour, scratching for a meal. An archbishop is said to have been beheaded by upstart yokels, though some assert that the head had been sliced off by a wind-swept slate.

Many, nevertheless, pray to the Emperor, convinced that, could he but know of them, he will redress gigantic wrongs. Queer reports abound. Some Cologne usurers insist that Jesus enjoyed wearing an ass's head; Franconian monks foretell a new Empire ruled by none less than the Holy Ghost, who will erase the sacraments, rewrite the Scriptures, replace palace and castle, Babylon and Rome with the soft commands of love. A king, though only of Bohemia, has wasted time and tongue on schemes to settle disputes not by faction and war but, scandalizing mature opinion, by a general council of honest men.

Too evidently, the world, overloaded with sin, is lurching into what Jesus called the Last Days, when redemption must be earned through blood-drenched torments. You must die horribly to live gloriously.

Sometimes, on a blighted plain, charred gorge, in a desolate tower, some broken knight, pallid virgin, or runaway serf stuffing his guts with straw, looks up at the ungiving sky and whispers, 'He will come.'

He? They can say no more. 'He' is as beyond imagination as new worlds at the end of the sea. Meanwhile petty fiefs are disrupted by expanding markets, surly peasants desert to towns, and bandits, some with great names, roam the hills. Plague lurks on dark roads, in privies, behind the altar. Against plague the best weapons are not ritual curses or doctors' hocus-pocus but red cloth and drawings so monstrous that the scourge flees: brandishing these, wise folk bang doors, clatter pans, ring bells, the uproar further rebelling the noxious.

Nothing, however, repels movement. Peg-leg Mark, reputedly the banished god Vulcan, bawls for the restoration of the Garden, of Old Times, applauded by vagrant goliards, jobless tailors, famished and dispossessed farmers, mutinous Bamberg weavers, renegade friars, creeping towards him under the moon. Garden-loving Jesus the Kindly is now Christ the tormented Avenger, though in balance the Virgin becomes taller, stronger, more beautiful.

At Augsburg the town clock has been ransacked in an effort to restore Old Times. A pack-pedlar from Trier has discouraged the meek by mentioning that Jesus was a thief who had stolen the birthright of his brother, Lucifer, and along the Rhine rioters hailed the Wronged One, licensing themselves to pillage. A town was inexplicably abandoned overnight, left empty save for a stray dog and rats gorged into immobility from food left half-cooked.

Another rhyme is whistled in cloisters, heard beneath street hubbub, repeated in stew and tavern, is found pinned to the bedding of the Arch Prior of Mainz:

> *The humble bewail their low estate*
> *The rich crouch behind their gate.*

In ornate guildhalls and frescoed mansions the leisured praise the wisdom of Leonardo Bruni during the Florentine glaziers' riot: *Let this be an eternal lesson to the civic authorities. Never permit the populace to assume political initiative or keep weapons within reach. For, let the people taste but one morsel of power, then they will never again be harnessed.*

Others chuckle over the Monk of Ulm who refused to teach novices to read, explaining that their first book must be a Gospel. Gospels, however, he continued, can blind readers, save those untainted by doubts, a test few would pass and fewer wish to.

All this makes the Empire tense with foreboding. But of what? Hungarians? Turks? None can precisely answer. Meanwhile the Devil casts gigantic shadows and the year 1500 approaches, heralded by the inauspicious: the usual comet, a small earth-quake. At Grinzing a sow has been banished for devouring a farrier's baby, rousing protests that she should have been roasted for the poor. Wittenberg savants are teaching that, since the heathen Roman emperors, Antichrist has been preparing an attack, now imminent. What remedy? A miracle? Unlikely, for Christ's miracles fatally diminished the earth's stock of them. Furthermore, a belief is abroad that when the rebel angels fell, some remained adrift, scattering evil, their dung causing foul dreams. It is said that cunning Satan, to confuse the devout, himself built Cologne Cathedral during seven days of tempest. More indisputable is the increase of criminals; their breath discharges impurities, further undermining existence, so that lords are saying that bad government is better than no government. There is no solace in hearing that ships are venturing extraordinary distances, safeguarded by necromantic instruments, carrying Milanese embroidery and Cremonan horses to sell to headless cannibals.

Wiseacres scoff at lords, tell of lions and Turks, foretell the world's end. Listen:

'Brothers . . . Christ, or Another, is almost due.'

'Roman kings pretended to be giants, treated steeples as equals. But they were only haddock thieves, fire-raisers, attempting wonders too heavy for them.'

'Verily. No doubt. Have you heard of Magister Schwartz, graduate of Nuremberg book markets? He knows all there is to be known, indeed rather more. He tells us that Christ's five wounds should be healed, not worshipped.'

'Sinful talk. He should be given to the Turks.'

Yes, Turks, circumcised and hideous, with swords curved as their smiles, still advance despite valorous Vlad the Impaler piling their damned heads like cannon-balls. Conceivably their Padishah, from his diamond throne three leagues high, throwing a poisoned rainbow over Europe, with his bloodshot gown and hundred dwarfs, is Antichrist, set to fire the Continent. Or he is godless Emperor Frederick II Hohenstaufen, long dead but sardonically haunting the Empire. Remember though, the ancestor

21

of the Turks was suckled by a wolf, which explains their savage impiety.

'So pray to St Sebastian. He hates the Infidel.'

'Bishops, though. You can watch them daily growing fatter. You can wager on the next inch. Fulda, Würzburg, Bamberg . . . His Majesty should girdle them tight.'

Pilgrimages, despite malapert bishops, remain plentiful, though frequently to shrines ill-famed, excuses for scroungers . . . friars, swindling indulgence-mongers, gippies. Monkish porkers, however, and university quacks are daring to maintain that the Saviour left his work unfinished, departing too early through grief, disappointment, cowardice or anger. Could it be, though, that Jesus was a joker, disrespectful to mortals like a cross-eyed Austrian seeing wrong ways? He offered caustic riddles about the triumph of losers, the powerless enthroned, the stupid addling the clever, the dead showing merry faces?

5

Beneath the Graf's stiff, fretted Castle, pilgrims, though slightly sparser, their cockleshells probably false, trudged south from Brandenburg, to pay, indeed pay lavishly, to glimpse the Bleeding Heart of Wilsnack and be cured of mentionable ills by a miracle, illusion or illustrious fraud. On a wagon-load of jades, 'King O'Spain's Daughters' trundled for public hire in towns. Wiseacres continued.

'We hear too much of these guns. Crossbows were sufficient for our Lord's father.'

'Nuns crave turds.'

'They may have to. Dirt seeks dirt.'

'Nuns! Dry as a pardoner's conscience.'

They could be scattered by a fearful cry. *Knights*.

Once the mainstay of the Castle, knights, the minor nobility, were now rootless, useless. The Crusades were ended, in failure, confusion, collaboration with Islam. The mighty Templars had perished in thousands for wicked secrets. German knights up north had invested, very profitably, in a crusade against heathen Prussians, but most others had lapsed into debt and poverty, to gross mortgages to princes and bishops, so that they must raid and plunder for brute existence. They were hated by peasants, bankrupted by new incomprehensible wiles, ravaged by pox, mocked by their faded names and forgotten exploits and had become, the Emperor said in his fine way, so much dung. In ever-diminishing circles the knights hunted game, which always diminished. They might die of hunger surrounded by resplendent armour and grandiose banners. Many had degenerated to mendicants, hucksters or mercenaries against Wends, Poles, Balts.

Here, by Broken Mountain, there had always been a Graf, beloved of God, high in the clouds, planted stiffly in titles and dues. Down below, few knew a Graf's age and name: simply 'He', or 'It', reigned on high. *At one time* the North Wind had hurled an eagle against a knight's shield so vehemently that its outline remained stamped on it and probably remains so. He became the first Graf, his domain founded on a smile bestowed by a Bavarian prince.

The Castle was sustained less by halberds, bombards, arrows, by gibbet, pincers, the fire, than by the Name and Honour necessary to rulers, though the Graf was undecided about the degree of respect due to a Spanish grandee of unquestioned Name and Honour yet questioned rather too frequently, who, on progress through France, had been welcomed at a succession of banquets, at none of which Honour permitted him to partake because the King was not present, eventually dying of starvation at Blors, surrounded by exquisite dishes and favourite wines, but inconsolably mortified by His Majesty's insult.

Grafs, like all rulers, have access to the unseen. All villagers believed that their lord rose and retired early to ensure the perpetuity of the sun. Unfortunately the present Graf possessed the Evil Eye, against which a man fondles his genitals and a woman a key or fragment of iron. Once, standing alone with this potentate, His Reverence the Confessor perceived not two human shadows but three.

23

The Graf's grandfather had precipitated a scandal by intro-
ducing the fork, an Eastern fad tainted by Islam. The late Gräfin,
rather worse, had collected mirrors, verses, drawings, all now
safely concealed, with an intensity that had forced her husband
to watch her like a spy.

In clear winter blue or August moonlight the Castle outstared
Broken Mountain and its brothers. In harvest glow it dwindled,
blurred as if in dreams. In frost-bound dusks and wet autumns it
loomed ponderous as its rocky, slanting, pine-shaded approaches,
all-seeing and despotic, a reminder that a shadow lurks behind the
sun, even behind God. The nervous recalled that in the deepest
dungeon, nine times bolted, the plague sits amongst piles of the
lipless dead.

Nevertheless, no more than God was the Castle all-powerful.
Trailing on Fate's Will like gulls following the plough, lord and
serf alike dreaded a Fimbul winter, night of the wolf, enduring
three years, the sun outlawed into darkness within which crouch
avenging devils or Antichrist. A cloak of fur and nine otter-skins
cannot withstand the Fimbul cold. Then the dead return, envious,
bitter, malicious: there are blinding gales, hail, famine, irregular,
terrifying thuds as though frozen chunks of wind drop to the
ice-locked earth. Wolves grow outsize, from the flesh of liars,
blasphemers, perjurers, themselves numerous. Throughout, emptied of sun, moon, stars, the sky is low enough to touch. Only the
mountains remain unshaken.

The Castle has survived Fimbul, and, through all turns of the
day, a man will pause, straighten, gaze up at the tight pile of
turrets, ramparts and gates, then cross himself in fear. He knows
its queer sounds and eerie lights. And, stark beneath it, the scowl
of authority, rears the Horse, the gibbet on which malefactors
ride to hell.

Notwithstanding appearances, the Castle had to maintain its
own on fewer resources. The Graf's tax-collectors, moving with
grave-robbers' stealth, were more cowardly, less devoted. Much
was unpaid, tolls were diminishing. Furs no longer arrived from
Lord Novgorod the Great. Vendors of Baltic hemp and timber
were scarcer, mechanical clock-makers' expenses had mounted

so that many nobles had reverted to candle clocks. The visits of the soft-spoken moneylender, 'Herr Don't Borrow', were ominously frequent. Visitors, within hearing of the Graf, loudly proclaimed his stronghold a refuge of pleasure, fashion and plenty, while privately agreeing that pleasure was scanty, fashion was absent, and plenty never came. The spider's web Graf flaunted no damascene silks or curled, cock-certain slippers, so indecently elongated that they had once angered heaven into sending plague into Plantagenet England.

Visitors changed, the Graf's entourage did not. Foremost was Reverence and Excellency von der Goltz, Confessor, Guardian of Seals, titular Treasurer, though daily administration, legal and fiscal, he left to his Clerk, 'the Sexton', retaining only the ceremonial. His spiritual activities of course assisted the secular, particularly as he controlled almost all access to the Graf. 'I have to be inspired,' he would tell penitents seeking favour, a declaration usually interpreted as an invitation for coin to change hands. If sufficiently inspired, he would effect an introduction to the Graf, or summon the dead, who did not always obey. In earlier years, before appointing the Clerk, he had, as Treasurer, been over-influenced by his beliefs as Confessor: from piety, he ignored the Arabic conception of zero, his accounts thus, quipped the Fool, Prince Narr, being unaccountable.

The Fool's office was hereditary, so that the ignorant suspected that, like the Graf, he had existed for centuries, had taught Christ and mocked Nero, an illusion, if illusion it was, that Prince Narr did not contradict, claiming indeed to have kissed Brunhild, Queen of Franks, thought to have murdered eleven kings, 'not considered satisfactory to all'.

Prince Narr considered the Confessor a time-server whose time served few. The Confessor, in return, suspected the Fool's mockery, if not heretical, was atheistical, which was almost worse. He mocked the stable, the accepted. Cardinals' hats, he remarked, too often, are flashes of hell. Very thin with womanish breasts, voice high but melodious, Prince Narr minced between rooms in a faded, multicoloured robe carrying a stuffed owl and a mirror, for reasons left unexplained. His whims too were womanish and his jests were seldom amusing, usually irritating, often indelicate, thus reputed to have discoloured his teeth and corroded his throat. 'What,' he demanded, 'is a pure, ovalled line imprisoning a colour?' None knew, none cared. He bowed his head as if to secure a prize: 'A fish.' He also possessed a fairground trick, seldom wholly successful, of appearing to speak through his elbow, a talent he enjoyed exhibiting on inappropriate occasions – funerals, executions, or the arrival of an imperial courier. 'I am,' he continued, 'a creature of many lights.' His complacency was thought unjustified.

The Confessor, as far as possible, ignored him and depended on his familiarity with the Scriptures, which few had read and none, save the Graf's uncle, could understand. Faced with some solecism, he would nod gravely. 'Our Lord cherished drunkards,' he might reassure at a banquet. The Gospels appeared to teach that whatever was, simultaneously was not, a juggling more appropriate to Prince Narr. Thus the Confessor was sometimes referred to as Greaser of the Text, which he assumed was complimentary.

Actually, von der Goltz had small capacity for reading, and relied on a multitude of quotations learnt from a long-dead monk. He had been appointed by the Graf's father but his ordination was suspect, the elder Graf being boastfully irreligious and much approved a rejoinder of King William Red Face of England, when told the death of a Pope: *God rot him who gives a damn for that!* In youth the Confessor had been a mercenary paymaster, which, he said, gave him experience of men as well as of learning. 'I cherish the simplicities,' he would say, always genial, pleasing the Graf, who disliked mysteries. The simplicities were coin, wine, easy ways, fresh bedding, and boys, about whom vows of celibacy were not, he maintained, very strictly attached. 'As Christ so often said.'

Small, bald, small eyes bright as a beaver's set deep in parched, wrinkled skin, he would, as it were, rebuild himself, never with decisive action but with unexpected words; each given a different colour by his Rhenish dialect and uttered with some grandeur. 'Heaven,' he might declare, adding to the simplicities, 'has nine mansions . . . God indulges in eight names,' his smile suggesting that he recognized the slight discrepancy and could, if sufficiently inspired, interpret it.

The Graf's relative, called 'Uncle' by everyone, even by those, the majority, who never saw him, had been both conceived and born under Virgo, thereby observing life with exceptional clarity. Prince Narr said that, like the blessed Ephraim, he fed the winds and ran after shadows, the joke being that Uncle rarely left his turret.

An unusual word, or the refurbishment of an old word, *News*, had arrived. Like all novelties, it contained danger, for it was always dismal, usually disastrous, save when the money-swilling, sty-defiling Lord Abbot of Karlein, a puny swab scarcely filling his own skin, got drowned in a pool of filth, very appropriately, for, the Confessor related, Jesus always declared that in much money was much mud. Yet all desired news, like lechers seeking release, a craving fostered by the new printing: books, broadsheets and pamphlets were surging through the Empire, to disrupt, revoke and confuse, querying lawful authority and divine order.

Receiving few travellers, Uncle could yet always provide news, disconcertingly immediate. 'Venice,' he informed the Clerk, 'enriches herself by arming the Turk. Soon she may enrich herself too extravagantly, and pay for it.' His roundish, curiously smooth face between neat white hair and short trimmed beard was quietly pleased, even amused.

Uncle collected both old parchments and books newly printed in Ulm and Augsburg. None were obsolete bestiaries, saints' lives, vapid romances, but ancient teachings and recent philosophical dialogues. Not only Virgo, but his green Venetian spectacles permitted him to see much that was hidden from others. He knew of times when men flew through the sky, addressed each other across continents, ranged seas without oar or mast, chatted with dolphins. At the forebodings about the year 1500, his seasoned, superior smile was tinged with pity. Lately he had been deftly describing imperial Byzantium with its poisons and blinding irons, and could discourse on Moorish discoveries to whoever cared to listen; almost none. Unconcerned with the flesh, he would quote Aristotle, a Greek, probably dead. *Women are a*

27

deformity, though one that occurs in the ordinary course of nature, adding that Venice, preferring money to morals and wedlock, was a paradise of harlotry, this not obviously distressing him. With a slow, indifferent chortle he scandalized a devout monk – some few of these persisted – by murmuring, 'God indeed is by no means perfect. Witness the Creation! He does not always claim to exist, being too busy.' Again, Uncle's subdued, ironic satisfaction.

The question was less whether this was commonplace truth but whether it was as suggestive as his unicorn's horn which could detect poisons and which concealed runes, undetectable without green spectacles, which could explain everything, even a secret that now oppressed the Castle like a stench or Black Things, local demons, doleful as Turkish onslaughts, banditry, price rises.

The Gräfin, the Graf's young wife, had, as the Confessor would repeat, withdrawn. Only her exalted husband could reveal more. She had not been seen since some mountain dog had howled on three successive nights. Moreover, the White Lady of Blundersheim had trailed the valleys, always inauspicious. Prince Narr had reflected, unnecessarily, 'Some dead are less dead than they seem. Others are more dead than the dead themselves', which reassured none. The Graf was known to have plunged a flaring torch into the Castle well: as token of devotion, desolation, or as a precaution. Against what? To answer that was risky.

Whatever the truth, she had been seen less and less, her youth dwindling, her laughter – laughter was always a strange sound in the Castle – decayed, her eyes, once flowery, now raw and distressed, pleading for what her voice could not, until finally the Confessor, in a darkened hall, summoned the council: 'Her Excellency has been succoured from her maladies, withdrawn by the Lord's blessing.'

Maladies? What maladies? Sharing a bed with the Graf? Some chatter followed, clumsily oblique, about the identity of the benevolent Lord. Unspoken was a suspicion which, if true, could affect the Graf, the lands, the very seasons.

Unpleasant tales were soon exchanged. The dead girl's robes had always been damp, suggesting that she had been a water sprite, ambiguous in her affections, possibly with webbed feet,

28

unbefitting her station. The Confessor hastily mentioned Christ's detestation of such creatures, 'as the Book declareth'.

She had inspired few supporters: these held, though from a safe distance, that her sweet smile would open the gates of paradise, might already have done so. The others, whose condolences to the Graf resembled congratulations, held such a supposition inopportune and subversive.

Since her withdrawal, Castle amusements, never numerous, were rarer. She had welcomed music and verses but her husband disliked, and was wary of, both. Some wagered with cards, 'the Devil's library', or danced when the Graf hunted or made his solitary rides. Prince Narr cackled at his own jests and recalled the harsh voice of Blessed Paul. Strangers brought gossip and *News*. Ladies complained of monotony, lack of colour, often died young, few bearing children. Only from guardroom, gatehouse and kitchens came mirth, brawls, lustful games of foot and trot, hide and kiss, and round oaths.

The Castle acknowledged the necessity for peasants, hard-working and docile, but deplored Black Things, effluvia of mines, graves, charnel-houses, disguising themselves as gippies, charcoal burners, grave-diggers, hooligan youths. A Castle official, as hangman, guardian of the Horse, was reviled as a Black Thing, but, nicknamed the Ostler, was also much respected. The small church, above Findlestadt, had actually, for whatever purpose, been built by Black Things, though chroniclers prudently record its miraculous emergence overnight.

Peasants knew plenty about Black Things, flitting about the stacks and byres, riding with desperate, haggard knights. One, perhaps, was Hans the Shepherd.

6

Unlike the rich, who wear green spectacles, who dream in Latin, luxuriate in privacies and privies and whose wives withdraw, the poor have few secrets. Beneath the mountains, huddled in rain-drenched huts, they live in each other, at one in speaking of Emperor and Graf, harvest and midwinter, shuddering at Turks, belching at a friar's lewdness, shrinking from plague. Their children are akin to animals, and with their own rites and groupings, mouthing foul jests, growing up swiftly, then lusting without mercy and, joining their elders, seeking to overthrow them.

Hans, though sharing much of this, was an outcast, allowed a decrepit shed outside the village by the middens, doorless, and where the sheep followed. Deeply, however, he inhabited himself. Sometimes a hen-wife allowed him an apple, hunk of cheese, mug of beer, then asked him to foretell the future, which must be happy, or describe a princess. In the next village Crazy Meg prophesied, but only gloomily, and preferred hags to young princesses. A preacher, she groaned, a miner's brat, would convulse the Empire, cannibals would rule, the Turks . . . but enough.

Hans was a foundling, some said changeling, thus of witch blood from Fray Hörsel, Swabian Lady of Sighs, best called St Ursula, surreptitiously invoked at stiles, fords and under the Hörsel Berg, near the Wartburg in Thuringia where a cloud had once bred adders. Supposedly the unclean goddess had fashioned him not from honest-to-God spunk but from a mandrake, the man-shaped root growing from clay oozing beneath a gallows.

Witless, he spoke as if recalling sights behind the common air. Of a fugitive knight vanishing into his own shield, of the sea, blue field unknown to all, where ghosts with hands of white foam bestrode waves which at a glance transformed to meadows of blue and scarlet. His words were as if from the crucifix in the churchyard, fixed deep in rotting mould yet not wholly dead.

The other children, whooped on by Heiner and Johannes, scorned and tormented him. His tongue stumbled, his mouth was too large, his eyes too small, his back crooked, his freckles stupid, his hair outrageous and, belying his meagre body, his cock, his Little Pike, dangling from its tawny shrubbery, was immoderately long, longer than the Jackdaw's, even than Heiner's, and he could jerk it so that it spurted farther than anyone's. This, so perverse, was praiseworthy, but that hair! Hues of blood and hatred. Their contempt mingled with unease, for all knew of a red-bearded devil with magic hammer who could hide in a glove. Red, with white and green, betokened the Friendly Ones, mischievous but less malignant than Black Things, merely stealing milk and tricking wayfarers into marsh. In some regions red-headed infants were drowned, especially twins, and Hans allegedly had had a twin, disposed of in the river. Fortunately, lacking a name, the corpse would have no soul, thus preventing hauntings.

The children usually excluded Hans as they might leper or gippy, but were always aware of him. They would hear from fields a high, slow pipe, tremulous but obdurate, then grumble, 'That's Hans.' The sounds were thin, as if pleading, distinct even through wind and rain, slightly eerie. Whatever his origins, he was guileless. You could make him forfeit his bread for a fox's cough, a ghost's wink, the Virgin's secret name, unwholesome, indeed libellous. Periodically, however, driven by an urge inarticulate but imperative as hunger, the others ceased to pelt him or jeer at his stunted form, his squalor and accursed hair; they then clustered about him, smiling, clamouring not for his bread but for a story, threatening to maul him if he had not one ready, and afterwards running away without thanks, indignant at their own desire.

He could pick stories from nothing and, telling them, lose his stammer, finding easy streams of words, at which the listeners sat open-mouthed, motionless, though the stories were moonstruck and, in retrospect, silly. How could a prince be born twice, a blind dwarf see to the ends of the earth? Stupid, like a girl without a twat. Yet, a few days later, they must return. 'Hans, go on . . . a story.'

One day, of course, they would chase him away or, if tedium oppressed them, more angrily, hang him, as they did dog or rat. Meanwhile at festivals he was allowed to join the Jackdaw, Scarcely Seen, Big Hilde and the rest, when they swam, chased, burnt an outhouse, though he lingered behind, downcast, even squatter, when they destroyed a bird or ferret. At any cry of pain his mad tears started.

His stories saved him, gave him wispy radiance, chiming with villagers' lifelong ignorance, answering their curiosity for what moved beyond the mountains, clouds, stars, the air itself. From them a Stinger, an Ant, learnt of sunlit, incredible lives, winged princesses, singing flowers, talking trees, the small magic of Friendly Ones. Stories were slits into the wide realm of transformations, enchanted tunnels, gold, which youngsters could crave like apples, eggs and ale. Only Hans provided them, older folk only gossiped about Manfred and the cowgirl, the priest and little Helmy. Stories could be effective however well worn, like a curse or coin. Hans, puny, defenceless, absurd, was yet a sort of magician; rubbing one word against another he created several more, which made pictures on the air. Like his piping, stories shook the body, ruffling hairs and pressing the nerves. Stories about belches becoming silver, farts changing to birds, a girl born of a turd and a shriek. Stories of proud margraves and pretty goose-girls, of shining palaces, of lords, clanking bits of the Graf himself, master of the visible. Hans told of the tiny dove hidden to flutter between a girl's legs, and the erratic, piercing cockyolly bird, sharp-beaked, thickly shrubbed, fixed to all men. He knew of *sea*, of *ocean*, and though even he could not say whether these were identical, they were nevertheless wondrous. He told that demons were dreams which never got finished and, angered, broke away from the body, usually spiteful, sometimes jesting, but always tormenting mortals and themselves.

He knew much nonsense that was not always rubbish, explaining that at one time the sun had been a giant eagle, still retaining wings, for how else could it keep aloft? The richest man ever was not the Graf, not even the Emperor or Father Pope, but a *Persian* merchant who flew on a scarlet mat. He had not yet flown here. Dead grandfathers could reappear as trees – and, listen, at dusk, an ash or alder do actually whisper and follow you.

True, Master Wilhelm, Castle Bailiff, denied this, growling that all Germans, save Hunnish giants, spread from Erman, whom some called Japhet. They were no trees, many, especially the giants, yelled and writhed in hell. Wilhelm, in his rare good moods, could point to Erman's Path, that trail of stars behind Broken Mountain down which the dead glide to the Underworld.

Master Wilhelm would have liked to tax them all: giants, grandfathers, Huns, trees, stars.

The priest rebuked all story-tellers and talk of the past. The past meant temptation to pry into matters best left to authority. The Devil loves mischief: knowledge, curiosity, old tales incite trouble. Life is a cruel joke played upon mankind, the Crucifixion redeemed little and made the Devil snigger. You learnt this from the priest's sour face. No priest, however, would deign notice of a red-headed simpleton with feckless make-ups about a legless singer climbing sapphire steps into the moon.

For the children, of course, nonsense allured like midden stuff. They jeered but could not forget the tale of a cloaked man, one eye blue, the other green, sitting in a tree and laughing twice: at a starving beggar unaware of treasure stored beneath him, and at a rich youth buying shoes, ignorant that he would die tomorrow.

Peaked, thickening, oafish, faces pitted and soiled, boys and girls demanded more, fiercely, like dogs, the outcast beguiling them with bright tricks of speech which soothed his tormentors into awe, no longer choking on words as if they were nuts, his piggy eyes light blue against soiled freckles and head like shredded carrot, as he described sights visible only to himself. Afterwards they would resent their submission to this deformed babbler with a tongue like wild honey, be again jealous of that animal cock which made them stretch their own, farther and farther, to overtake it, never succeeding. The girls teased, the pleasure was pitiful.

Before rounding on him, chasing him away and terrifying the sheep, they might prolong the stories with questions. 'The Green Stone. What is it? Where. . . . Tell us. Tell us at once.'

They suspected that he had found, then lost, this marvel which all sought so vainly. Whoever left thatch and hearth for the Green Stone was seen no more. A passing friar, all piss and wallop and stink, Heiner said, less foully than usual, had said that the Stone was a tooth of Anael. Anael? 'Ah!' He crossed himself, soothed his chops, gross with vanity and much else, 'That's not to be told. I can tell you, however, that he might be an angel. No less.'

Such fellows had to be paid to reveal more, with coin, girls' thighs, a night's bed. No villager, though, would admit being able to pay even for the most magical of secrets, God's most hidden name. A groom had been thrashed, on the Graf's orders, for revealing that the name was Chief Ram.

'The Green Stone. . . .' Hans's smile was ingratiating, with a flake of cunning. 'Climbed mountain, a sheep was lost.'

They chuckled tauntingly, especially the girls. Who but an idiot would lose sheep on a mountain? But he heard nothing.

'Saw a tower, Lady standing. She-belly. She's be silver, she's be gold. No clothes. Babby-bare. There, I saw all. Big chunks. White buns. She smiled, was kind. Gave out cake, milk, then Green Stone. Very green, very deep. Grassy. Shiny. Like 'er smile. Must reach for it. Then thunder, tower cracked. I was with my sheep, nothing left, only thistles and trees. An' munch.'

Quickly, the lady bored them. They imagined little, saw less, the Green Stone produced only common thunder. They jumped up, threatened to make him bleed unless he found a better story next time, and ran off.

Hans feared only that his fellow-ragamuffins, sons of cowdung, daughters of ditches, might scar his beauty. They were scared of darkness and the wandering devils, but, sleeping, he saw himself tall and perfect, rimmed with light. Only by day was he little Hans the Shepherd. In the dark he was envied; he piped, the cripple danced and carried off mountains, the blind saw, the stones happened.

Questions broke into memories, what those others called stories. Clear bodies swam up from brown waters; beneath marsh were swineherds who had once dazzled and, when they stirred, filth rippled, sometimes showing rotted babies, priests' spawn, sometimes tied together like arse-lovers. Certain memories had no words; forests without trees, fierce rivers without water, cold flames, all distinct and lonely, inside nothing. Like a footmark, a stile. Messages were everywhere: in a fallen twig, on bark, in maggots stuffing a dead sheep's eye, on a scab like a red snail to be explored as it dried and sucked for its salt. A cloud signalled to him alone as it blotted out the sun, like a gryphon. He knew what the rest did not. A pine might imprison a blanched spirit wailing when the moon turned black. In fair moods the earth opened, surrendering a leather sheath, silver hilt, a greeny coin from which, smeared but still implacable, leafed like a plantain, stared the Lord of the World.

He had treasure known only to himself; a stone under the river, now pale, now bright, sometimes friendly, sometimes a frown. Occasionally, leaving the sheep, he dared roam the mountains, and, from tree roots and caves, might find an iron ring, a bone, a dulled scrap of blood.

More often, while the sheep cropped, he sat upright, very still, staring. Grass, thin and discoloured as if by a devil's hunkers, concealed ants who, like elves, had once upon a time been men but had got little so that few now feared them. Though clean, the boar left a stench by three trees. The black goat down there could lead him to the Underworld, a white goat restore the sunlight. The quick hob-thrush would settle amongst the sheep, angered if they gazed at its sparse feathers. Ravens meant danger, sensed by the sheep before seeing them; they had been white, blackening when the dying prince on the cross cursed the world. Snail shells calmed an aching ear, as would talk of a girl's cockle. Seeking a mate, she-otters left tiny reed crosses by water.

Hans, solitary, piping or watching, saw grey goose and gander do it near the green slime and frog-spawn, then rear their brood, quarrel, but stand hissing and flapping against fox or cruel boys.

In the mountains lurked Loving Father, Welcome Brother, Abbot Fur Coat, savage bears, to be killed only with very ancient spears, twisted like hunters' horns sounded over the fallen stag. There also glared dead grafs; the wind rose, they groaned in anger and sadness. The mountains themselves were monsters slain long ago: at nightfall, Broken Mountain could move, heave itself elsewhere, returning with the light. An emperor had been buried under Broken Mountain, later bursting through earth, a vast shape split like girls with the men, scattering trees and rocks. Or perhaps no emperor but a mountain spirit masked like a Black Thing. Some parts of the mountains had silence that touched the skin, others were never still. Some mountains stood in the head, cracked by blood, to be climbed, or fled. They could change to emptiness and falling.

Sometimes he piped in the mountains and the rocks called back. Sometimes, from a height, he looked down on himself asleep amongst sheep far below. Then he might tremble deliciously, feeling wordless sensations different from all that grew.

Thus, solitary, he was not lonely. Wet or fine, he was searching the sheep for scabs or murrain-blotch or examining an egg, yellow striped with black, which might reveal a sign. Fondling wool, he might feel his joy-rod prickle, then tighten, or tears sprung up as if from the Bailiff's whip. A sheep had once carried two children across a sea. Reaching safety, vile as Johannes Ox-Face or the branding iron, they had killed the kindly animal. He wept at Michaelmas and Christmas when his sheep were rounded up for the Castle, where screams for meat harried the Lenten shortages. Each sheep was his friend, each memory offered other friends. Albrecht might come, bestow him a nod, or pass unseeing, eyes high.

He was crowded, he could see through the entire world. The one-eyed hunter in broad hat galloping between stars on an eight-footed horse. A lady waits on a glass hill, pointed like a giant's ram-mast, a queen fades to nothing, smeared with pig-shit.

Villagers wondered where his memories came from. The wind? Demons? No monk had taught him letters or numbers. Counting sheep, he could manage only, 'One . . . two . . . and those.' He had discovered that certain words – *rope*, *coil*, *shut*, *lurk* – were best hidden. Like a hanging, they lay alone and deadly. *Honey*, *water*, *glass* should be uttered very often. Words were part of the earth, clay, to be changed into shapes and colours. They could be jealous of each other. They could wait, they could fly, like screech-owls. They tumbled out of darkness, were all around him, and, ranked together, became a story. They dropped from the jangle of bells, scarlet, purple, black, the bells that chased away devils and delighted angels. Tree, bird, shit, a bead grew words like moss or rust; the words moved, often escaping before

36

he saw them whole, like fish. To where? Why? What next? Words descended on a bridge, edged from shadows, or the cracked statue that sweated blood at Lammas. They bubbled from wells. A leaf dazzled, within the light was a ring that dropped more rings. In water boiling in a pot a face, ravaged or tender, glimmered, went, too swift to leave words trapped tight.

All was endless: the wind blew, the sheep shat, colours glowed on branches, fell to earth, the mountains pressed the sky, the Castle held fast its wonders.

Hans would close his eyes, peacock spots, gold and green bands, all shimmering, on a farther haze of silver and blue. *Peacock.* Villagers had gaped when that slow, sparkling bird, spun as if from Hans's stories, had been escorted up to the Castle in its greens and purples, its glittering foliage and myriad suns.

He had flown, seeing the far, the wide, all that shines; also, he knew the dark secrets in the earth, like a mole, like rain that fell into blackness, returned in silver pools. In rain, he was safe, none hunted him.

He watched the sun, a giant's supper, swallowed by Broken Mountain, firing the Castle, smearing the dawn hailed by tiny voices heard by no one else. In the long winter he felt the lost sun was within him, so that he saw more keenly. Pines leant back in the wind, the fox dissolved into autumn leaves, new stories rubbed the air clean.

Dwarfs might be at hand, lured by the damp stench of hollow oak, or old Broad Hat push from mist, he who had never been a child and understood ravens; one of those who grow tusks and shield but become shadows if you approach.

Hans sat with his pipe within diminishing frames of light, the sheep intent on him, vague in the desolate twilight; and as if expecting a story. He could tell them that Archangel Michael's real name was Merky, that Friendly Ones used only milk and saffron yellow as a hawk's eye. Instead, he grasped his pipe. As he played, the dim air curled into leaves and faces, the sickle moon cut the sky where a fighter was trapped in ice. A blue flame on a heath showed that riches lay beneath.

Sounds changed with the sun: at noon, thin and pale, by night larger, darker, very clear. There was else. He hankered after flesh. His own, and Albrecht's, forbidden though it was. Still playing, he thought fiercely of men swimming. He would crouch behind a tree, secretly, emblazoned by curved arses and drooping fishlets. Riskily, he spied on women, wondering, never satisfied, for he could do no more than watch. Not for him any touching, exploring, digging. Desperate, he could attract only himself, uncover that famous Little Pike knobbed like Toad King's stick, streaked as if with blue rain, and now straightening, poised to Make Fire, Polish the Spade, Plough the Pond, Pull the Pig's Tail, Dance with Little Fritz, Beg the Red Cap. His was Little Pike Marvellous, springing from its duckskin jewel-bag. He plucked the tip as he would a mess of strawberries, charming it, watching it uncoil, juicy as maggots; the sting, the throb, then swamp, pierced by visions of Albrecht helpless, imploring rescue from water. At such an instant, now held tight, now released, he was inside a song, in his pleasure master of the village, perfected. But the white gush must not touch earth: it would lay eggs of danger.

Lying, complete, fondling, naming each part of himself, he kindled his secrets, his night being. He was a cleft tree, a dripping wave, magpie's nest, island, sun rays, a fountain, bog; he was hills, undergrowth, hidden river, path to a baker's hut; like the sky he flowed, dropped filth, struck fire, sheltered the stars. Fields were hooped with bridges, only he could see them; he would cross to where the Marsh Woman dwelt: her hut, above, here, below, was wretchedness, her platter, famine, her knife, greed; a boy, laziness, attended her, with a girl, sloth. Her door was ruin, her curtains fire.

How did he know? He could only crease his muddy face, close pale blue eyes, and begin stuttering, 'I remember. . . .' He remembered a hill turning, pulled by the sun, but was unconcerned with questions, could seldom answer, accepting his lot when, sudden as a snake, the children, jealous, hating, rushed at him. He was seldom afraid, for Albrecht, in light and superior graciousness, would save him by no more than a silence or head-shake. Very occasionally he smiled at Hans, had once spoken, unsmiling but kind, 'Your ride is chosen', or something like. Lord in hiding.

Albrecht won without playing, gained without asking, mastered without commanding.

The Shepherd had a friend – not of course supreme Albrecht, protective but not loving, but Grete, small like him, bird-eyed, scrawny, a deaf mute, believed, like Broad Hat, to understand birds, permitted to do so by her inability to betray them. For him she stole eggs, cabbage leaves, scraps of fish, doing whatever he wanted. She would hand him the pipe, clean a sheep, fondle Long Pike Marvellous with solemn obedience, so that, gladly, he told her stories. She heard nothing, but her face, flattish under tumbled, black, rat's tail hair, was agitated if he halted midway.

7

From far below the Castle was barely measurable, hard, at one with crag and abyss. Newcomers, however, noted fissures and gaps exposed by winter hail or raking summers. Weeds sprawled over yards, rust already gnawed a bombard acquired from Florence by a dubious loan. An impertinent dock plant obtruded from Uncle's turret.

On so dominant a height several successive burgs had risen, *at one time*, the time of triumphant knights; all had been assaulted and plundered, only for yet another to shoulder up from the ruins, absorbing them. Halls, vaults, towers were jumbled amongst collapsed walls, roofless passages leading to piled rubble, crumbling storehouses, cracking yards, refuges for ghosts, dead birds and bats, aged, useless retainers and much too gross to mention. This was no Abode of Wonder, no haven of round table, enchanted cup, Green Stone. Better class singers mostly avoided it, its few women were indifferent to the latest soaps and paints. They produced a litter or two, then drooped helplessly, without refinements. They were said constantly to swallow pennyroyal, which forestalls pregnancy. The cries and jabbers of children were rare: children were usually ill, coughing themselves away.

Tapestries, linen, straw were damp and discoloured, the bath-house was seldom used, the dogs were surly. Apertures were too narrow, many lunettes and vents were boarded up. Little glass reached the Castle save for Uncle's spectacles and the Gräfin's mirrors, now hidden or destroyed. Thus the Castle was almost everywhere dense with shadows, some live though indeterminate, flitting between walls as if scared.

Unusually, however, the Graf enjoined tidiness. No rat or dog could be left rotting in corners he was likely to pass: even the high-born were forced to use latrines, however remote and draughty, Prince Narr murmuring that he had prosecuted a turd for trespassing near his bed.

Days were longer in the south wind, longer still when windless, and within the Castle, despite draughts, no wind, no freshness penetrated save in dilapidated outworks. Time was thus different here from that in the flat lands, where peasant and swinker counted hours by the open sun. The mechanical clocks surviving those dispatched from Milan and Augsburg to the Graf's father still chimed but were muffled by the gloom, melting in dim vistas which, lit by infrequent lamps, seemed depthless. Those passing under blotched tapestries or bare stone glistening with moisture looked discontented, often shabby, though this could be to delude tax officials and indulgences.

The Gräfin's departure, removing vital influences, had also thickened the air. If the Graf, to animate the atmosphere, had retained a bag of her hair, he had hidden it too expertly.

Throughout the Empire each man proclaims his poverty. The Emperor bemoans a purse emptied by his labours against Turks and Hungarians, the Pope casts around for dues and reprints indulgences tenfold. Bishops beseech new tithes and exhort piety, lords huddle beneath debts owed to untitled unsurers, long-fingered, unforeskinned Jacobs and Nathans, and merchants insist that their latest venture has been ambushed by Barbary scoun-drels. A fleet has sunk off Cyprus, a ban subverted by foul-bearded Levantine Christ-haters. The beggar flaunts his nakedness for profit, a serf professes inability to recognize a coin, though awaiting his chance to grab it. The priest berates stinginess as the worst of sins, and taxes, while ruining all, fail to reach treasuries.

The Graf, less ambitious than his father, had nevertheless twice reneged on debts, so that loans were seldom forthcoming. His grandfather had won territories extending as far as Prigsheim, but Father had flamboyantly lost most of them, announcing this as stupendous conquests. Other estates were disputed, or ingloriously mortgaged to a Wittelsbach prince, a Bamberg counting-house. The Graf sought redress from the fugitive Emperor, pleading that he had suffered more grievously than any, but no answer had been vouchsafed, save, as the Confessor put it, in the spirit.

The Confessor would tell the Graf that he was comparable to Hercules and Christ, in striving to maintain his own, for his respect for boundaries, his devotion to duties, his anxiety to keep all in their proper station. But news of the riches of Antwerp, the splendour of Bruges, did nothing to assuage the Graf's moroseness. Many ruffianly peasants slept more soundly than grafs, let alone knights.

'It is true,' the Confessor sighed, 'that Christ, whom but few of us resemble . . .' – he implied a loyal compliment – 'could never abide knights. The light of his countenance he does tend to withdraw.'

He spoke further, of the Unjust Steward, whom the Graf admired, and the Mammon of Unrighteousness, which he coveted.

The Emperor should come and see conditions for himself, if he could afford an escort. Depopulation, sporadic plague and famine, coin-clipping. Manorial court fees and tolls were daily more difficult to collect, ransoms had departed with the knights, even the sanctity of oaths had lapsed. Throughout the mountains agitators were denouncing serfdom, ordained though it was by God and Pope.

Yet – the Graf was puzzled – money abounded, streaming towards upstart monopolists along the Main who had doubled the charges of cloth, timber, and, would you believe it, honey! The Bishop of Würzburg had doubled his girth, not through godliness but from wines and iron.

The Graf's perplexity was more painful than any crown of

thorns, easily borne once you were used to it. The more he repaid, the more – those who presumptuously styled themselves his advisers assured him – he actually owed. You borrow, he thought, a ducat, spend it on behalf of lazy good-for-nothings, then get the bill. More precise explanations from the Confessor muddled him further, and the Clerk's intervention showed him only that matters were worse than he had supposed.

He sat with one adviser, then with another, gazing so long at accounts so methodically dispatched by Messer Florio, by Herr Kraus, and presented very respectfully by the Confessor-Treasurer, the Clerk-Sexton and Bailiff Wilhelm that the figures began dancing.

8

The Graf had been born a few years before the bloodiest peasant rising, reports of which had gravely affected him, and following an invasion of rats, repelled by an archbishop cursing them in a tongue hitherto unknown to him and to others. He was now over forty, though by how much he did not know, because, whilst attending communion but once a year – to do more, the Confessor asserted, was unnecessary, perhaps condign, and, by some bishops, forbidden – he frequently attended mass, assured by the same authority that hours spent therein were outside time, devotion thereby prolonging life. The Graf prided himself for his superiority over those Augsburg and Bremen clowns who thought that by destroying a clock they could delay 1500, and over those Englishmen, the mad men of Gotham, uncouth loons, building a wall around a sunlit garden to prevent summer escaping.

The Confessor nodded in his sagacious way, draped in furs from which his head protruded like a mottled parsnip, slightly pitted, his eyes small rims, brownish, moist, complacent, rimmed with what resembled dust. 'Even grafs can die. . . .' – he spoke as if making a jest amusing but inconsiderable – 'and have sometimes done so. Days,' he said, uncovering grandeur of thought, 'are plentiful, though years are not.'

He was standing, from respect. The Graf was seated in a pointed, high-backed chair. He had grey, wispy hair, a nose slightly too long for its small face – people said that a playful demon had tweaked it out too far and forgotten how to push it back. His pale, indeterminate eyes were set flat and too close together, the thin mouth as if drawn in dry charcoal and, like an afterthought, broken by a small, blue scar. Below, the barely finished chin was shaven. The illustrious body had the leanness of a rider, and a stiffness markedly defensive. His long, skinny hands were tapered to a fanwork of bitten nails, usually concealed within sleeves otherwise too lengthy.

He was apt to complain that his mother, dead from a screaming childbirth, had while pregnant betrayed him by staring too long at ill-favoured youths, thus destroying the graces appropriate to his status. At this, the Confessor would remind him that the Sybil, Socrates, Jesus and Blessed Paul the tent-maker had been the ugliest of creatures, designed to rely on wisdom alone, and safeguarded from sinful pride.

The Graf's movements were clumsy and, as now, he would sit motionless and watchful as a lizard, unwilling to reveal his thoughts by a spontaneous gesture, unconsidered motions, even blinks. This posture also suggested immunity from common habits, though reminding Prince Narr of a constipant at stool. From Prince Narr you recognized the difference between laughter and a laugh. As for the Graf, few lines cracked his face, and, as he neither laughed nor frowned, only his dry teeth gave any illusion of smiling.

Closeted soon after dawn with von der Goltz, he had rigorously tightened his mouth, having heard that his favourite hawk was moulting, probably cursed, that his favourite hound had died, almost certainly poisoned. The damp air reminded him that he had breathed too much rheum and winter fatigue, not yet ended. His companion's baldness was glowing unpleasantly even through this dingy light. Like Uncle, the Confessor always brimmed with unnecessary news: horses, with no such obligation, were better companions and took one farther.

43

The Fuggers, he now heard, great Augsburg bankers, were leaning too heavily on those too fragile to support them. The Confessor then mentioned the arts of leadership, from which the Graf expected some compliment. This did not come.

A mouldy fire drowsed in this low, circular room. Blurred by generations of smoke, a tapestry hero, thin and naked, wrestled with a bear or tree. The Confessor stroked his furs, his tone worldly-wise. 'In the Great Pilgrimage . . . we should not call it the first Crusade . . . leadership was that of the Holy Ghost, let majesty have say, disguised, strangely, we may think, as a honking goose, assisted, or I am inclined to surmise, merely accompanied by a duck. Scarcely, you will comment, very courtly, but as the Scriptures put it, all animals are finally unascertainable. The centaur has manifold implications, even insinuations. Our Lord said that he preferred a donkey to certain disciples. The difference not, perhaps, very distinct.'

The Graf's chapped, depleted features, like a holed bag, were querulous, his mouth loosened, then pursed; he was convinced that he was being compared not to Our Lord, which was permissible, possibly apt, but to a goose, which was not.

The two were disturbed. From some hushed recess, Prince Narr wandered in, unannounced, as was his privilege. His yellow-and-blue tunic was smudged like his painted face beneath lolling, scarlet cap; his grin was vicious – 'Mischief,' he rejoiced, 'warms me up' – though his versatile elbow was silent.

He had interrupted von der Goltz's account of a Galdenheim seamstress being burnt for strangling an infant. 'Then the fat's truly in the fire,' Prince Narr giggled. The others affected not to have heard, and he glided away, finger to his lips, doubtless sneering.

'You, sir, good shepherd as you are. . . .' But this, still tied to a suggestion of animals, did not please, and, cognisant, reading the signs, which was all he ever did read, the Confessor ceremoniously departed.

He was followed successively by the Noble Huntsman, who as always punctilious, marked his attendance by having nothing to say; by the Cellarer, appropriately bottle-nosed, who had too much, mostly complaints. With scuttling eyes and furtive manner, he was always mushroom-pallid, from too long sojourning in cellars. The Fighting Commandant, Ritter von Statz, who so seldom fought but flaunted a strenuous chin, eyes too heavy, slightly bulging, as if about to drop from interior struggles but possessing, as far as was discernible, little else, came but for an instant to raise his hand. Of simple tastes, the Commandant felt that one pair of choice buttocks outbid the claims of war, the skills of star-gazers and alchemists, and a tiresome saint's vision of ten thousand virgins. Uncle visited less often than a miracle, though his company the Graf preferred, as he might a dish not immediately palatable but curiously spiced, enriched by indefinable sauces, and delivered with teasing yet friendly lack of respect.

The Clerk was waiting. He was always waiting; for bad news, decisions, opportunities obliquely to denigrate those who, like the Confessor, he felt inadequate in their duties. These were plenty: laziness, mediocrity, lust and cupidity had their say.

Finally admitted, the Clerk stood, black gowned, hands folded, primed with solemnities: doubtless the betrothal of an infant heiress, a monastic scandal. Though still young, he had a bony, monkish face as if slightly frost-bitten, one cheek apt to twitch, as if touched by a moth. His eyes were already old, lustreless but shrewd. In lip, eye and stance his demeanour was courteous, though with the calculation of a diplomat not the humility of a menial.

He spoke: he spoke at some length, forgoing heiresses and lascivious clerics. The Graf's expression quickened.

'You are certain of this? You can find no other means?'

'None, sir. We . . .' – *We* implicated the Confessor – 'we have already delayed too long. From considerations of charity. But a tax is requisite, it is required. Urgently.'

A new tax, any tax, foretold trouble. The rich could now afford gunpowder and enjoyed using it, the poor still had sharp teeth and claws. Yet Jesus, as von der Goltz had remarked on the last tax levy, severely recommended the payment of taxes.

The Graf remained motionless as before, but his spirit slumped. Since Father's death he had quaked at visions of blood-streaked hands growing giant claws, rearing from hovel and barn: they must presage turmoil at the gates, the Castle in flames, outlaw knights uniting with rebels, mere drains of life.

Far-away rulers – that expensive fop in Paris, Squire Harry in England – at any unrest, in or out of visions, would pounce without hesitation. He himself had the fault of excessive generosity.

The new tax concluded the morning's business but the Clerk did not at once receive permission to depart. The Graf, while trusting his acumen, disliked his company, but still more he disliked solitude save when riding. Oppressed by the silence, he said reluctantly 'Last night, I dreamt. . . .'

The Clerk bowed, the first movement for some minutes. Shadows, fire, the tapestry hero, the Graf, the very draughts were alike suspended. The small room chilled further.

'Sir?'

'I dreamt of a raven.'

The Clerk shifted a foot. He looked uncomfortable, as though about to twitch. Earnest, conscientious, he had learnt some Greek from Uncle, but though versed in New Knowledge, he retained much of the old. Ravens, he recalled, are by night unlucky, less so by day. He lowered his head, fluttered one hand as if signing, attempted reassurance less by words than by their quietly authoritative tone. 'Only an eagle looks directly at the sun.'

This was barely relevant, untrue and persisted in the unsuitable theme of animals. Yet the Graf was appeased: no sheep, no shepherd, he might, figuratively, be an eagle, he might even be the sun. Nodding with considerable pleasantness he inquired about news, less from curiosity than to withstand his own thoughts.

The response was immediate. Ambitious behind outward meekness, the Clerk kept himself informed.

'Little of moment, sir. . . .'

This too lacked substantial truth. Unknowns had hacked to death a Westphalian baron, though the Clerk's concern was not much evident. One baron less, his smile suggested, was no great matter, though to the Graf such a demise was unseemly, exposing the vulnerability of lords, possibly reinforcing that disturbing prediction, 'He will come.'

The Clerk hastened to produce further news, speaking with mild relish, though the last traces of youth left his papery face: 'Wolves have increased around Cologne, magnified, so to speak. Slobbering with hunger. This cold . . . they devour children, girls when possible.' He gleamed slightly, disapproving or envious, a funereal presence in his black robe. Then, to dispel unwelcome prospects of wolves, he continued, neutral, official: 'Venice strives with Genoa . . . though when does she not?'

He paused, then extracted an information more exceptional.

'They say . . . that is, we are told . . . stones have been found. Outside the Castle.'

'But there are always stones.'

'Certainly, sir, yes. Finely expressed. Without question. Nevertheless . . .'

'But what, man? Come out with it.'

'They have already been removed, anticipating your commands. But they were seven. Seven stones in a line. A straight line.'

Seven! Very inauspicious or very promising. An arrow of stones, pointing this way or that. The Graf remained expressionless. 'Did they point towards the walls? Or away from them?'

The Clerk closed one hand, then opened it. 'Assuredly, they did both.'

Annoyed, the Graf stared him into nervousness and the Clerk left him.

Remembering some nonsense about Saturn and Venus glaring at each other across Taurus in the seventh month, the Graf rose, eased his limbs, shivered, drew in his cloak, crossed to a ledge under the tapestry where a dulled copper bowl was filled with pepper and leaves. As he inhaled, his streaked, meagre face lost some of its strain despite the unpropitious stones and insolence from regions below. If only he could dispense with dependants, as God had with Sodom and Gomorrah, though these had surely threatened no castles and must have provided much pleasure, though of course damnable.

Amid stone, hush, damp he stood at a chipped lunette. Gazing down through clear, steep winter light over his domains, so many lost, he saw the river like a crooked trail of pewter, sorry hamlets submerged under smoke, thin cattle, minute at this distance, the highway, crowded in his boyhood but now forsaken save by armed groups of traders, ecclesiastics, thieves, vagrants. Under the bleak scrub sloping into the fields were other stones, ancient boundaries, disturbing in their reminder of magic hidden but infectious.

Turning, he noticed with further disquiet a patch of red on the naked floor. A dead butterfly. A live butterfly foretold death; this one was death itself. He crushed it at once, rebuffing death, then kicked the fire, more to show feelings than to excite warmth. Resuming his chair, he reflected that he should inspect the stables, condole with the hawk, but was disinclined to move. The Clerk's disclosure had worried him, also the momentary glimpse of the outside. Heights always sickened his nerves, only rides and hunts assuaged such queasiness: speed and intensity left him supreme, at one with earth and the wind.

He sighed, convinced that his head was too small for his exceptional thoughts, a prison trapping him. Yet it could sometimes be excessively large so that he would lose himself, as though riding too far. At this lack of control of his own head, he winced, then called a dog; a shadow stirred, but no dog came.

Thoughts should be moved like chessmen, deliberately, in design, but they flew at random; he needed to steady them with plans, hopes, orders; with desire, for a stable brat, carter's bawd, scullery slut, but beneath the girdle he was inert, shrunk to an acorn in this abominable winter. Once it had been scarcely controllable, roaming free in Franconian stews and bath-houses, but now it was mutinous even when, so to speak, manhandled. Yet God himself was not quite perfect. There was a tradition that he had lost an eye, and that the true Grail was the cup in which it still lay, to be rescued by some immaculate seeker. The Graf, however, laborious toiler, had insufficient leisure for such an enterprise.

He remained thinking of brute desire, unsensationally, for he had lost hope and ardour. His own wife had refused her full duties with scared protests, shrinking from his sharp member as from a leper's sore. At once there intruded the unwelcome parable of the tares, which, the Confessor maintained, smiling as though he himself were not part of it, was the common lot. Judgement, disapproval, the oven.

The Gräfin had early told him that he was brave; good. But then added, as if to an unseen witness, that he lacked courage. He had wanted to beat her but found himself irresolute.

When alone, he feared hearing his own heart beat, falling like a dangerous hammer. Now it was loud, very menacing, he really should leave for the stables, but he did not stir. Thoughts chased each other like starlings, the world was sinking into a morass. Malign stones besieged the Castle, men were not brothers. In Mainz, discovering their plague blains, they did not kneel in prayer but scurried to embrace neighbours, to contaminate them so as not to drop into hell alone.

At this, he pulled up a sleeve to examine himself, not for blains but for acne. Uncle considered that skin reflects the health of the brain and soul, a disagreeable thesis, for while his own skin was pink and smooth as ham, the nephew's was unhealthy, apt to turn yellow as the basilisk found in Halle, where huntsmen had forced it into seeing itself in a pond, so that it died of horror.

Uncle, while commending the brain, had small respect for the soul – a concoction, he said, of Greeks who misunderstood Persian, and of Arabs who misunderstood Greek.

The Graf, perforce, reverted to the Gräfin, mindful that in old songs certain women periodically shed their skins and slithered away into holes and rocks, a skill unadvantageous to the marriage bed but which she had very possibly acquired.

The afternoon waited, empty, forbidding. He would have hunted, but the Noble Huntsman, an inefficient lazybones, reported that all game had vanished and that mountain tracks were dangerously iced.

49

9

This Graf was regarded as a considerable thinker, particularly by those who did not know him, or avoided him because of that Evil Eye. Undeniably, his brows, his eyes, were often fixed in painful intentness, though little of moment emerged in his utterances, themselves few. Aware of his reputation, and though habitually self-mistrusting, he was yet inclined to believe it. Ill-read, seldom encouraging discussion, uneasy with Uncle, he did know that all was connected, simultaneously simple and intricate, like a map, lines at first confusing, then revealing roads and bridges, rivers, forests, frontiers. The massed webs of the universe must meet in God, the reconciler. You could link Uncle's chronicles with an old Greek demon, Cronos, blood with the sun, water with the moon, and with I, which in turn affected the mirror, a Three in One, thus a reflection of divinity, again reaching to divinity itself. Ordinary life, however, he discerned as a gigantic and aimless swarm, requiring most rigorous disciplines. To countenance change, novelty and disrespect would, by fostering rebellion, imperil the world, thrusting it into the chaos which he had heard, on excellent and near at hand authority, Christ had called the Last Days. An empire should grow castles like forests, holding the land firm. A tall tree gives shade, and moreover is fine timber.

To such convictions the Graf clung as he had to a branch when his horse stumbled in a forest. He never doubted them, only his own will. In boyhood mock-combats and tourneys he had suffered fears of retaliation, of hitting back, always seeking some smiling, indeed deferential escape. This was, he later understood, due to a fastidious refinement that Christ would have understood, even applauded, yet was unreliable against mortal breakdown. He was unlike mighty Charlemagne, wielder of armed righteousness; unlike the godless, merciless, spectacular Frederick II Hohenstaufen, whom none dared resist. He had always been in the shadow of such as they, his Name was obscured, on sufferance. He was praised only to his face, with his prayers unanswered, his labours unacknowledged.

Harassed by responsibilities daily more exacting, he had no time for scholarship, and, like any peasant, feared books and profound knowledge, which might release suggestions powerful enough to jar the world, maintained as it was by balance, and overseen by princes, the best of them German, under God.

Uncle, with supple smiles, had quoted some deplorable clown, Dirk of Delft, *An uneducated ruler is an empurpled ass,* but education, the Graf felt, though silently, too frequently excuses laziness. Look at monks, scribblers, lawyers – Uncle himself, while formidable in an inexplicit way, was too imprisoned in books to assist government, the building of dykes against turmoil. He enjoyed the incomprehensible, the unexpected answer, audacious supposition. *To strive after knowledge* – he shrugged his flabby shoulders, indicating a pile of newly printed books – *is sin, if it be knowledge other than of God.* His eyes suggested a joke, not in the best of taste. 'The words of Aquinas. Thomas Aquinas.' He frowned gently, patiently, as though elaborating the joke, inferring that the blessed Thomas had been mischief-making, though playfully, not maliciously, leaving Uncle undeterred from salacious Ovid, tiresome Virgil, heretical Ulysses.

Reading, the Graf now believed, was a conspiracy of those who shirked work in what Christ called the vineyard, and possessed unwholesome potency. The Fighting Commandant had once, very properly, jailed for something or other a fellow unable to read; yet, chained, tormented, he became content, then enraptured by endlessly unrolling a scroll, peering at it as if enchanted, though its margins were bare of fantastic beasts and lecheries. This was a destruction of justice. Writing invited retribution. A Gailersburg monk wrote so much that his hand withered, some said had dropped off. A Bulgarian king, renowned for writing a treatise, touched a sick child, who promptly died.

The Graf, then, despite weak shanks, long nose and settled expression like three weeks of rain, was virtuous, an example to the Emperor, approved by God. Striving for cohesion, he saw himself as the wise spider spinning to unite the lands; as the assiduous fireman extinguishing flames tossed by the fearsome wind. He was clear-sighted. Anti-clericalism was rampant throughout the Empire; the Pope was unworthy, though not for worshipping Mammon, which was not. Never to be forgotten were the horrors of criminal kinghts and peasant risings. These he could withstand, but the burrowing, insidious energies of print – sermon, song, lampoon, pamphlet – could destroy him. Temptations to disorder, books would never reject the influences that had bred them. Greek, a most suspect tongue, also the Turkish, Arabic, Hebrew, noxious and pestilential, with occult allure. The Gräfin had murmured that verses healed more readily than physicians. True, the latter were impostors, perilous as angry herons, but easier to restrain than were books. Words, faded on crumbling parchment, were yet stable, like oaths had formerly been, and faltering only at the barbarous edges of the world, befouled by dragon and centaur. Through words the dead, infidels, heretics, sodomites and agitators could outmatch the live and virtuous. Words, cunningly arranged and planted, had powers inaccessible to lay rulers. By a ritual curse, the Pope had ensured that King John's England had three years of famine and during that time none of his dead subjects were allowed into heaven. A poet on Elba, by his bitter mockery, had made boils sprout on rich men's faces. Like Jews, bones of Satan. The Gräfin had further declared that words on a page changed the light, then uttered more nonsense about carving from the air, from water. Such stuff changed neither the light nor herself.

Save for title-deeds and treaties, the Graf allowed himself only maps: maps of extinct Rome and Carthage; maps, mostly blank, of Arabia and China, and of Mongol lands, entirely blank; maps of England, France, Burgundy, Spain, Italy, and of the ever-encroaching Ottomans. Maps of heaven and hell, much subdivided and precisely detailed, in circles, oblongs, straight lines. All maps were victories over chaos.

A poor sleeper, the Graf, to remedy this deficiency, would count and peruse his maps, a distraction so interesting that they kept him awake.

Books! That paper was made from disgusting old rags was very fitting. Yet he, Graf of Grafs, an axle of Providence, a pivot of Christendom, had stood in full armour, helmed, vainly nerving himself to thrash the Gräfin's book of devotions, stuffed with insubordinate beliefs, but had been scared off by the thunder likely to follow. To each reader, the very Bible alters its teachings. Identical words can nevertheless be different. Uncle, von der Goltz and Prince Narr might read aloud *Love Your Enemies*: the first voice would be jovial though sceptical, the second sententious, the third a screech; none would render it less than a puzzle.

The Graf liked to remind himself that Jesus, disgusted by books, wrote only in the dust.

There had been the Templars, gross with learning and secret knowledge . . . but a thought of them, the first and most outstanding of the knights to fall, made even the virtuous dread being alone.

Like Uncle, the Gräfin too had collected books, though frivolous ones. They had done her no good. Involuntarily, tempted beyond himself, the widower would sometimes unbolt a great chest and pick out a volume, often a collection of songs by Walther von der Vogelweide. What a name!

> *The world is fair to see, white, green and red,*
> *But see within it; it's black and wretched as the dead.*

Hard to gainsay; it harmed nobody, but to write more attracts bad company, mingling the solid with the absurd. Truth is a White Wave, and so on. The Gräfin's contribution to marriage harmony had been to introduce an Irish vagabond with a pack of insolent songs. The Graf, submitting to no book, as behoved his dignity, had thereby developed an excellent memory, and could repeat the oaf's verses should he wish to. He did not. Let others judge their idle boasting.

> *I am the sea wind, ocean wave, surge murmur,*
> *I am seven battalions, a strong bull, eagle on a rock,*
> *I am a ray of the sun.*

The Irish degenerate was none of these, but puny, sottish, while claiming himself a sword-swinging champion of the fair and oppressed and with some heritage of bardic magic, able to transform himself at will. Unlikely, undesirable. At best, an Irishman will transform himself to dung, a stoat, a pot of bad ale, having seduced wives with gibberish about the land of the ever-young. 'I enjoy the good,' he hummed, after declining a challenge from the Fighting Commandant, 'I enjoy the evil. Both are equal in my eyes.' In Thuringia he would have been hanged for such heresy. Nevertheless his songs tricked women. Music sank into a different part of the head than did books, doubling the risks. Fools bleated about music straightening unicorn's horns, fertilizing barren cows – though the only such cow thus rewarded was a Hungarian queen who, listening to minstrels, gave birth to a frog. Only tax-collectors were thought to be totally immune to music, fortunately in view of the new tax. Mysteriously, these were notably cherished by the Saviour.

Over-familiar with the Gräfin, this Irish fellow addressed her as Sister Champion, speaking unctuously of the Virgin, greedily of beef, ingratiatingly to the Cellarer. Slimy, he knew too much about women and, though feigning not to, the Graf found himself listening to those wheedling tones, flimsy but incessant.

'Gracious madam, revered lady, respected spouse, I tell you this. Of a French lordling, call him Jean, Pierre or Louis, who lived, did he not, in a forest, and why should he not? He loved the chase – boar, prime boar, best of boars, accompanied by his rich cousin. Did I say rich? Why then, he was seigneur of the province, master of wherever he saw. Then, on a day of mischance, Jean, Pierre or Louis, saw, *espied* the ripest of boars. He sounded the pursuit. A view, a view, indeed a view! Praise be! With his cousin he galloped, he overtook, he struck, but, may the holy Virgin witness my truth, by the Devil's craft, by wicked ordinal, he slew the seigneur. His terror was lightning swift. He stretched the body flat, then fled blind. At a fountain, under noonday sun, there was a girl, beauteous as a running spring in June, as a forest glade in Connaught, as light on the sea. She besought him to return home, and proclaim to far and wide, to near and far, that the boar had gored the young lord. Well enough said, in a voice lovely as all the bells of Tara, and she then permitted him to strip her and they lay together for the blue bliss of paradise, before he rode away at her command. Riding, he forgot the dead, could see only her hair, finest spun Silurian gold, eyes deep as Solway waters, her nakedness throbbing like the sweet lyre of Orpheus. She had consented to be his betrothed. Matters, I mind me, were of course less simple. How else could there be a story? For she was no natural mortal but the water-sprite Lusinia.

'Meanwhile, all in fair France believed his account of his cousin's death, and he succeeded to his lands. Lusinia soon joined him, but at their wedding, three days and three nights of splendours, she warned him never to set eyes on her on days when she displayed a ball of red silk. In return, by skills known only to poets, in truth to Irish poets and not all of them, she built him in seven days the castle Lusigan, to be seen to this day. She bore him seven sons, very handsome, yet sadly deformed, an eye missing here, a finger there. Only the youngest was without blemish. . . .'

The story twisted on and on, the Gräfin not impatient but wide-eyed and tremulous. The shabby narrator was trespassing on forbidden knowledge. All women were slippery sprites. Their souls, if they had any (it was disputed), lingered over their corpses longer than did men's, sometimes refusing to depart. This might explain the fretful humidity of the Gräfin's empty room.

The Irishman had finally said 'Sister Champion' once too often, had been thrashed and sent packing, though he had, on leaving, packed a prized silver bowl. He had been proof that poets, like dancers, jesters, musicians and those who pray secretly, are like demons, bandits, snakes, upsetting natural order. Song, it is said, though on poor evidence, can topple mountains and freeze hell. They are particles of chaos. A Prince Narr will jest amid the blood and fumes of Troy. Rhymes cock snooks at castles.

The Gräfin's demands for privacy had been intolerable, yet, despite her weakness and folly, the Graf had, in a manner, feared her, as he did darkness and ambush. He had learnt from Uncle that women, long ago in colleges of nine, had trained boys in weaponry and later, unforgiving of their lost powers, were forced to rely on sorcery and blandishments. And how had that hooligan saint, Bernard, described woman? Ah yes! *Her face burns, her voice is the hissing of serpents.* A Frenchified braggart, nevertheless, this Bernard, though Uncle had very gently remonstrated that he had in truth been born French. His words were not wholly true of the Gräfin whose face, before marriage comely enough, afterwards resembled sour wine, her voice barely audible.

There were days when, striving to be unobserved, keeping close to walls, he would sidle to her apartment in West Tower, forbidden to all others. Dust gathered on tables, embroidery was threadbare, mice crept through decayed rushes, moths bred in robes piled in darkness. The silence was as clammy as the walls and air.

Pondering, he would stare into a tarnished mirror, the last of those she had so loved to collect and which, like her clocks and books, he had thrust away or destroyed. His unfortunate nose crinkled disapprovingly, alert for the scented drag of her soaps. Not for her the customary slabs of mutton fat and ash. Sometimes he tried to outwit the mirror by very swiftly kissing his own cheek therein, but had not yet succeeded.

She had cherished mirrors for what she called their conjuring, evidently descrying what was denied him – spirits, souls, the outline of a future lover. He himself, in this deranged, perhaps haunted atmosphere, might see, or think he saw, not only himself, blurred, tight-lipped, suspicious, but, very faintly, her face too, colourless, impervious, disobedient to himself and God.

Marriage had brought him the left bank of a river, five unprofitable villages, a muddle of obsolete grazing rights, some forfeits, unpaid, and eleven horses of unknown breed. Most of her cash dowry remained undelivered. Furthermore, despite his commands, pleas, even exertions, she had never allowed him to see her naked, a privilege doubtless reserved for Irishmen. Never had she willingly opened to him her silken purse, and when he managed it, he found only obstinate dryness. The only portion of her body, slender, boyish, with which he had been thoroughly familiar, was her neck, not a resounding conquest or the most appetizing of regions. She had resembled the Rhine, flowing for ever over a pot of gold which a thief would steal. Only, she had not flowed for ever.

The dead can have an aggravating ability to express themselves more fully than they did in life, and this with female perversity was true of the Gräfin. A year after her departure he was imagining her more vividly, hearing her more irritably and, often at untoward moments, desiring her more savagely, though to summon her would risk his soul.

He had not secluded her jewels, which he would finger as he might at least her neck, though the poor light diminished their radiance and perhaps their potency. For they too were more than they appeared. Being, Uncle liked to say, is more than seeming. Like love, he would add, oddly, for he could never have known love and would have raised a brow at its approach. These glimmering heaps were also entangled with stars and tides, night and idiocy, sunlight and rose, the gold, with kinship to blood, which signified, very tiresomely, both wisdom and temptation. Emerald enclosed faith, though gräfins needed faith mostly in grafs. Sapphire meant hope, though her own had been for a disgusting, low-born Champion. Ruby was charity, though why should she have stored rubies when his own charity had been lavish?

Similarly, flowers had further existences, seldom wholly consistent. A daisy was sacred to the Virgin, yet had been stolen from shameful Hörsel, Fray Holle, Ma Go-to-Bed-at-Noon, or whatever impious hobbledehoys called her. Shortly after marriage the Gräfin had shyly given him a bunch of daisies. Hastening to the hunt, he had been angered at the delay. She had wept. On his return he had complained to Uncle, but the older man, though not despising but disliking the young woman, probably all young women, had in mild rebuke explained that the horrid flower's gold meant love and pity – love was a graf's due and pity an insult – and that its white symbolized purity. Damn all symbols, and anyway his own purity was famed throughout Germany. The petals, Uncle continued, relentlessly, not proud but secure in his erudition, represented glory, another insult, for, times being what they were, he had been allowed too little.

Such multitudinous inferences, like those of numbers, increased his grievances. Why could not things be as simple as he himself saw them? A table was, very properly, a table, not a platform from which to jump into holiness, a higher degree of chivalry, belief in circles. The Saviour himself had constructed a table, just that, no more than a plain table, still to be seen in a monastery near Bremen, made well enough but a trifle unsteady. Much thought, despite Uncle's learned exposition, must be mere fashion, unbefitting those who maintain the actual world, thus with richness of being.

Unseen, the Graf allowed himself a smile, for the phrase gratified him, awoke in him his singular merit. The Emperor's Man.

At the mirror he saw a dim patch lingering behind his head, which he almost convinced himself was a halo.

His wife's drawings had exasperated him as much as her reticence, her disobedience in bed, and her daisies. She might have made pictures of himself, which enemies could capture and distort, thus crippling him. Damaging good sense, drawings were like music, scarcely distinguishable from witchcraft. The Gräfin had, treacherously, listened to music unheard by others, as if she were a saint who alone hears music from dancing planets. He had once found her half singing into a cedar box which she hurriedly closed, then locked. He had not dared break it open, but, surreptitiously, he had it burnt, and that week a gale cracked a rampart.

Incapable of lying, she had nevertheless uttered much falsehood, murmuring that jewels could be glad and – no physician would agree – that the heart could be golden or leaden.

As though clutching a secret name, wandering in places she jealously concealed, she knew of the queer Green Stone, gabble of menials, peasants, drink-sodden trulls, all that was wayward and irregular. Dark corners, winding paths, half-glimpses of what he could never discern. Life in a shroud. She was a crazy-jane for whom long-legged youths are swans. She would gaze long at the horizon or at the twin peaks of Broken Mountain as if expecting wonders. The horizon! Whoever else contemplated anything so worthless, indeed imaginary, and, to a capable man, an actual danger concealing Turks and unspeakables, not forgetting Hungarians and French. Clouds also engrossed her; always the fleeting and vague. A busy ruler, like himself, is at ease only with reason, with straight lines, obedient horses, tax returns, dignity, which the Confessor interpreted as the gist of Christ's teaching. Even heathen, crow-swatted Romans had understood that: His Holiness spoke of little else.

He had seen the Gräfin, thinking herself unseen, kissing her own lips in this very mirror; never had she freely kissed him, accepting his own like a peasant greeting demands for just dues.

From curiosity and sanctified but frustrated lust he had once offered her body for one night to a visiting Lombard banker, whose eyes at once glinted like florins but, after one glance at her, he had covertly crossed himself and returned to his balance sheets. As if suspecting an insult, he had, on specious argument, added more to the amount owed him.

Familiarity with his wife, if it could be so called, had only deepened his unease and suspicion. Only with Uncle had she showed some friendliness, and Uncle, smoothing away boredom and dislike, nodded pleasantly when she told him that the Lord's mother could be blamed for being too good for her son's good. It could be said, the Graf indeed had said, that wise Uncle and the foolish Gräfin despised the good sense of Signor Cicero, in jabbering, rapacious Italy, that activity is the whole glory of virtue. The activity of both was negligible; he seldom looked up from his books, never glanced at the world outside, she never allowed herself to produce an heir, however often he turned her over in bed, as God ordained. Such behaviour left him to scatter seed elsewhere. Twice, after a barren struggle, he had dreamt not of joyous love but of four young pigs, very long, very pink, corded together, lumbering helplessly on a cobbled street.

At this, arresting as a single footprint in dust, he at last desisted from the mirror, noosed by a further thought, so harsh that he had to seat himself in the shadows and lower his head.

Victim of her tight, depraved nunnishness, she had appeared to prefer death to banquets, bed, relieving the poor and so on, turning for relief only to songs, scribbles and tricksters. Forbidden to leave her quarters, she had rejected luxuries at times offered, he in turn refusing her rations more ordinary. She existed on air, moonlight and, no diet, a substantial pile of verses, until, praise God the Avenger, he had found her, gaunt, almost bald, stiff with cold before the empty grate, dying within the hour, his bounty, his magnaminity repulsed. She had been about twenty, the noon of Venus, people said.

He had waited some days before announcing that God had summoned her for his own special purposes. During this interval ample meals had been delivered her, which he himself ate. Her funeral had been perfunctory, justified by Lenten fasts, and, these over, black banners removed, the apartment cleared and purged, he had prudently made a penitential journey to a distant cathedral, leaving the Confessor and Clerk to supervise the Castle, under the nominal authority of Uncle. Despite his indolence, von der Goltz, like his junior, was trustworthy, preferring bad justice to no justice, disorder, dissonance. He had once advised pardon for an influential, well-endowed murderer, and the hanging of a youth innocent but with riotous followers who had dared hail him as Christ of Last Days.

Entering the high, misty cathedral, though a nobleman, he had immediately felt lost, insignificant in a night world. Its least adornments travestied reality. A stone tortoise carried a ship's mast, a blindfold lion embraced a mermaid, a cowled fox preached to sheep. He recalled the four elongated pigs in his dream. Kneel in prayer he did not: prayer might contain energies to blow apart cathedrals, but most prayers were vulgar attempts to cross God's hand with silver, and these would smirch his Name and Honour. He had, though, inclined his head to a tooth of St Peter, while noticing that it was somewhat canine.

A man, then, of suffering, plagued by ghosts, the Graf knew that no cock would crow away his dreams of pigs, of a bloody hound chasing the moon, the bleeding head of the boy Conradin, hope of thousands, last of the mighty Hohenstaufen, beheaded by the French, vomit of hell, in Sicily. He had several dreams of a swan, another forecast of death. But whose death? Or did dreams look back?

Throughout last year he had sensed, within the drone of events, in Castle routine, on landscapes over which, as if in further dream, he rode, often alone, that much had halted, was suspended with unspoken expectations that boded ill, like a fear of scorpions that yet might not exist.

The Gräfin's death, he told himself, was no more than a dull void. He had displayed the remorse required by his rank, which heaven would respect. Furthermore, the Confessor had disclosed that to relish one's wife was by no means certain to please God. This should suffice. It did not. Fate's awards defer to none, however honourable. Rumours were now being heard that the Gräfin had been a saint. The slavish and doltish, greedy for miracles, were praying for her return. Miracles, the Graf considered, were respected most by those who never saw them, and most saints had, very enviably, perfected a way of assuring their absolute authority at whatever cost. St Constant had procured harvest at freezing yule-tide, thus ruining numerous fishermen, bankrupting nineteen millers, caused many to die of over-eating, while securing his own glory.

Huddled in indignant despondence, a thin smudge in the gloom, like a forsworn creditor, the Graf sought what he would have reluctantly admitted as salvation.

He encouraged himself not by unrolling a map, mumbling to God about a dead, impertinent woman, appealing to the Emperor or convincing others that he had won glory against the Turks. Leave the dead to bury their dead was a handy precept. The living remained, and there remained one, simultaneously near and far whom, at this instant, with all his power, courage, titles, he could not bring himself to mention, yet who existed in proud light; too proud, but in all truth, light. Like the meanest cowman, latrine drudge, or any clawing for survival on the flatlands so far below, His Excellency the Graf, remotest shadow in his own Castle, a speck in the towering gloom, now resolutely lifted his cold head against all dangers and said aloud the three words by now universal and almost mystical: 'He will come.'

10

A queer, sickly apprehension always followed yule-tide festivities, as if from ashes of forgotten sacrifices. Yet spring flowered as ever, defying glum prophecies, rumours of a new tax that made honest folk cross themselves at the thought of the Sexton and Bailiff. Torches had flared at Candlemas, Feast of Light, by the priest to our Lord and his mother. A wax image of the Virgin, Gatekeeper, Lady of Birth, Guardian of Taurus, of Pasture, had been garlanded, token of green glamour creeping up the mountains from fields starting to glow. Frost had been routed not by priestly spells or Castle edict but by immemorial communal rites, hunger and resentment briefly forgone.

In wood and meadow, nest and hole, in bodies, sap rose, irresistible, wandering students sang, as keys opening the new worlds of blossom and bird-call. In dreams and on the wind the surge was unceasing, a hymn to plenty and increase.

Roads were again astir, with mercenary bands from Italy and Switzerland, margraves and ecclesiastics from the Rhine, merchants from Ulm and Mainz, monastic and banking emissaries, with armed escorts whose slitted casques made them faceless and inhuman. If all these were less numerous than formerly, there were more actors, mountebanks, jobless weavers, radical agitators.

Some great ones demanded hospitality from the Castle, more hastened on, for the Graf's hospitality, though punctilious, was more formal than pleasurable.

Village celebrations lasted four days, belauding the All-Highest Trinity and, for this one season, a shadowy but awesome 'Just as High'. Mountains, the very Castle, were forgotten. In Great Barn, children, freed from work, pranced on crude hobby-horses, clustered to pull apart a bat, tear away a girl's girdle, watch Heiner kick a three-legged cur. They sang to a spider, while destroying its web:

If you seek to live and thrive
Let the spider stay alive.

Under blue sky painted eggs were tossed, circlets of leaf and May blossom were dropped into wells, on to boundary stones and stiles. Clumsy dancers stamping around a tall, beflowered pole bawled of Ostera, the Spring Lady, Virgin's daughter and at night clear, unearthly voices sang from woods. Three naked girls were said to have been watched through dawn mist by youngsters jigger-jaggering with stallion ferocity in see-saw ups and downs while the girls leapt and rolled in dew. Unseen, the witch would be crawling in a circle, casting a wolf shadow on the damp ground, while the breeze blew fresh seeds farther than men sailed or pilgrims ventured.

No precaution or delight was overlooked. Good Friday fennel and salt were rubbed into ploughs, against famine, whilst older folk muttered 'Frigg, Frigg' for Amlothi, son of Teut, a lord of the fresh sun, regularly slain in the grass in wicked times. Certain children were thrashed to fertilize the earth. 'We must make weep the fields.' A pedlar sold 'A Letter from Heaven' to three different women, though he departed before producing it.

For these days the blacksmith was much hailed, thick-bearded, grimed and, though none knew why, feigning a limp. He beckoned girls, who feared to disobey, and was begged by those visibly ready to drop their calves to threaten men into marrying them. Several such marriages he himself performed, according to custom. 'Idle misbehaviour,' the priest muttered, 'blasphemous rogue. Thinks himself Pope.' Horseshoes and iron rings were polished for the blacksmith to bless against Black Things, though, the priest continued, he was one himself.

From the dimmest chimney-seats stole the blinded, hobbled, maimed, some in small carts, wooden blocks strapped to limbs long severed. A sack of live cats was buried by Felon's Stream.

The fair was in Two Shoes Field, youths already whirling fresh-leafed branches assaulting a mock-castle of turf and logs. Scraps from pipe, zither, hurdy-gurdy and drum flaked above shouts and yelps of pain. Mendicants, buffoons, tinkers, pimps

– Keepsake Jacks – swarmed, many from none knew where. Pond-swarm Harrys, Meg If Onlys, Virgin Not Likelys. Villagers paraded in tatterdemalion finery; faded ribbons, freshly lumped coifs, cleaned kerchiefs, brass armlets, painted feathers. Dirty tents had appeared overnight like swollen mushrooms, stalls were heavy with the tawdry, gimcrack, broken, not worth a groat or a kiss. Wonders were yelled on all sides: strips of the tanned skin of the hanged, useful talismans against fever; a swarthy girl without feet or ears was exhibited as an Amazon, chained to a log; also a morsel of Moses' rod which could bend and stiffen at will, provoking many jests. In a booth striped with purple, smeared with foreign lettering, sat a learned sow that could read through her feet and count with her head, and compared by a stable-boy on leave from the Castle to His Excellency, Uncle. Capering in and out of small, jabbering crowds was a figure in a donkey's head pursued by a live skeleton with nose-bone long as a dagger, the pair, now in chase, now dancing arm in arm, gaped at by the Ants, Jackdaws, Scarcely Seens, Big Hildes, and imitated by Heiner and Johannes, Lords of May.

But Lords of May were insufficient. 'There must be a king,' young voices clamoured. 'King of the Green.'

The Ant waved a crumpled hand, shrilled madly, until cuffed by Broken-Tooth Heinrich, who, over-satisfied, scuffled with Johannes Ox-Face who knuckled his fist and jammed it into him, to much delight. Some older people had repeated the earlier demand. A king was necessary in a custom-bound region. For this one gap in the year the children ruled, ready to elect the bravest fighter, richest copy-holder, the blacksmith, even the Miller. Such names were at once bawled, yet all were disputed, howled at with increasing impatience, each raucously shouted down. Change was in the air, spring promise, with expectations vague as the Indies but as tempting. Finally the Stinger, pale, aggrieved at the perpetual ascendancy of Heiner and Johannes, risked a cry: 'Silly Hans! Hans for King!'

Unexpectedly the clamour wavered, then stilled. Startled, the

Lords of May glared at their followers, then at each other, and all looked around for Albrecht, their elders puzzled, oddly submissive, and at once he was seen, in a porch apart, in his fine shoes and dainty coat, high-boned features as always coolly reserved, thoughtful as a master mason preparing to instruct an emperor.

Ah, Albrecht! If the Saviour arrived, in wrath and extravagance, Albrecht would be there awaiting him; he would dispense that faint smile and remind him, with innate courtesy, that he was a trifle late.

His approval was eagerly sought, though most were braced for that trim brown head to shake dissent, but, as if hearing nothing, absorbed in his delicate thoughts delivered in neatly winged language, he made no sign, so that at once old and young were turned to his composed, negligent form, his face neither very young nor old, one hand dangling a feathered cap, which, though soiled, resembled that worn by so many of those who grandly rode from the Castle.

With the silence about to break apart, Albrecht, as though recollecting something, forestalled it with a gracious nod so that, as if at a shot, the shouts started: 'Hans for King', 'Hurrah for Hans the Piper'.

Hearts must have changed, joined New Times indistinctly prophesied from a Bremen soothsayer with mutters about 'A Thor-headed great one', and many remembered that hoary, jovial, outsize Thor had been red-headed, red-handed, red-souled.

Albrecht had disappeared but the larger boys, cross-bred bruisers, were scampering to the sheepfold where, seated amongst his trusting flock, was Hans, absurd, incomplete, the babbler. He had already jumped up, arm timidly raised, ready to ward off the stones and torments, and the fleeing sheep were quickly white distant blobs. But the faces, rough, inflamed, were yet friendly, glad: Big Hilde, at her heels dirty, stumpy Grete, was holding out a band of plantain and clover, those behind bowing in mock-solemnity, exhilarated in the merry reversals of springtide.

'King Hans . . . the King. . . .'

He stood in their centre, crowned, pleased but not wholly astonished, hearing no mockery or threats within the plaudits. He knew his secret beauty, his visions that could enchain them. The flowery prince killed in the thicket, the wanton princess of glass country, the Green Stone showering lights. His smile was weak, but he was neither timid nor grateful, accepting his acclaim like tribute. His under-sized blockishness, probably louse-bound, his uncouth, blatant head, his spotty face and small eyes were the disguise once worn by God himself to avoid blinding the world. Did not the dwarf crush the giant, the last of all win the chalice?

Rapidly, hilariously, he was escorted to the noisy fair, welcomed with stolid greetings, awkward but elaborate obeisances. Urged on by the children, villagers shoved him pots of ale, cheering as, with his chaplet jauntily crooked, he blinked, gulped, choked, swayed slightly, gulped again, a squat St Bacchus. In the half-drunken medley of sensations his head was no longer a blistered carrot but Thor's gold, Asa-treasure. Dazed, gratified, he was suddenly thrilled by the sight of no less than Albrecht, almost within reach, standing in quiet, imprecise complicity. Everyone recognized this. Hans, in his worn jerkin and bare legs, was a grotesque parody of whatever was so indisputably possessed by Albrecht, thus linked, as beauty and ugliness, saint and devil, maiden and monster are linked, bound together by necessity of complete being.

Cheers rebounded. Hans's eyes, part of his messy grin, brimmed with fealty to Albrecht, in whose light he grew in stature, submerged his spots, his inane grin on a loose mouth. At Albrecht's unspoken will he was showered with tributes from those usually callous, envious, fiendish. Now, as they stripped him, they praised his lovable shape, willowy limbs, the girls screaming at his top-heavy balls and incongruously lengthy dingle-dangle, woodpecker in a russety bush. Swiftly draped in green strips, bespattered with blossoms and hedge-drift, he chanted tunelessly as they rushed him to Dancers' Wood, leaving the sheep to regather cautiously at the old stoop. There, as was the custom, in a grove glossy with sunlight, they left him.

At sundown they returned, more rowdily, many ale-sodden, half-filled John-o-plentys, festooned with leaves, banging pots, waving cloths, the wood resounding with hunting cries, urges like the dance of gnats, at one with the lewd rhymes and puns of the season. A few, swaying as if blind, attempted to dance an Easter carol, soon collapsing, exhausted, laughing, then joining the others in song.

> *Hans, Hans, King of the Spring*
> *Pull down your breeches and let it swing.*
> *Count, Count, Count of Desire*
> *Count your desires,*
> *Hans the Green*
> *Must have his Queen.*

Queens enjoy spunk, they chorused, let them drink deep.

He was soon tracked down, dozing, still crowned, under a tree, soggy with ale almost always refused him, but happily stirring, to receive them as a hero should, gobbling their wild friendship. They hoisted him on a blind donkey, its neck covered with daisies and dandelions, and led him out of the trees back across fields to the gaudy lights, over chilling grass under the darkening sky. From the Waude Oak, standing alone on waste ground, leapt a Black Thing, charred, tailed, furred, easily recognized as Ploughboy Fritz, and then routed by the yelling troupes. Hideous winter, farewell.

At Waude Oak, though they were too hectic to remember, wide, antique, though flourishing with new leaf, no name could be spoken, for reasons which, even if known, must be kept secret. Old women held that it was the centre of the earth, and at night it sometimes faintly gleamed, bluish and white, even without a moon. On such a night, doors were bolted but gates left open. For this night, however, each child knew that he himself was the centre of the earth, and several shouted 'Hans, Hans' as they sped by.

At the little fairground more tumult surged. A considerable crowd parted to receive them, waving torches, many in roughly assembled horsehair steeple-hats. A young moon floated across the deepening violet sky. 'What a fine hoof-flinger,' they anthemed the donkey, 'he earns his holy oat', before, led by a squad of older people, greetings swept up for the Dandelion King, the mob turned away to fill the nearby churchyard. A drum, its thuds a controlled riot, sounded from the arched doorway, from which a chipped old gargoyle grinned as very much part of the game. The uproar would muffle the priest's maledictions as, in riotous baptism, more ale was offered the king, greedily accepted, the small flushed face at once looking about for applause.

Under the torch flames people were boarish, even tusked, hands swollen, feet monstrous, the church dimmed yet haughty behind them. Many had one eye blocked by a black patch, an allusion to some story long since lost, yet wordlessly lingering like a spectre drooped over a grave. Renewed shouts struck at the blacksmith, broad and swart, like Lord Herod in a mummer-play, beard as sooty and shaggy as his speech, as he limped with grinning ostentation, mantled in black and red, towards Hans, now seated on an upturned gleaner's cart.

Aloft on a tomb, he brandished a smelting-iron, his coarse voice lunging through all of them. 'Choose your Queen, Excellence. Frigg. Venus. Best-belov'd. Bed-toy.'

They chorused encouragements.

'Oats and barley for a queen . . .'

'The virgins stuck with a waiting hole.'

Under the jackanapes moon, attracting the dank stare of the dead, now lit by flame, now phosphorescent in a mirk of darkness, the donkey-head and skeleton still pranced, now separate in rivalry, now entwined, parodying stately Castle dances in a prolonged jeer at life, sardonic doubts of existence. Then movement ceased, belches, callow gestures, exclamations were reined in, waiting for Hans. Distorted by the rank lights, taller than usual, head like massed sores, he stammered, in tones churlishly assertive or defiant.

'I . . . choose . . . Queen . . . Grete.'

Thrust forward, scared, bewildered, gratified, the little mute stood with him, shouts resuming as he grabbed her hand as he might a bun, the donkey nosing and prodding between them, then nodding, as if accepting the din for himself.

The stammerer and the mute. Verily, the last shall be first.

Jollities mounted. Birch twigs burnt against witches, children leaping naked through the fire, dancers impassioned, leaping higher and higher as though the ground was too hot, their rags in the quivering glare transformed to glitter. Lord Herod married two couples behind a thorn-bush, broomstick lying between them, and demanded a lord's right to bridal access, which, genially enough, he did not get. He was said to have later coupled two aliens, a pedlar and a gippy lad.

In Great Barn rye loaves, black biscuits, honey-smeared scraps of pork, more ale and quickset brandy lay on trestles, the jittery candles making them appear more ample and lustrous. On benches girls swarmed about prone, barely conscious men. Still ahead was a promise of blood: that of torn, baited dogs, their ears sliced off and stuffed with stolen pepper, distributed to the hungry; the goat's horns sawn away, ground to powder, for love philtres. In reeking fumes the revellers, bondsmen and copyholders, latrine-ghouls and whores, goodmen and hen-wives, stupefied, over-loaded, vomiting, a swarm of pot-house bellies, ploughed-up cheeks, gummy eyes, blubber-lips, blained fingers, were rocked by drink and lust, blown by a dream of luxuriant hours far from the impoverished, rancid, threatened. Music aroused songs and hoots. When looking up they could discern, in a deranged medley of broken-off insets, fumy, dishevelled light, lamplit fantasies, the inert, tilted figures of Hans and Grete, throned aloft in Mayfly time, dollish, barely sensate, at times as though jerked by hands not their own.

11

In the wake of spring people sagged back into drudgery, the pains of back and knee, the whip, the red groans of birth. And worse. The long expected punishment for existing. The snot-infested Master Wilhelm proclaimed to all feudatories, petty tenants, stewards and elders that all in the Castle's domains must deliver the new tax, the one-eighth.

Over the valleys protests raged, less to the unassailable Castle than to heaven. Wails ascended Broken Mountain and Virgin-blue skies; sumptuous leaves and foamy blossom were naught. A resplendent harvest, a light gust of fish, were liabilities overnight. Old men pleaded, women grovelled and wept, children chucked dung, chanted insults, but Master Wilhelm on his black stallion rode them down and was said to have bought Scots archers to reinforce the men-at-arms, and flayed an outspoken journeyman.

Little work was done that week. Under the Castle, which in early mists floated soundless and inexorable between black trees and summer sky, men loitered at gates, collected beneath walls, gathered in pine woods and behind the alehouse. They grumbled, then cursed, as though obscenities foul enough to blind the Virgin's ma would demolish oppression, and dispatch Black Things into the Castle. More often they stood staring, baleful but hopeless at the mud.

Their women, bulging, prematurely lined and scarred, had rare spasms of tenderness, hearty or wistful pleas for love, for the lilt of the wild rose or the mendicant's wink, the brother-in-law's grab for a tumble, a 'straw marriage'. In resistance to the Tax they were no help, and help could be nowhere expected. The Emperor was as invisible as God, and both High Gentlemen loved taxes.

The idle week ended when, one warm, cornflower forenoon, led by the Bailiff, Castle overseers, horsed, dark and harsh as miners, strange men of the earth, drove the men back to work. Tufted, red-eyed, snouted, toad-souled, Master Wilhelm uttered hoarse imprecations, reminding them that the Castle Horse awaited malcontents and that the Ostler had complained of under-employment.

Opposition was futile. Within these slabbed, laboriously hewed faces, the sullen eyes and grooved, gristled hides, was conviction that God's hands scalded, were merciless to rebels. Also, that behind him was something else, inexpressible, a cloud heavy with inert but live thunder. A slaughterhouse providence which had overcome sweet intentions of Jesus. Such are the ways of fate. Out of the priest's hearing some called this *Orlog*, which identified nothing but, being a word, must be true.

Their young, however, were less easily mastered. They could not remember the last revolt: the gibbets, braziers, stabbings.

Cowed throughout long, monotonous winter, then excited by the spring japes and delirium, they could flush into helter-skelter moods vivid as plum-stains and free of the Castle and its eternal Graf. They had no concern with the Tax, and that cakeship the Sexton, robber master of the all-powerful Bailiff. Their fathers' agitation pleased rather than worried them. Scattering at the Bailiff's hoof-trots, they quickly regathered, sneering at his thick back, daring each other to chuck stones, betting on the behaviour of his horse's rump.

Few could easily explain a tax, save that it was a sort of theft, pictured as nails hammered into life by the Castle, goading Father into extravagant rages and beatings, and digging deeper into Mother's face. If you dwelt with pigs, were at close quarters with hunger and death, you owed taxes.

The children had little with which to find succour. Albrecht, as so often, had not been seen since the May crownings, absorbed in his unimaginable secrets, and, without him, his followers were disconsolate, adrift, despite loud, brawny Heiner and Johannes, who could easily tread them into the grass. Albrecht could not, but that this feat would never occur to him made him the more powerful. They gave only kicks, slaps, crack-arm behind the shed; Albrecht bestowed his brief, superior, small and indifferent smile, and won adoration and a little fear.

The girls hovered in a single group, noosed by unfailing curiosity but keeping out of danger, committing themselves to smiles but fleeing bruises. Amongst them was Grete; her sunshine reign was over, if not quite forgotten. Whatever she was thinking, she remained as before, plodding away with bits of food for Hans. As his favourite, she might indeed have the privilege of a bird who sees into heaven but can divulge nothing.

Early summer heat slowly baked the earth, tied down stones, stilled the trees, split timber. The river sank, lazily trickling towards seas known only in Hans's tales. Prayers for rain had already been sent upalong, to damp-eyed St Swithold, fossicking in paradise amongst languid angels naked though without charms. Grievance brooded over the valleys, smouldering but ineffective, about that tithe to the Devil, the Tax.

71

'That stew-faced Wilhelm . . .'

'His mam was a fart from the north wind.'

'He . . . and those others. A waste of eyesight.'

All life was listless, purposeless torment. Mountains, Castle and woods reduced men to insects crawling beneath the flinty stare of Jesus the Judge on a hell-bound earth. New Times might come with 1500, but no sign of them flickered over sick faces propped on huge, obedient bodies, no sky-pattern unravelled to convulse the world. Given his approaching chance to put his hand to the plough, the Holy Ghost would find the ground very rough.

Children overheard fathers and uncles, leered, spat, sped away, grouped now at the pump, now at a stile, lured by some image that readily dissolved at their approach. They stood, hesitant, awry, tensed. At any moment they would be rounded up for digging, carrying, cutting, and for the lash. They were nerved to savage each other in this large, yellowy emptiness in which mountain and wood, thatch and wall interrupted nothing, were no more than parts of the drowsy, dreamless suspense clamped on the plain from which colours were slowly draining, save the parched and rusted, the air itself ceasing to quiver. The young, wizened by the glare, hemmed in by what could be felt but not seen, tightened helplessly, with no bird to stone, no beggar to chase.

Desperate to win favour from Heiner and Johannes, Dolf, farrier's cast-off, called out 'Hans'. The usual remedy. That sheep-minder, sheep-witted thing! But though browned, scraped faces looked up, their response was feeble. No one looked for a stone, bramble-switch, cowpat. Life, still vile, was not quite as before: the delirious flash that had crowned him Spring King had not wholly subsided, still lighting their uneasy awareness that the red, unshapely head, demon-shot though it might be, had poked into uncanny realms known to none else save, very possibly, Albrecht: the far, far away, past Anthony Cleop, Archduke of Egypt, past Babylon built of gold where the giant tree grows anew each dawn, filling the sky with a blackness that overflows into the night of our German Empire, despite the Emperor's efforts.

As though agreeing, piping called them from the fields; low,

dreamy, elfin, now faltering, now climbing, never wholly mastered, never surrendering. Familiar, it was yet reassuring, and,
in herd unison, they spread themselves on dusty grass, to listen.
Ugly shapes and sizes, they were far from grace, but, silenced,
under a sun massive and brazen as Asia, they were hearing not
beauty, not hope of succour, but again the unworded, the signal
from that *far away* which might summon them as if by a torch
from the dead.

Fimbul terrors, which even the Pope's stockings would never
warm, make you breathe badly, causing boils and bad dreams.
Fear was astir in the valleys. The deafest churl, even Grete,
knew that a high, unpainted carriage, shuttered, drawn by a
pale horse gaunt as rib-bones, had been seen simultaneously
in villages leagues apart. It harboured that other tax-gatherer,
Death. Inevitably, a crop of demises followed, which summer
calm could not avert. Five horses were killed by lightning in
the same field; a healthy young woman, skilled cheese-maker,
was found dead, though unmarked, on a bridge. This gave Prince
Narr cause to snigger. Dapper in the sunlight, blue-cloaked, one
leg scarlet, the other green, he recalled another trick he had seen
played by Death.
　'There were three sisters, as there so often are. A hundred
years ago? Two hundred?' He smiled, over some secret. 'God
alone knows and, as in so much else, has ceased to care. One
sister died, smiling, caressing herself, in her youth and beauty.
Her body lay on its bier, turning jaundice-yellow, as might be
expected. Well now, keeping watch over it, waiting to observe
the soul escape like a bird, butterfly or, I grant you, bee, all
precious little in the blank gaze of eternity . . . were her two
sisters, who had much prized her beauty. Nothing else, she
had only this to prize. Many have less. Fearful of demons, they
barred the door. But they were as brainless as birds, butterflies
and, yes indeed, bees, for they had imprisoned both the soul
and themselves. Neither one soul, nor two, nor three, beat itself
against oblivion and mortality, for the door remained shut, they

dared not open it, so died of want and lack of wit. For many months the three bodies lay there, mouldering, and as for their souls, there was probably nothing at all. A tale of love and death and folly, no longer than the silence of an April cuckoo, as a tale should be.'

Nobody laughed or offered a gift and, offended, Prince Narr stalked away to repeat it to Uncle, always appreciative of words deftly and truthfully assembled.

Dirty children below were, with no deftness, quarrelling about the Green Stone, avoiding, when possible, homes raddled with drunken angers at the Tax, Father breaking a jar on an infant's head, Mam cursing a hen that refused to lay. Heiner's ham-boned face under its matted clump was strenuous in unaccustomed defence of Hans. 'He told us it throws light. Falls on . . . what it chooses. There!'

Johannes Ox-Face, stubble glinting, bristling, cheeks florid as August, grumbled, 'Where's light? How's it done? Eek!'

'Eek'. The Stinger stood on tiptoe. A few gibes were heard, and cowhand oaths, until a shout from behind a stack called them to work. Heads lowered, a brief resolution gone, they slunk back into unremitting heat.

By sundown, however, their need to dispute, to stand big, had returned. Their minds were slow yet fickle, liable to sudden change by incidents trivial but provocative. Barely heard, yet unmistakable as curfew, bells had sounded from none knew where, a warning or summons. They helped in what, years afterwards, was remembered as the Pot Roast.

Joined by most of the girls marshalled by Big Hilde, the cow-girl, without spoken orders but urged by some undeclared purpose, the boys had drifted to Great Barn, nearer the mountains than the village, from which it was invisible. On the mass of beams, clay and thatch sparrows twittered, the stork nested and owls called, surrounded by untended grass. The building had once served a hamlet long since destroyed and was now abandoned to the covert and forbidden: night strippings and explorings, furtive killing, occasional offerings in rites best unimagined; a circumcision that, starting as a game, a gippy pretending to be

74

Jesus able to transform piss to wine or perch on a sunbeam, ended in gruesome blood.

With fifty or so children gathered outside Great Barn, night stole from the mountains, warm and moonless, the stars sharp, one occasionally flaring downwards before vanishing behind the mountains. The Barn, within a very wide field unevenly fenced by a hedge of bramble and pollarded larch, reared like a gloomy fortress, its slanting roof touched with starlight like the adjoining stream; its doors long shattered, the interior dense with dry husk-smells and folds of dinginess. Amongst the shadows moving around it was Albrecht, at first unnoticed, then, by merely standing quiet, he imposed a hush, completing the occasion, everyone seeking a chance to obey.

He said nothing, but his presence at once gave impetus. Unless he forbade it, all was permitted, even the bullies strove for his attention. In the near-darkness his expression was hidden yet extraordinarily encouraging. Hurriedly some bundles were unwrapped, Heiner extracting a jar of tarry substance, several showed flints, the Jackdaw a bag of shavings.

'Ah-h.'

Fumbles, an impatient cry, then delight and the south end was smoking, with a rapidity that scared and transfixed them, then, renewing their greed for sensation, already the Barn was sheeted with flame. Roofed with dry turf, packed with a residue of dead seasons, the old structure burned easily, fiercely, flames leaping along rafters, striking, gulping, in giddy hopscotch as the revellers stumbled in through eddying smoke-plumes, standing appalled, triumphant. Above them birds and bats, shrilling in panic, were dim, spiralling shreds chased by fires and pallid cowls of fume, many falling choking and in agony into the furnace. Wonder changed to mirth at a sparrow, in terrified flight, shrivelling in its own fire.

At the first crash all rushed to safety, whistling and cheering. All Great Barn was aflame, reviving the thrills of watching Father cut a pig's throat, the blood spurting like piss. All around, the air was swelling, gusty with sparks and scarlet shadows, in carnival frenzy. Thuds, small explosions, moans and hissings raced with

75

the flames, in which some would claim to have seen queer shapes, transparent, mottled, wavy. Flowers, snakes, towers, a grin, a vast tooth soaring, gnawing, crumbling, as smoke blazed and the sky reeled aside. By himself, at a distance from the blasts of heat, the spitting timbers, satanic lights, Albrecht watched.

The younger were capering in giddy craziness, joining hands with the red night, with the streaming, blazing pyre fiercer than stars, pouring themselves into the fears that intoxicate, that dazzle with the blood of others in a world without grafs. They were giants, horse-headed Black Things, they could dance for ever. An Albrecht could perhaps sense a magician's flourish transforming tatters and decay, the half-devoured, the fiefdom of woodlouse and mushroom that feeds on rot, to unearthly purity.

Heiner, with others running from one end of the fire to the other, then shouted an obscenity against the enemy, not Great Barn, but the Tax. The others groaned, yelled, made erratic sword-passes. 'The Tax. . . .' May devils drink out of its eye.

Grete had been dancing alone, gravely, deep in herself, but, as the roof finally collapsed, to demented, rippling whoops and alarums, the sight of her reminded them that, despite Albrecht's impassive, guardian presence, their company was incomplete. Spontaneously, voices sounded the clarion, all mockery gone:

'The Piper . . . The Piper King . . . the Piper.'

12

From a village, mountain slopes, the Castle, people had seen the sky bloom infernal petals, heard screams and the rush of a blistering wind. At morning Great Barn, familiar for so long, was a blackened heap. Only the thick, irregular hedge had been out of reach of the fire.

Early rumours insisted that it had been destroyed on orders from the Graf, impatient with nocturnal meetings, conspiracies, the politics of stealth. Quickly, however, missing faces betrayed the truth, or some of it, though townsfolk far off heard that angels had swooped to destroy the godless, that children, bewitched by a piper, drunken on fungus and on broom-tea, had broken their necks in attempts to climb into heaven, deluded by extra but imaginary arms and legs.

No child dared return home, even the swaggerers finding excuses to remain by the ruins, Albrecht still with them. Though exhausted, many were too restless for sleep, continuously reliving the momentous dance of flame. The stars paled and dawn glimmered, but they still boasted, began songs, dozed a little until, the sun clearing the mountains, shadows leaping free, they rose, looked about them, sniffed the ashy air, contemplated the still smoky wreckage and groped in a changed world, in which fears could not stifle muddled hopes. Beyond them, they realized, nothing had changed. The mountains, the ogrish Castle, woods and pasture, their homes, save for smoke, visible only on exceptional days when no wind blew from the heights.

They were relieved to find that Albrecht had remained, taller than any, stronger, by grace of being, blue fixity of eye, fair brows which, if raised very slightly, could condemn the most brutal of them. He was sitting on his cloak, unperturbed, comfortable, as though but just arrived from some scented arbour.

He was graciously familiar, surprisingly responsive. Now on his feet, he was the decisive leader in what was not yet ascertainable.

'You will need all you can find. Spades, stones, an axe, plenty of wood. Anything to strengthen the hedge. Also pots, knives, anything that holds water, cuts, binds together. Poles too. And, when it's dark, food. Crawl in and grab whatever you can. . . .'

His manner was calmly assured, incapable of rashness, he might have been planning a holy day festivity. His face, under dressed, glistening hair, was like the signed warrant that can reduce a rebellious province to obedience and terrify a traitor. He added, negligently: 'You must defend your Troy.'

Troy. Depthless archaic name, or magic password hung with half-tales, midnight dreams, ill-recollected challenges. *Troy*, headland or chasm, place of giants, or sonorous names – Alexander, Hector, Charlemagne, Siegfried and Brunhild – overcome by no mortal but by an enchanted horse. *Troy*, undying after thousands of years.

They clamoured, shook fists, exchanged amiable blows until, stilling them with a glance, Albrecht smiled. 'A dance is best led by a piper.'

Within an instant they recollected their outburst as the Barn fell and the fire scattered. They understood. They chanted, 'Can we get him?' And several were already speeding up the mounds, down towards Dancers' Wood where Hans lay with his beasts, mouth open, eyes closed.

Hands pulled him up. 'Albrecht's sent us. He wants you. Albrecht himself.'

He looked at them, smiled foolishly, then whispered, 'Albrecht'. Summons of love, deliverance. Everyone nodded. The name, uttered aloud, made Albrecht one of themselves. Grete's grubby face was straining to break from her silence, her eyes besought. When Hans had rounded up the sheep, he was led back into the exuberant commotion where scavenging, stacking and ranging were being hurried forward for the defence of Troy.

Tousled, bare-legged, his smock torn, Hans stood before Albrecht as before a vizier. Unsmiling, features carved very distinct, the leader said nothing, but Hans shook with childish joy, giving a short, ugly laugh when Johannes gave him a bow, ordering him to shoot an arrow at the sky, for luck.

Hans shot. The arrow trailed to a surprising height, vanishing in brightness. Albrecht, missing nothing, retained mature, reflective approval. Unexpectedly, Hans heard himself addressed by the young gentleman of affairs: 'Guard the sheep.' The cool eyes looked past him. 'They too will be needed.'

By sunset, many poles had been sharpened: grass, mud, stones, thrust into the hedge, had started a rampart. Some bread and dirty ale had been collected. Nothing threatened from Castle or village. A small fire was made. What else was needed but a story? They thronged about Hans, begging and, as ever when they favoured him, he grew in stature, was fluent, part of warm, thriving Trojan earth.

Backed by a heap of stakes that slanted outwards from thorn

and branch, the children sat round the fire, night enclosing them, with all else but Troy discarded, reduced to magpie sameness: parents, Bailiff, bleeding shoulders and buttocks, the Tax, were absorbed into the lively radiance, that of the Green Stone itself, the crystal of longing. They sat agog for Hans, the changeling who had grown from nothing to something, whose hair was dangerous but who had powers very close to those of Albrecht, as a trudging, defenceless harpist can yet stand upright before a baron. Before Troy, such a being as Hans had named the trees and flowers Bride's Skirt, Mishmash, Old Men of the Earth, Bareskin, Flock-Shade, Nix Nought, Waude Oak, and pulled stories from rock and shit and bubble. He performed no miracles but his tongue could let fall magic colours.

Hans was secure, feeling his authority, aware that Albrecht could hear him. In singsong accent, sly complicity, holding his pipe as though measuring his achievement, he began taming savages, quickening life, as if stone and wood would rise at his words and verily build Troy.

'God made 'isself into a bird, a flyabout. 'e thurt another thurt, made 'isself int' an egg. Egg was 'ot, very 'ot, 'otter than fiercest trees in old 'ell. Then egg burst. Ten thousand bits an' shivers.'

His over-large mouth twisted happily, he treasured some remote but jewelled occasion. The breathing forms around him sighed with content, trained on him, not daring to distract him, with no thoughts for other than the bird, the egg, and hell.

'Ten thousand o' them. From then, did ye know, flew up whatever's in the world. My sheep . . .' – he fondled a rough, fleecy head beside him – 'bees an' leaf, water, dragons.' He giggled craftily. 'Girls, don't forget . . . silly bits an' all afright of what they see, an' 'unkin' friars.' Transported, his skin looked seamed, scheming, part of *at one time*, anxious to forget nothing, fervid for importance, for disclosures which struck delicious shivers, exclamations of wonder. 'Beasts had great wings, they went there, they went there, to one day when they rushed together, there was thunder, louder than thunder, like the mountains doin' it, and, see it, 'ear it, they get smaller, smaller, smaller than berries, than

79

seeds, and are all back in an egg, today cold, tomorrow 'otter than old 'ell. . . .'

13

The province was becalmed, the respite of summer. Untroubled skies looped the peaks, the Castle no longer the baleful storm-cloud but radiant, benevolent all-father.

Yet within the sky much might be watching while men laboured, swilled, lusted, waited until darkness to spy on the truants' absurd encampment, from which, however, nothing could be seen save the long dark rampart, behind which rabble-mouth songs were heard, occasional orders, also deeper tones that none could identify.

A few villagers recalled the fearsome Frederick II Hohenstaufen denouncing Moses, Jesus, Mahomet as wily impostors, enslaving all Sicily and paying children to report on their parents. Cursing, they trooped back, refusing to answer questions from women and inquisitive strangers, the last more numerous than usual and untrustworthy. People thrive on signs, rituals, whispers, daily enlarged and distorted as if by Venetian mirrors clutched by sleepers.

A Castle armourer announced at Midsummer that King Alexander had been seen. When? None knew. Where? Somewhere. Everywhere. Soon every tongue in the region was chattering about virgin-born Alexander, scorched Asia's charioteer, invincible, from whom even Turks sought cover. Alexander, now amongst them, who had flown to the top of the sky, sank in an enchanted boat to the ocean's depths. A flip of his beard had routed thousands.

Life was sustained not only by what was, but by what was not, like the magic Grail of the knights, like Jerusalem, the princess sleeping in a maze of thorns, like the Green Stone. And now, all were exchanging absurd tales of mischievous children calling themselves Trojans.

Few suspected that the Graf was taking notice. In the Castle, the makeshift camp had first attracted only high-nosed ridicule. Some bastards of impious pudding-creatures, crowding in armpit squalor in a rickety toy fortress, were travestying their grandfathers' rebellion. The Graf, however, had not laughed. He was withdrawn and glum, having found in his bed a strip of willow. What of it? Remember, that pernicious tree signifies love rejected or mislaid. Neither maps nor sealed documents solaced him, nor the candied jibes of Prince Narr, the Confessor's texts, which showed Jesus roundly cursing all families, which must include children whom he might have loved but more probably feared . . . nor Uncle's mellifluous chuckles. Goaded by vulgar, exaggerated report of unruly manikins, sleepless from that other unpleasantness, he thought it best to summon advisers, without seeking their advice.

'I shall,' he addressed them as if charging them with indolent lack of foresight and valour, himself showing unwonted resolution worthy of his ancestry, that majestic procession of grafs, 'take these affairs into my own hands.'

This prompted an aside from Prince Narr, which he ignored, and he quickly ordered the Fighting Commandant to select the best oiled bows, heaviest bolts, most seasoned archers and the most swaggering, moustachioed men-at-arms, then await his pleasure. Ladies, barely visible within recesses, under dim arches, glanced at each other, uneasy yet also inflamed. They too could find a use for their own hands.

For a while nothing further was known to occur. The armed men remained expectant but leashed. One could only wait, imagine a harvest ripe for cutting . . . slicings, castrations . . . imagine the Ostler rehearsing his knots. There was talk of a sheep's shoulder-blade dropping into a fire and showing cracks that showed the future. But what was it? None could say, as if there were no future. Undeniable, however, was the Graf's good humour, his confident step and brisk manner. Some thought he had received a secret message, the Confessor was convinced he had, though was reluctant to speak of it.

*

The Trojans had forgotten the Graf. They skipped and sang, grinned at saws teasing with double meanings – four skins make sausages, old fellows foul the nest, Squire Stand-up in his peaked cap drops into the velvet cup. Around them, under Leo, in superb summer, the camp had already swollen, its tremors had penetrated the outlands where for so long discontented cottagers, shamble-fellows, pigfeed vagrants, donkey-drivers, nightsoil carcase-wights, had obeyed the overseers, morosely, bitterly, looking only to the sky and the grave for escape, mistrusting sermons about 1500 and conspiratorial exchanges concerning New Times, which were of no more value than Friendly Ones, huddled by marsh or flitting in mountains and seldom friendly to mortals.

The camp, this Troy, however magnified in the telling, promised more. It appealed to the blood, it hinted at vengeance, in a challenge to dare all. Its call was more downright than that of Holy Church, though perhaps Jesus had been forerunner of New Times.

Trojans now ate at common tables, sharing bread, cress, sausage in criss-cross unity, without tax or whip. They ventured outside with impunity, scorning thoughts of home, noisily welcoming the growing import of strangers. First to seek entry were two gippies, horse-robbers, with long black hair like Poitevens, eyes bright and black-slitted in blacksmith skin; dead flies under their fingernails, as millers say, and they were slung with small, metal pots, at once commandered for the whole camp, as Albrecht had ordered. They were soon showing deftness at snaring rabbits and fish. To confuse demons they had secret names, then delighted the children by wearing rings in their beards and by showing themselves circumcised, allowing the curious, Hans to the fore, to finger the blue, gristly vein leading to the red, tilted mushroom. To much giggling, Big Hilde hung a shell on it.

There soon followed hungry Bohemian runaways, several students from Ulm with intentions unknown and bags stuffed with pamphlets, many with strident, vindictive woodcuts. These caused suspicion until Albrecht, for whom a small shed had already been erected, covered with fresh ivy, explained that books could trap words but also release them, which contented the worried ones, and he was soon conversing with the students on rare matters.

Albrecht's poise, merging the casual and the mannered, never faltered: like Parsifal with his charm, or the Graf never relinquishing his Evil Eye, he required neither bludgeon nor dagger to exert mastery.

More arrivals. Wanderlust felons, geniuses of dream, escapee prentices, gaunt scavengers, jobless suppliants were grateful for refuge, all fleeing perils seldom confessed, or confessed truthfully. Many had seen sights and events more extraordinary than child rebels and an aristocratic youth, courteous but ambiguous. Meanwhile, food was steaming, older girls could probably be lured by beads, bracelets or even less. They set themselves to be agreeable. One revealed himself as a surgeon-barber, able to remove boils and knock out teeth; another was a master baker. They acknowledged Albrecht, accepted Hans as an oddity, a mascot natural to such a place, understood 'Troy' without mockery, took their turn at sentry-go, latrine-digging, building shelters, refrained from rivalry and quarrels, joined in with the singing and story-telling, and agreed that the place was like a nun's temptation. They winked, giving jovial laughs.

Across the land, folk envisaged this Troy as a fortress, sanctuary for angry marsh-dwellers, club-men, mountain bandits, some with women fierce and brawny as themselves. They were not wholly mistaken. The square hedge, now a sturdy rampart of mud, stone and wood, with ditch and enclosing a brook, within a fortnight had attracted over two hundred, many armed. Tents, rickety lean-to cabins, trestle-tables, crowded yellowing grass: to the solitary elder shaking out leaves in the warm breeze several horses were usually tied. Donkeys, and great dogs, roamed, nosing and scuffling. Tramps, chipped and bald, left over from fabled expeditions against Turks, sat good-humouredly explaining the mechanics of crossbow and pistol, the technique of feint and stabbing. Children were engrossed with such voyagers from afar, were awed by missing hands, strapped-up legs, empty sockets, gashed cheeks, tokens of wild adventure, and saw themselves as tyro Attilas, Siegfrieds, von Etterheims, even, a fancy from

83

this torrid month, as sultans, while, out of sight, Albrecht was winged Alexander planning the breakthrough. At ease with all, he was familiar with none: his tones, his high stance, kept distance, yet his smile appeared grateful for favours from natural inferiors. Coolly supervising those thrice his age, he devised activities for the entire camp, so that by sunset, after devouring newly received eggs, honey, dried eel, berries, carrots, beans, the swigging of ale and milk nightly stolen, most were glad to slump on to palliasse or sacking, while guards stared from the rampart, weapons ready.

Albrecht suggested that bark should be stripped from Dancers' Wood to lay on wounds. Recruits were brought to him, and, with intonations precisely measured, he learnt that here was a thatcher, here some who could caulk, daub, plane, cook, entwine for rope. Wooden shafts and blades were being fashioned from ash, toughened by abstruse smearings. Hearing Hans speak of the Waude Oak, powerful Centre of the World, stronger than an Erman column, a burly freebooter who spent most nights foraging returned with a branch of it, and staked it against lightning, misfortune and a famed Evil Eye.

Meals were more plentiful than in the rag-and-bone days; noisy plungings, grabbings, gobblings from those to whom forks were as alien as confession. Darkened villages were scoured, travellers waylaid, the brook ran untroubled. There were also the sheep, though these had to be taken while Hans slept or roamed. Unable to count them, he knew them by name, and snivelled when he missed one, though a crop of new lambs soothed him. He was like the others, befuddled in happiness, clapping when brought a baked apple, a hunk of cheese, a carving, though, once presented with a butterfly, brilliant but dead, he was stricken with sudden grief, with angry, stuttering reproaches, so that all fled in terror. That he had once been their scorn, their butt, the idiot, was already forgotten. Never approaching very close, Grete watched him like a diminutive nurse. He had little to do, save to be, his presence was a shred of the bizarre, the inexplicable, requisite for Troy. They saw him standing on the rampart, intent on what they could not see, or, seeing, did not understand. Perhaps the white path in the mountains, always narrowing towards a hidden place where might await him a tower, a wooden horse, the bright rim of the world. No one brought Albrecht butterflies. Such as he drew sparkle from themselves alone, he was deferred to as one sexless, immune to age, fear, greed, as if he had stepped down from a church fresco. He needed no nickname, no pipe. He was a magician who disowned magic; like sultans, a hypnotic exhalation of summer.

Each day was a pageant, sliding perfectly into calm night. Adrift in timelessness, threatened by no tomorrow, the youngest had never known such play. New friends appeared incessantly. A ragged, caustic fellow was found to be a fairground juggler, veritable miracle-monger. Albrecht in his bounty gave new life to old games, encouraging almost everything and leaving alone all else. They rushed to sport at Nick Nock, Fly-away Peg, Stealing the Apples . . . enveloped in a Hans story, a Garden of Delight, offshoot of Troy, where all comes true, all is simple, only the fantastic is real. Jowled faces softened, greasy hands applauded, as tumble-hatted strangers joined the game, shouting, singing, starting a dance. Young and old wagered plums as they watched ant or beetle races. Sores had healed; toil, thrashings, hideous births, sickening broth, scarecrow apparitions had been swept away in the helter-skelter of games, tavern songs and mirthful feastings. Posts had been rammed into the hard ground, stained with bilberry juice, badgers' blood, lichen, a make-believe Trojan Maze through which to chase, dodge, leap, then run back into the swarming Garden of Delight. One child would sit through long, shining afternoons, dreamily intent, knocking two logs together, lost in her own music. Not only the young could be noosed by a bird-cry, a flash from mountain, and, again, by distant, unknown bells, while Prince Alexander and his adopted council completed plans, preparing the gigantic leap over Broken Mountain into the green impossible that Hans had known. He was piping less in this continuous uproar of pastimes, building, wagons lurching out of the distance, drinkers' choruses, but had entranced almost all with a tale of the Man Who Never Is, which, constantly repeated, was repatched as 'Nevis! Hero of Troy', as yet unseen but nevertheless about to appear, an irresistible fighter.

Between Troy and the village, grass was sallow but barley ripened and glistened in July stillness. Few cared if the Castle begged for its stupid tax or knew whether Turks were gathering, joined by shattered knights seeking respite from spectral hunts. Free cities, bishoprics and margravates might be seething with the workless and workshy, back-alley saints and would-be martyrs, but they could be left to the torments of the Last Days, while Trojans luxuriated in a season lavishly fruitful, which a chronicler was to describe as a cauldron heated by the Devil.

One evening, after a long communal supper of crows and hares baked in cabbage, there was another sort of arrival. A youth crept from the mountains beseeching asylum, guards informing the others that he had escaped from the Castle. He stared bemused at the long, crowded tables, the hilarity and ample provisions, and at Hans, smiling under his startling mat of hair, enthroned on a pile of freshly dug turf, a summer lord. He saw knives and pistols hanging from belts, twilight glinting on spades, flails, sickles, picks, axes and scythes as shadows deepened and moths flew.

In a silence delayed but now stretching over the whole camp the fugitive stood before a mass of suspicious faces. Still a little breathless, wearing a copper breastplate, clean sword in one hand, a basket of loaves and fruit in the other, he could not at first speak, provoking more suspicion. He deposited the basket in awkward tribute, looked at Hans's harmless smile, then recognized at the end of one table Albrecht, of whom he knew many curious reports and conjectures.

Albrecht's brief gesture was a guarantee of safety and a mild command to explain himself, so that he took breath and spoke, in valley dialect.

'Young master . . . all of you . . . I've got warning.'

The words chilled, with a fateful question. Was this but a phantom Troy dreamt by outcast lives, defenceless against Castle and Turk, the sovereign mountains? Attilas and sultans must sink back into mud. But Alexander? Even hardened veterans of warfare and beggardom were already turning to Albrecht, in query, appeal, even demand.

Albrecht made no response, though those nearest him saw his small, fleeting smile, by now well known, instantly replaced by a willingness to hear more.

'They are preparing. They . . .' – the young man dared not say *The Graf* – 'tomorrow they will come.'

Hans, picking at cabbage leaves, seemed not to have heard. Several tables away Albrecht heard everything, perhaps somewhat more. The deserter pleaded, 'I want to be with you. To fight. I've known it.' Pulling up his sleeve, he displayed ripped skin, still purplish. Cheers, profound relief joined with shame at brief misgivings and incipient disloyalty were awarded Albrecht as, without haste, he pushed away his stool, his reply ready. Perhaps a few more thoughtful newcomers thought of a prince drowning his woman through love of himself.

14

Prospects of fighting stimulated the blood, strengthened the flesh. Grunting, battle-cast warriors abounded, Nevis was at hand, Albrecht had spoken. Anything was believable. A young woman, probably a whore from Bremen, laughed sharply. 'She opened her eyes and saw nine moons. She closed them and saw thirteen.'

In celebration, on the next day, while all remained wakeful, weapons to hand, hens were killed, eggs cooked, blood-puddings made, jars of rhubarb wine hauled from a stack of timber. All day the Castle remained tightly closed, no soldiers were seen, the young fighter bowed his head, imploring patience, cheerfully granted, but doggedly insisting that attack would come. No complaints. The Graf could be booted to hell, his household ransacked, also every jot of its women. Every sight was propitious. Harvest was being trampled at the edges by those still urgent to reach the fabled refuge. A fox was trapped and roasted, a rat very slowly hanged, with novel, exquisite refinements taught by the gippy brothers, inducing a fine measure of agonized squeaks, tiny appeals, quivers that rippled from eye to feet, to cries that such a fate awaited the Graf should he dare molest any Trojan. Heat was building a new sky, promises of victory, the New Times, while, seen from afar, feigning disdain of their children's marvellous doings, bondsmen bent in immemorial stance in Break-back Field.

No village mother wailed aloud, there was little to lament though a bundle might be tossed over the rampart to relieve imaginary hunger, ale be found in the ditch. Fathers cursed, yet some had secret shame, believing that a protest had been made against the Tax, better made by themselves. Others remembered that the souls of dead children were demanded by wild hunters riding the night sky.

On his second night the deserter joined a group to hear Hans tell of Schamir, the deathless worm that could gnaw through all roots and foundations, even those of the Waude Oak. Despite trumpets and flutes, horses and carriages, its witchfinder's traps and callous scribes, no castle could withstand Schamir.

Afterwards boastings resumed, and jokes about the Ostler and the Stallion. The cowled and crested, the gowned and armoured, purloiners of rights, thieves of pigs and women would perish atrociously. In his turn, the young man told them about Castle life: the Fool mincing from room to room in outlandish colours, the Confessor like a woman in man's clothes, Uncle in green spectacles, the Graf moving very slowly like a man under water. He described them well enough but his face seemed worried.

'I was mistaken. They didn't come. But I know those men. They will come.'

Albrecht was not present, nor any of those who could be relied upon to defend the camp. The group, silenced, was hesitant, without lead from above, until they were unexpectedly rescued by Hans.

Misty in the near-darkness, no Great Captain or Marshal of Horse, he retained the moonshine potency of a May King. He seemed to be suppressing some glee. 'I've seen them go away.' He nodded, screwing up his eyes, doubtless at the sight of a regiment trailing away in defeat. His eyes and mouth were moist. Then he spoke again: 'The red. Redness. . . .' Then appeared to lose his thoughts, be about to swoon, his head suddenly too heavy, deranged by whatever he had meant.

A girl shivered, exclamations were stifled, pangs of uncertainty began. Redness suggested his own tawdry head but also much more. Under the ramshackle dwellings, near the tree where horses shuffled and tossed heads, they shared thoughts which veered away from Hans. They imagined the Ostler's hands, and that long moment when hangman and trussed victim gaze into each other's eyes: and slaughterhouse redness, red banners, red sunset streaking the mountains and promising tomorrow's sun. Some know of red salts in an alchemist's crucible, others had heard of red wolves, somewhere in the Empire was an emperor's city built entirely in red.

Anything more? Heiner, now with a straggly beard, ruffianly, holding a long knife with a decorated handle, probably stolen, confided, with unwonted slowness, even shyness, that his mother had believed that 'red was happy', at which a self-important student announced that it was also wisdom. This was less pleasing. Wisdom meant nothing here, the word was unknown or associated with priests, scriveners and other cunning rogues, and loiterers at dodgers' corner. Probably scandalous and certainly dull. Not even a squirrel needed wisdom, or a rabbit, who at least knows his way about the moon. Children overheard some words about red added to white and conjuring up the Devil. Another knowing voice murmured that a red horseman could be devoured by frantic lust, spurting jiggery-jaggeries. This, even for the very young, conveyed more than wisdom, one of life's blots. Everyone was at once more cheerful, grateful to Hans.

He had indeed spoken well enough. His instinct, or whatever, was sure, for early next morning, the sky obediently red, shouts from the rampart awoke the camp. As could be expected, Albrecht was already up, clad in thin leather, consulting with his chosen: two club-men, an experienced mercenary, Tough Jake, and a

Swabian fire-raiser, known as Donk, now examining a crossbow with professional care.

Out of mountain mist men, though cumbered with heavy, old-style Nuremberg plate, were descending briskly, indeed with swagger, yet their small, straggling formations suggested a slackness of command. No Fighting Commandant was deigning to show his prowess. At this distance they were small, catching bleared streaks of light, the Castle and peaks louring above, but, at the critical instant, the shock of collision, they could become giants. As they reached the plain, thus free of mist, sunlight, first edging their metal, swiftly enveloped them, perhaps thirty, molten, glaring, all archers, cheapest, least dangerous of the Graf's resources, now clanking on the stony ground, each root, bush, rock lit sharp.

Troy was motionless, suspended, dependent on Albrecht, now under the rampart, gazing through a gap, unarmed, unperturbed, as if at a play mounted for himself alone, one of those protected by saints from a few brutish fair-weather archers, cabbage-stalk menials posing as storm-princes and knights. Offshoots of bran and dung-mast, residue of Old Times.

Out of range of arrow or shot, the attack halted, bulkily ranged in irregular lines, visibly laughing, supercilious with braggadocio confidence, fingering weapons, prepared for little more than mere tinkles within the clamour of life, and a muster of degenerate, broken-backed carpet-warriors huddled behind their haphazard wall, about to flee on demand.

They were unprepared for the impertinence of Donk, now aloft on the rampart holding a crossbow. He grinned murderously as the Castle men resumed their advance, lowered it, upheld a hand to test the breeze, aimed, then discharged his rusty bolt. An archer recoiled, slumped to his knees, grabbed madly at nothing, jittering like a spent tallow-flame, then lay scuppered.

The Trojans whooped, only pikes prevented Heiner, with his knife, and Johannes, clambering over, yelling for others to join a demented charge. Men, however, joined Donk, with bows and slings, most discharges falling short but fanning up small dust-swirls, an effect of danger speeding. Below, there followed incoherence; unlimited ferocities were wrenched and confused by the tumult, by sensations of white light falling on red petals, of salvation, of meaty surges of spirit. Already the assailants were backing away, first cautiously, then, as another half fell, but recovered, more rapidly, stooping, seeking cover from the first wedges of pine, before a climb too stumbling to be called flight, too obvious to be anything but retreat.

Behind them, a carcase lay in its blood, flies making a black, quivering coverlet over a face changed to a swamp.

The noise subsided, now awed by the sodden lump of gristle, the perfection of red, envisaged within its casing. The quiet was broken by an urgent cry. 'Look!' It was from Hans, standing with his last sheep, and pointing to the sky farthest from the mountains. Flying towards Troy was a white bird, soaring and dipping in oracular benediction.

Cheers renewed for Hans, bringer of luck. No longer content with milk and water, he joined in the furious gulping of wine lately dragged in a sledge by a local poacher. His face creased into foolishness, he held out a mug not yet emptied, crowing happily, then choked as he swallowed, pleased with himself, as though he could stuff the wind in a bottle, and had perhaps done so, he who saw trees breathe and the stone wink at him in the river. Very soon, nuzzled by his animals, he was curled up, happy in vast, careless sleep. A tall, bearded Bohemian paused, looking down at him. 'That little fellow . . .', but at once looked perplexed, unable to continue.

The victors hopped and flourished, joined hands, embraced, exchanged exuberant conceits. A Swiss recruit's longbow was strung with human sinew, mutiny was already rife in the Castle, the white bird had been wafted from heaven. Mountain woods were bloodshot, the sky wounded. At midnight celebrations still raged, dancers flapping, clucking, neighing in barnyard anthem, Donk so drenched in ale, so laden with praise, that he sprawled motionless as the wretch he had felled. A falling star, scratching the night, was applauded like a showman's trick. Certain girls, kindled by the brute energies of the night, were surrendering behind wagon or tent, men fighting for their chance, Ants, Jack-daws, Grasshoppers, sporting, whistling, begging further delight from a passion that, clanging from Troy, seeping into mountain and river, must be making the lords shudder.

15

Not only must the Gräfin not be mentioned, and, if High Folk referred to Albrecht, it was only as 'the Hopeful' or 'Master Stay-by-the-Door'. Few ever saw him, his status within the Castle was undefined, not all were convinced that he possessed any. Suspicious, hostile or resentful, they maintained that his balls were sugar, his disposition wax, his prospects null, that he was neither boy nor girl but a neat accumulation of the worst of both. That he was mixing with, nay leading, a herd of snottish, vile-born ditchlings pleased them, for this surely condemned him. Yet he was simultaneously considered the solitary love in the Graf's routine, and though this love had been unaccountably frozen, it might yet be restored, the Graf being . . . well, himself. It was granted that Albrecht was scarcely a lice-ridden churl spiced with pox and vampire bites. He could, objectionable though it was, be destined as Heir. The Graf, who had never been youthful (none could remember him as a child), was scarcely designed to endure many years. He too would turn putrid, not worth a thaler.

Throughout the Castle there was by no means disorder, certainly not chaos, but fretfulness and apprehension. A visiting prior wrote that the Graf loved nothing but nothingness, before hastening on, speeded by the hazards less of an absurd camp governed by children than by reports of a rebel army approaching from the Rhine.

Most lords and ladies shrugged contemptuously, though affecting to sniff vile stenches drifting from the camp, thickening atrociously by sundown. Children required scalding penalties, better a useful nag than a young upstart. More men-at-arms were about, together with a rank suspicion that, if not quickly given their wages, they would desert to the so-called children's army. Heavily determined, the Fighting Commandant had several times been closeted with the Graf.

With the archer's sad accident, the Graf, again pared down to indecision and grievance, summoned his advisers, to whom he said nothing about the Hopeful, Master Stay-by-the-Door.

The council had opened with an unnecessary report by the Clerk that some scullery hand, with an ear too big for her, had heard hoofs in the night, very high up. Seldom propitious, as the Graf knew, seated still as a hare, very pouched and wintry in the drab light, despite the warmth. None cared to meet his gaze, never ingratiating, though his complaints could not be gainsaid. One sensed that more than his hapless archers had oppressed him, revoking the vigour of the previous week and some surreptitious rumour of a secret message, and the Confessor found himself reminded of a disappointed lover. More publicly, the Graf was being ridiculed, his Name and Honour bespattered by fishpond imps, lumbering clodhoppers, hod-carriers and criminal wastrels. The Emperor, Roman and majestic despite his tribulations, would have been told.

The children should have been sold at birth or poisoned by roots gathered under a full moon. No precedent existed for a camp so infamous. Despite intimacy with remote ages, Prince Narr could recall only the foolish Children's Crusade, a doomed transaction challenging not lords but infidels, very properly ended by slave-traders and falsified geography. A prime instance, the Clerk ventured, of misbehaviour begotten by error, fraud, disobedience, bizarre as a camel.

However true, this brought no comfort to grave officials ranked at table under high, smoked vaultings. Outside, late July sunlight was flaying the walls but here, squeezing through a thin vent, the light fell away, limp and ill. No tapestry hung, the walls were bare save for stains, the august chamber, therefore, could be by no means mistaken for a mere provincial *Landrat*, with its superfluous, middle-order comforts and trappings. Covertly they wiped their wrists, both to remove perspiration and conceal their unease. On the table lay not documents but a strip of birch against headache. Several empty stools somewhat derogated the occasion. The Noble Huntsman was hunting, the Cellarer doubtless occupying the cellar. As always, a special chair carved with inappropriate lions was reserved for Uncle, who seldom came. Prince Narr's slashed sleeves and frilled collar gave colour to the lax air. The Clerk looked uncomfortable; his duty was to pay the soldiers, but he could not yet do so.

The Graf waited, but loss of the archer worried them, particularly the Fighting Commandant who should have swept the rabble to perdition but had miscalculated the odds. Porcine, barrel-shaped, mastiff-headed, one hairy nostril higher than the other, with blue unsteady eyes, a radish-hued skinful of grunts striving to remain awake, he did not speak, though knowing how to and indeed he was reputed to have withered a vineyard by the grossness of his oaths. Today he had merely muttered 'God's womb!', then chewed his nails without relish.

Sourly, his mouth nipped and dry, nose in the blur looking longer than usual, his cheeks shaded by stubble and as if boneless, the Graf glanced at von der Goltz, who had already mentioned that the best way to treat children was to refrain from having any, an example set by Christ himself, who had other tastes, involving followers scarcely – he deferred gently to the Graf – of the highest lineage. He sighed, rubbing his bare, placid head. 'These bratlings and kennel-sweepers . . . to get rid of them should be simple as laying an egg or making a wheel . . . we could laugh, indeed we do laugh. . . .'

None were doing so and he himself contrived only the outskirts of a smile, and the Clerk twitched as if in pain. The Graf, though fixed in his customary immobility, yet conveyed impatience, and the Confessor spoke more hurriedly: 'We should look further afield. At Bamberg and outside Aschaffenburg . . . I need say no more.' Nevertheless he did so. 'This trouble may be the spark – how shall I put it? – leading to a blaze, a conflagration. One can harbour misgivings, anticipating the worst.'

'The worst' – Prince Narr's words were soft and, as always, taunting, drifting through plump, tinted lips – 'never occurs. Only the very worst.'

On his left, growling followed, the Fighting Commandant summoning his own resources, barely audible stuff about the offspring of cabbage and garbage. Few attended. They were thinking of children speeding through valleys, down rivers, with messages stitched into tunics, nailed into clogs, inciting rebellion throughout south and west Germany, where hobble-dehoy conflicts still raged, and in its turpitude the Sublime Porte gloated, awaiting the final Islamic conquest. Bamberg peasants had sacked a half-empty monastery; at Aschaffenberg pilgrims had been murderously ambushed by knights. Such outrages might be connected, in black conspiracy against a social order approved by God himself. Across the border, in Florence, a crazed friar had led mobs and expelled the ruling Medici, and had organized children to inform on the powerful, the art-loving, their own parents, then intoxicated with pleasure, heaping paintings, carvings, books on gigantic fires. Many citizens had perished.

In himself, the Confessor cared little for the Empire, its diminution would reduce the sin of pride. For the Castle, and the Name, however, he felt the responsibility of a trusted and chosen adviser; no one could feel affection for the Graf, a half-starved boar peering at an empty trough, but a confessor, spiritual aristocrat, would mourn the overthrow of grafs. Only Prince Narr remained unperturbed. A reference to the red-headed shepherd monstrosity amused him. 'Whoever knows of a tall man who is wise, a small man who is modest, a holy man who is chaste, a child who can reason, or a redhead who is faithful?'

The Graf, himself small, and who considered himself holy, inspected Prince Narr as he might a map of rogue territory. The thin paste on the Fool's skin was cracking in the stale heat so that he appeared plausibly antique, his very eyes old, even decrepit. Others could sometimes believe that he had indeed walked with Nero, observed casual miracles from Jesus, deplored the cut of Charlemagne's beard.

This did not relieve anxiety and fear. Tales, earlier laughable, now became unpleasantly credible. Peasant delegates had been received in guildhall and stronghold, seeking alliance with the mighty, a stage in the process which had already demolished the

95

knights like snails under the hoe. Restless townsfolk might soon join hands with barbarous rustics. A new and threatening word was abroad: *confederates*. The first to suffer, Florence notwithstanding, would not be archbishops and imperial princes but the lesser nobility of which the Graf was – the Confessor stated, anxious to erase his images of wheel and egg – so illustrious a member.

Talk, unsettled, with little direction, veered back to rebels nearer to hand. Humdrum millers, always planning, foreseeing, foreclosing, living in the future, anticipating change, were thought to be supplying the rebels with flour.

'A rabble . . . children, to call them no worse, are children.'

'Assuredly. Just so. Rags and tatters, not truly human. Nevertheless. . . .'

The Clerk, careful to maintain deference to the Confessor, who was often offended by suggestions other than his own, had patiently awaited a chance to speak.

'Let us assume that these kidlings can do no more than dance in a high wind. Blown on the tide like dirty sponges. Disowned by their parents. Left to themselves, they will accomplish nothing. So we must peer a little deeper.' His scholar's face looked at the others, convinced, secure in his knowledge but wishing to please. 'We must examine leadership. There are leaders who lead, leaders who think they lead, leaders who are thought to lead, by those, the majority, who know no better. These children . . .' – he was very careful to avoid mentioning Albrecht – 'have a leader of the utmost insignificance. A babbler of infantile fables and midwife fantasies. A piper. Story-telling and piping. Here, here alone, is his power. Yet it is dangerous to despise them, as we all know.'

Though he privately told himself that few of them did know, he was mistaken. They had different degrees of thought, but realized that a piper, however runtish or weasel-muzzled, was not always negligible. Even trundling, hurdy-gurdy traipsers could attract a following with their uncouth music. All Germany had learnt that Satan himself had invented the pipe. The Clerk had spoken well. Leaders, whether rebels or idiots, luckless or demonic, were pipers, overcoming edicts and customs by enchantment. From the

Rhine to the Vistula pipers were notorious. A hermit by Lake Lorch had charmed mice away from the harvest, a charcoal-burner at Lenz had expelled plague by piping. In the Hartz Mountains a vagrant piper in star-spangled cap had played tunes so devilish that villagers danced themselves to death.

The Confessor then invited them to remember that Christ had called himself a piper, rebuking those who did not dance. Prince Narr said that sounds of a pipe could mean death, frequently the death of children. The Fighting Commandant recollected that at Duisburg several children had been executed for robbery, 'while music played'. From his swollen throat struggled a suction sound, not quite a laugh, presumably not a groan, which reminded the Clerk that cannibals were not extinct.

The Clerk again intervened: 'Can we but remove the shepherd, we will disperse the others. Confederates, trouble-makers, Jews . . . who snare fledglings with subversive promises. To accomplish this will save much of the Empire itself. So much is on fire beneath. Contumacious, condign. With permission, I shall read you this.'

Permission was neither granted nor withheld. Afternoon heat, the arguments, the morning's wine slowed responses, only the Graf appeared to be disregarding drowsiness as the Clerk's monotonous voice began, vainly hoping for indignation and perhaps action, reading from a cheaply printed sheaf with a woodcut of a crowned figure crouching from a flock of crows, disguised confederates. It illustrated a text not from Satan or some Haarlem agitator but from the blessed and saintly Thomas à Kempis.

For though thou dost know by heart the entire Bible, and the words of the philosophers, what doth it profit thee with the Divine love? Surely a lowly husbandman that serveth God exceeds the worth of a proud philosopher who, neglecting his own being, struggles to understand the movements of the stars.

Silence. Those who felt anything at once saw themselves not as lovers or star-gazers but as lowly husbandmen, ordering the land on behalf both of His Sacred Majesty and the know-nothing stumpledons buried in sloth and ignorance and believing that snow was caused by the Virgin making her bed. Prince Narr had apparently witnessed Kempis's birth near Düsseldorf in the previous century but he now did no more than hum lightly through the last of the paste:

> If all the world was mine
> From sea to the Rhine
> I'd give it all
> Could the Queen of England lie in my arms.

A goliard snatch, most of it too improper for the Graf's ears and the Confessor hushed him, so that they were suspended in grandee nothingness, breathing with difficulty, perspiring, yearning to go but unwilling to depart. Men of the Empire, to be wakened only by the unexpected.

This happened. There was movement from the darkened arch, a visitant from above, slow, ample, swathed in Saracenic silks, glimmering sashes and Spanish slippers, his rings, even in this dusty twilight, winking colours. The bald, elderly personage acknowledged them with subtle geniality, green spectacles giving him a Merlinesque aura.

Even amongst these stolid men Uncle evoked quiet pools, space, fountains, opulent leisure, happily funded guests and equipages. His pink face, very smooth, scarcely lined, with comfortable, slightly sagging folds, had the long family nose, slightly coated with Neapolitan powders, his grey eyes, even from behind the spectacles, politely ironic, as if shrugging under heavy, rather lazy lids, friendly enough but always holding much in reserve, possibly too much. If questioned, unthinkable of course, he might confide much about young Albrecht hitherto inadmissible.

Before moving himself forward, Uncle glanced around, noted each man present though with little sign of personal recognition. Then, ignoring the Graf, he pulled out his chair, awarding the lions as much deference as he had the councillors. Very little. Settling himself, he resembled an ornate galley at low tide.

The atmosphere had immediately stiffened, not with hostility but realization that Uncle possessed an authority, curious, indefinable, that his nephew lacked, for all his dispiriting silences and statuesque poses. Even Prince Narr demurred from tweaking Uncle with ill-judged witticisms. Uncle had a tongue free as his own, though more fastidious: his presence rebuked bawdiness and libertinage as markedly as the Graf's shrank from disorder. Neither man was imaginable craving a fleecy dancer's pirouette, back-alley twattishness, jakes' assignment. Uncle's consequence was reckoned the superior, his observations, if sometimes too abstruse, reached further than the Confessor's and were less bleak than the Clerk's, a verbal contest between him and Prince Narr would be welcomed; but Uncle, while enjoying his own remarks, was disinclined to endure those of others. Immersed in books, he was known to be currently concerned with Enoch, who long ago had seen intercourse carnal but not gross between men and angels; with superstitions about the Last Days; also with the disciple John who tempted Jesus into practices that had ruined many knights, whose skeletons lie bleached in Palestine.

Uncle, hands on the table, contemplating the birch strip as he might a rarity of disputable value, loosened his robe, passed a hand over his nose, warding off the frowsty air, then sat waiting, a portentous master of life anticipating a pleasant discussion of no very great importance, not approximating that of Enoch, more delicate than that of John, his smile soothing, herbal, dispersing tension. Misled by his inspection, outwardly benign, the Fighting Commandant found speech possible, his gobbish words finding their level, very low, like beer in a leaking tub. 'We shall attack. A battle!' he rumbled with a wistfulness at odds with his cumbersome frame and as if recalling some earlier, wonderful day.

Uncle's tolerance had professional ease, his voice, with its small lisp, somewhat too bland. 'A battle?' He deprecated it as a trifling oddity, 'We live in unregenerate times.' His curved smile implied that this was not wholly disagreeable. 'Battles could in former days be won by fasting, curses and godly example.' The same smile inferred that he was sceptical of such battles. His sigh was playful, and with elaborate attention he caressed a long peacock sleeve. A scent, sweet but not sickly, was faintly drifting from him, another call from the far-off and exotic. 'Wars are tiresome necessities, are they not, like women? Very like women. Thus, though seldom lacking absurdity, not demanding the capacities most true to our being.'

The absurdity of women might be construed as a compliment to the Confessor, whose preference for boys was long known and, in some quarters, envied.

Straight as a coffin, the Graf showed neither agreement nor disagreement. Listening to Uncle, he always felt unschooled, too apart, even disinherited. The Gräfin had admired him, yet complained that he despised her. At times she had feared him.

The Graf feared things but not people, yet at this moment he knew that he was disregarded at his own council-table and could do no more than preserve dignified unconcern. Missing his old friends, maps, disinclined to attend to practised maunderings about battles, he realized that Uncle's face was itself a map, showing a rich land of secure frontiers, untroubled roads, clear gradients, seasoned though without seasons, without peaks and abysses, but with each crease, tiny wrinkle and minute indentation a landmark. A land complete in itself, welcoming no intruders, needing no faith, satisfied with its own language, particular knowledge, inviolable routine. With some grievance, the Graf reflected that such a figure enforced no tax, incurred no blame, was afflicted with no insurrection, no imperial demands. Prince Narr remembered Plato, wisest of all Greeks – a contemptible people notwithstanding – dying of mortification when unable to answer when some common sailor asked him why birds fly south. Uncle was a Plato, all smiles and fine words, scarcely more useful than lords of mischief like Prince Narr, who, like thieves, poets and children, upset authority, smash boundaries and leave the mess to be cleared up by others.

'Absurdity!' Uncle was savouring some glittering experience like a gift proffered by Enoch or John. 'You are all mindful of the Englishman, My Lord of Suffolk? He was captured by a French cowman who'd stolen someone's weapons, a precaution that stood him well. To preserve his honour, the high-stationed Suffolk had to dub him knight.'

Save for Prince Narr, they tittered obediently, but Uncle had not finished. 'A rose, you will remind me, is both more or less than a rose.'

None did so remind him and not all believed it. Uncle, himself healthily roseate, was undeterred, speaking as much to himself as to them, with the self-indulgence of a mature abbot. 'A rose, you will tell me, combines the four elements, though perhaps most of us do that.' His inspection of the Fighting Commandant suggested an exception. 'Moreover, it is light, sun and rebirth which we are all granted though too few of us seek. There can of course, I do not expect to be reminded, be death before or after life.'

His *of course*, a favourite qualification, hinted the esotericism garnered from unceasing study. Uncle knew what no one else in the Castle could dispute: why Christ wore horns, gippies hate ploughs, what was the infamous crime of the Templars. He must also know that man had learnt writing not from God but a devil, a certain Penemue, though this, despite being adept at writing, he had not been known to mention.

He added conversationally, 'God, in his glory, I have often considered the result of the Creation rather than the cause.'

Again, with rather too pronounced condescension, he awaited scholastic discussion, literate debate, erudite appeal to the Fathers, citations from Pliny or Lucretius. They were not forthcoming. Motioning as if to depart, he nodded to them as he might to students finding a lecture too difficult.

Now he was standing, his head, with its thin streaks of white, glowing, his plump face wearing a smile like an honour, one hand, knuckles as if polished, uplifted, magisterial, even papal. Very contented, epicene, in oriental hues, he allowed them a departing text as a traveller might leave a purse while departing from a hostel, only Prince Narr, leaning away into darker shadow, feigning a weariness too overwhelming to permit him to listen. Feigning, so to speak, to feign.

'An angel, Let us imagine him? Her? Do angels have gender? Let us cease to imagine! He, she or it was sufficiently displeased with a devil that, from his pellucid eyes, there leapt a monster, to devour, to consume the diabolical menace. As might be expected, the devil – I forget his name, which can scarcely be considered wholesome – implored mercy, alas in Hebrew sadly ungrammatical, though prudently pleading love of Our Lady. The angel, in that spirit of righteousness so commended by the excellent prophets, agreed to restrain the monster. But, in his turn, the monster made his plea. I am, quoth the monster, very hungry, exceedingly famished. I could say, I do say, starving. Angels themselves eat no food, their, dare I say, stomachs are too etherialized, so require but spiritual sustenance, so this one could only suggest that, to relieve his pangs, the devil, a personage by no means interesting, should go so far as to eat his own flesh. Devour himself. To fill one's belly with oneself has implications adumbrating the philosophical, which I shall leave it to you gentlemen to develop. An unsatisfactory remedy, the devil considered, but perforce had to accept it, consuming all but his face, which now, I am told on not quite the highest authority, hangs outside the gate of paradise, which one day we, or some of us, will almost certainly see for ourselves.'

16

Uncle's notion of advising in crisis left his associates inconclusively ruminating about meanings probably unintended. The Graf soon left them, with nothing decided, preferring to sit alone in a small room known, too grandiloquently, as the chancellery, a single candle illuminating an unrolled map. Behind his head was draped a dark velvet pall, ragged at the edges, as if bitten, noted by the disrespectful as an image appropriate to himself.

He could allow his expression to weaken, and sought reassurance from his favourite ally, the medley of scrawled lines and coloured patches, though unpleasantly aware of regions that no map delineated, no document or armed force could dismantle. The jewelled, imitation d'Este dagger at his belt could disperse neither ghosts nor omens.

Uncle had once spoken of a Roman emperor who had expunged

reports of African rebels by simply, superbly, denying that the tribe existed. Not magic, but a sublime effrontery of soul. The Graf knew, however, that he was endowed with no such soul, and Uncle had also undermined the validity of the Castle by asserting that Wotan had built Valhalla not as a symptom of might but as acknowledgement of weakness.

The Gräfin too had a wilful tendency to rate castles of no more consequence than a shroud, though, in a limited way, this showed some prescience.

Uncle was a labyrinth without a centre, confusing, tricksome, irritating. Uninterested in food, women, prayer, enjoying gossip but bored with government, he enjoyed only his own recesses, abstruse as a pentacle. His words glittered but did not illuminate. The future, he had said, was usually mistaken. That led nowhere. His life had been no more credible than a silent market, a lean friar, an honest beggar. Like a lopped tree he sprouted too many shoots, not dominating but entangling.

Disconsolate, he pushed away the map. The stonework enclosing him wavered as the flame jerked in the draught, shadows piling under the walls with an effect of weight. Outside, summer was beating against the Castle, but he tightened his shirt against chills.

He must again, of course, take matters into his own hands and, though he had only the sorriest outline of a plan, he knew with dowser's conviction that he would succeed where a Fighting Commandant had not. He had patience, self-mastery, a rider's endurance and skills of improvisation upon which Uncle depended, while disdaining them.

Despite Uncle's cleverness, a rose remained a rose. In much learning is much quackery. A graf needs neither a rose nor learning: he is like a brilliant statue secure in a high niche, beyond reach of dirty hands, controlling by being.

He was not disturbed by lack of cleverness but by a concern more intimate. Albrecht had been favoured by the Gräfin and, though not appearing to respond with noticeable affection, he had, after her passing, refused first commands, then requests, to enter the Castle. His defection to the farmyard turmoil and its dung-shot, red-haired idiot could be seen as resentment, though his disposition had always been independent. Nevertheless he had, a few weeks back, contrived to send a package for the Graf alone: it contained but a small silken purse, neatly stitched but empty, perhaps opened by the thieving bearer. Perhaps a taunt, a threat, or a petition for reconciliation, and Uncle might justly hold that, like that aggravating rose, it was either more or less than itself.

Whatever it meant, it had caused the Graf's earlier satisfaction. Better a jeer from Albrecht than dark silence.

The Confessor had had to announce that Albrecht had been abducted, but none believed it, preferring to blame what they called his perverse appetites. Also, without legal status, backed only by their own ability and their father's whim, such youths were necessarily ambitious, though to seek power amongst scabs, idlers and arsonists showed either misplaced subtlety or ludicrous judgement.

Suspicious of shadows, hearing that distressing heartbeat, perplexed by Albrecht, desiring his presence, his beauty, even the uncertainty of his attitude, even his insolence, made alternately downcast and hopeful by that empty purse, the Graf, gazing into the candle glow, felt a small knock of the fear originating in boyhood dreams in which fanged beasts had threatened him. Men had once been animals, then became human at the cost of acquiring sin. In dreams scraps of many primitive lives, deposited in you at random, lively as Flemings, revoked the formal round of oaths, contracts, obligations, kisses of peace, grand alliances. Albrecht, not headstrong, but with the vanity of comeliness, the self-possession of one guaranteed by another's love, was meddling with such lives, using a subterfuge of intelligence to conceal what the Graf could see as a deplorable frivolity. He thought of a clown whose streaked, grinning face might turn terrible: then of a young sultan, shining, but as if through drizzle.

He attempted to steady his thoughts, rally himself from the disarray so often prompted by Albrecht, though they rioted through him yet more haphazardly. Both the founder of Rome and the first sultan had been reared by wolves, and kitchen talk was now insisting that Hans, the impious shepherd, had been born of some heathen slut, within a hill where she held vile court, in which, their lusts unreined as tempest, the Devil's minions danced and sang. The Devil was slender, neither young nor old, beautiful nor ugly, clothed nor naked; he had a poet's shallow fluency, was coldly jealous of God and man, was sometimes more powerful than either, strengthened by the armies of dead sinners, whereas God must rely only on the virtuous, some of the priests, women, mostly silly, and of course crafty Jesus, with whom Uncle might share more than either would relish.

Of Albrecht, he dared not think further.

Could a priest, like that wall-eyed village mumbler below, living in muck, still retain some dusty magic, like a jewel in a leper's privy? Priests and doctors conceivably did more harm than good, inventing illnesses which they demanded payment to cure, though fleeing at the first rumour of plague.

The Graf, as he did frequently, examined himself from outside, and at once saw the Emperor's Man, loyal and assiduous, then dodged his own eye, loaded with melancholic humours. He weakened intolerably, saw the Gräfin and Albrecht conversing together in special language, despising his inability to understand it. She had corrupted the boy: like a hound or bird she saw shapes and heard sounds unknown to proper folk. Uncle had a drawing of a black crab clutching a yellow butterfly, an Eastern symbol, he explained, trifling but amusing, of marriage. By day, the Gräfin could display butterfly levity, but when the sun vanished, she grew some undesirable features, only too likely crabbish. She would have been at ease with a graveyard ghoul, less than a man, less still of a woman, and, at noon, casting no shadow. She was liable to hysteria; Albrecht was invariably cool, unhurried, ambiguously polite. Strangely, in complexion, hair, even eyes, he had some resemblance to the Gräfin, with whom he was wholly unrelated, whilst in appearance and qualities he shared nothing with his father. He and the woman were best separated, in a manner which, the Graf was certain, would one day be considered statesmanlike, invaluable to the survival of the Empire.

After dark, pressures of mood drove the Graf to the ramparts, where he stood knowing himself master of all he saw. Actually the night was moonless, the stars misted, so that he saw little. The dim, petrified heights and black woods were scarcely slavish, nor were the fires of that shanty town where, amongst madcap urchins, renegades, hideous and damned, Albrecht would be doing – what? He was unimaginable there, joined with those who tore up maps, looted and burned, the degraded cripple-heads who believed they saw Christ's thumb-mark on every haddock, and were as unnatural as brothers and sisters rutting with each other on church altars, to horrify plague into flight.

During his nuptials he had stood on these very stones with his young wife, under just such a sky, the mountain peaks very close. They had had hours of silence, covertly watchful, knowing nothing of each other, until, quietly, as if alone, she had said, 'Loba. Loba'. At his question she had been startled, then shook her head, with no further response, an unmannerly and inauspicious disobedience. Months later, from a chance pun of Prince Narr's, he had traced Loba to a loonish southern poet, racked by love of Loba the she-wolf, himself howling in the night with woodcut starkness and eventually degenerating into a prey for hunters, chased naked, abnormally hairy, over heaths, until friends found him exhausted in ferns and led him to the forest, where Loba magnanimously licked him back to health.

She should surely have devoured him and rid the land of a pernicious nuisance. Could the account be true? So much was unknowable. Once a giant Tuscan braggart had hurled a spear into the sky and eventually it fell, thick with blood.

The Graf, no man's fool, knew that he, *he himself*, would contrive means to disperse the witless, recreant and bestial, but more urgent was the need, not only to rescue Albrecht from spendthrift follies but to win from him not an embrace or kiss, of which the boy was incapable, but a respectful glance, or a smile of forgiveness despite, of course, there being nothing to forgive.

17

'Lively Barter.' 'A pear for a tussle. Two for a fiddle.' 'Three for anything I like.' 'Suck my Our Father.'

Amongst the children, new games were displacing Nock Nock and Fly Away Peg. Always the first to show boredom, having, as it were, to be regularly stoked like an oven, they remained unflagging, keeping pace with the sun, renewed by the constant influx of strangers, so many exotic and fierce, and sensing that under Broken Mountain history was being cancelled by a dispensation utterly new. Rapscallion frolics, lewd riddles might stale, but they were free to boil live thrushes, attack an anthill, steal a bag of oats or salt, then retreat to the citadel, the primal Troy they themselves had founded on the wreckage of Great Barn. In Lively Barter older ones traded themselves, on tariffs prescribed by Johannes and Heiner, instinctive bawdmasters, though they were usually with the men, swilling, fancying their chances with women, occasionally training to shoot. The Ant, priest's bastard, hopped and chirped, raised her skirt, fingered herself, for any man who passed. Others were more canny and resourceful. Scarcely Seen sold his footprint to a credulous girl, the Jackdaw a sacred toenail, actually his own, though a jar containing a sigh from the Virgin, open to barter, remained unpurchased.

Gangs formed, competed, fisted, dissolved, re-formed in the fever of a constant holy day and its immediate sensations. They imagined blue, imagined scarlet, then stepped into a Hans tale.

He was now heard only by the very young, though this he scarcely noticed, nor that his sheep had gone. Few bothered to notice that he gobbled mutton stew and gnawed a bone as greedily as anyone. Overlooked, he was not, however, openly slighted. Even the last arrivals realized, without being precisely told, that he had uttered the unbelievable, which had now occurred, a topsy-turvy realm where cripples led the dance, goose-girls were princesses, shit a ball of pleasure. Only the ribald and unexpected were real. Had not Brother Jesus worshipped an ass and cursed lawyers and all the clever? A blind Saxon, reputed a seer, kissed

Hans, assuring him that he was tall and handsome, and was reputed to have said that Albrecht was different from what was thought. Nevertheless he soon departed, telling no one why.

Heat still trickled and dropped, though for some days the torrid blue was periodically tarnished by rough clouds that promised a cleansing rain, which did not come.

The slain archer had been stripped and thrust underground like a sacrifice. His blood had been worn as a badge of deliverance, washing away Tax, Turks, Graf. Troy was a victorious township. From distant Trenz and Frankleheim families and cattle, scores of the ruined and dispossessed, of dissident scholars and unruly apprentices, had been lured by the wild chance, the mountain sanctuary of a young squire of Hohenstaufen hauteur, doubtless winged, and of a red-headed dwarf, conceived in an acorn, born in a rook's nest, who could exchange talk with trees and beasts and had piped a dove down from heaven. An invincible pairing of pure souls.

The first rampart now enclosed only the citadel, from which, spreading far outwards to a high stockade, had grown a mass of roofed wagons, handcarts, canvas huts and tents, frayed, discoloured by rain and frost, badly plastered wattle cabins, awnings, together with tripods, cauldrons, barrels of salted herrings and malt. Horses and cows wandered on either side of the stockade.

Light had redeemed the suffering earth. A suspect monk swore that the blessed habitations would endure twice five centuries. It exposed wonders grander than the footprint and toenail and the Virgin's sigh. For a sojourn in straw with an Annie Behind the Hedge, a Tom of All Fingers, a Five O'clock Meg, a toothless, rather fungoid, unintelligible Pole with a tiny knife would prick out designs more perfect than perfect, of a flower, tree, eagle – on a platter, a buttock or thigh, a strip of lime wood. A rival claimed to transform a song into a jar of butter, though none had the means to pay for it. A piebald dog was supposed to play the tabor. Shrilly greeted by children, some bald men strode in, their heads atrociously scratched from butting and killing rats on fairground tables, and there was soon a rush to catch the animals for them. Also much admired was a Scot, Half-hanged Jok, once strung up for rape, but the cord broke and he escaped, to claim he had seen the flaming borders of hell.

Planks on stumps made rudimentary taverns where jokes, wagers and ancient broadsheets could be swapped, squabbles flared, familiar ditties were droned:

> *Jesus dead and gone to glory*
> *And the mill has dropped a sail.*

From bare windows, through wheels and irregular alleys, Albrecht could be momentarily seen, long-haired, fastidious, unarmed, in pale-blue cloak, dappled in sunlight, negligently contemplating men guarding the stockade, a woman skinning a rabbit, a fellow with a glinting belt examining horses. As always, unblemished by the heat, he had soon vanished. Brutish outlanders, at first incredulous or suspicious, quickly acknowledged his ascendancy, sensing lineage and more. They had not hitherto encountered an Albrecht, young squire of the bright brow. Hans's lolling tongue, childish grimaces and antics were less extraordinary, yet appropriate to enchanted Troy and burly Rhinelanders' hard tack. Switzers and gippies were soon doffing imaginary hats, making jocular obeisances, calling good-humoured greetings to the queer little creature who was at least as credible as the tarted-up idols in churches which made holy miff-muffs and wormy mugwumpers frig themselves into heaven and spit out mad litanies.

The alliance, seldom witnessed but which all knew, between a dotty shepherd and the young squire, was, when you thought of it, natural. Jesus had his whores, dancers, bumpkins; without wicked Satan and feeble Adam, God would have no story.

Albrecht's self-appointed retinue of students, Balts and tough river-men was scarcely needed; beside them he looked almost frail, yet his disdaining to carry a weapon diminished their swords, pistols and knouts. The less he spoke, the more he was heard. At his approach, the seething exuberance calmed, a crowd would divide, blessings were called upon him which, in unobtrusive sleight, he contrived to acknowledge without appearing to notice. One student quoted a Mainz poet: . . .

109

fresh light is nevertheless older than the world. Talk was rife about Albrecht's refusal to accept a crown, that he was treating with the Emperor, negotiating a loan.

Such a one does not love or hate; he might hold a feast but despises burnt offerings, is pained by incense, shrugs away harlotry and, like a graf, looks neither to right nor left, and is not tempted to applaud the spectacle of a bull mounting a heifer, to the frantic, mock-animal bleats of children. Endowed with more than unshowy arrogance, he has the alchemy of a new word, from the south, *charm*, or rather an old word braced with a fresh inflexion, which states no law, conforms to no title, but silently exerts a passion to submit. Unquestioned, unquestionable. A battered, punch-up *Landesknecht*, all scars and bruises, whom even the children feared, and who spat at Hans's very name, at his one sight of Albrecht, found his savagery wilt, and, though the words sounded like a foul oath, he mumbled in grotesque helplessness, 'He's only to lift his hand. . . .'

Daily the atmosphere thickened from stewpots, steaming fish pans, charred wood, from animals alive or dead, loose dung, offal, mounds of peat and rotting vegetables. Older women, grunting about Last Days and Better Worlds, absorbed themselves in establishing homes, but the younger were disinclined to wash clothes, assist communal cooking and care of children; when not lackadaisical in sunlight, they sought to join men in night raids and ambushes, swag the Graf's deer within bolt-shot of the Castle, silent in its dung-heap of glory, as if deserted, though one morning a basket of loaves, cabbage and cheese was found on the edge of the woods, apparently dumped by some traitor to old Poke-Nose. An encouraging portent.

The role of Trojans was to await whatever was being planned: the break-out, the Emperor's largesse, even the Last Days. With insufficient to do, greybeards reverted to the games abandoned by the young. When not sleeping, they would be tossing logs, playing tag, staggering blindfold in a circle, or, sweating, gasping, striving to race between the crudely daubed pegs. They squatted over dice or gippy cards painted with numbers and oriental courtiers. One fellow, caught cheating, lost a finger, though such an outburst was rare in this expectant brotherhood, for whom the future was a cherished part of the family. Others rolled ill-made balls, threw a dried bladder between themselves in a play of complex rules and imposts, and made indecent proposals to women who winked, chuckled and withdrew.

Old and young shared contentment. Each day was a continent of small surprises, helter-skelter adventures, disputes and lavish reconciliations, and meals which, if irregular and unpredictable, were extravagant. *Take no heed for tomorrow* the Lord had taught. Experienced freebooters from cities, however, took care to salvage pickings which might be useful in whatever tomorrow – a trashy jewel, beaded shawl, a foal, a net, a top, a stray orphan flaxen-haired beneath soiled lousiness – but for most the idle steps of summer, pot-house good cheer and indulgent liberties were unsullied respite from lifelong pursuit, vagabondage, bloodshot labour, and silences diseased and merciless. The lessons of past centuries had been wrong, cruelly distorted. Escape was possible, sin and hunger need not rack you for ever. In this empire of Polly the sun-god, the ordinary had lapsed. The Christ who loves the misbegotten and wronged, and lambasted snivelling rulers had led them here, to rest protected by the young squire, the redhead in whom absurdity was wisdom, and 'Nevis', invisible as the Holy Ghost, potent as 1500.

The Camp had transformed to Troy, and now, in this August furnace, Troy had fully merged into the famed, so long elusive, Garden of Delight where nakedness had begun, and was at last doing so again, beginning when Kick-the-Dog Heiner, flushed and swollen from drink, perhaps goaded by an older man or a girl, pulled off his shirt, then his breeches, standing vaingloriously naked, like a smirking tyro, master of ceremonies, buttocks raddled with nettle-rash, thick cock askew. At once an outsize Bohemian, his own member lengthy as a gosling's neck, did likewise, and in nothing but his boots, chortling, rampant, he plucked the unresisting Ant from her startled companions and hurried her away, leaving his mark on her to much merry acclaim,

111

and excited giggles from the Ant herself within the constant song and chatter, neighings and snufflings, the sizzle and buzz and shouts.

Mottled, marbled, cheesy, caky, wounded, unblemished, slender, brawny, shy, flaunting, nakedness was the true attire of a Garden of Delight, nature's gift. Soon it was commonplace, students repeating a Latin tag that truth herself is bare as Eve. Men and women strolled golden in sunshine, vanity gratified, enjoying each other, fondling, laughing, between carts, on open grass, lying embracing in dust, jig-jagging by the brook, happy in the marvellous relief of marriage unsanctified but sincere, consummated, though a few roger-rogues more coldly, more methodically, humped their kitty-frees and demanded payment, indifferent to whatever finery-winery Albrecht might think. The word being made flesh, an educated voice said approvingly. Children, ever-watchful, cackling arse-hole jests, played statues, posing lewdly, and imitated the lovers strutting like Irish sacred swineherds. The names of other primeval games – Find the Treasure, Down the Cave, Beware the Neighbour – acquired new meanings.

Many sported belts of ivy or larch-leaf or in teasing humour covered their breasts and loins with transparent gauze plundered from high-road merchants. Elderly women, draped and kerchiefed, affecting not to notice the carnal hilarity, were making gardens, scratching out strips for beans, cabbage, devil-green parsley, carrots, mixed with sparkling queen's thoughts, marigolds, purply-mallow and daisy. They quickly sprouted in alleys between wagon wheels and tent-pegs, huts and steaming midden pits and in the ditch outside the Citadel's rampart. Simples were pulled from outer fields, then replanted, as remedies for suppurating wounds and insect bites. In the molten heat plants, upright at dawn, by noon were trailing in dust, though thistle and dockweed roved undeterred from between planks and in cracked walls.

More pasture was being fenced, where cows and goats munched peacefully, carelessly supervised by volunteers otherwise exhausted by New Times. An attempt to plough had been frustrated by the baked ground.

Foragers, bragging raucously, carted in from the mountains a squat frith-stone which gives forty days' sanctity to whoever sits on it. With such a possession, such confident noise, spontaneous love and generous couplings, the authority of Pope and bishop, Graf and tax-gatherer could be mocked with epithets jaunty as cup and ball. Even the staid old women enjoyed hearing of a tinker confronting Speyer Cathedral where bearers of great pomp are buried, so that miracles are common, and the tinker saw one. Praying, he muddled the words so that an imperial mausoleum abruptly changed from stone to glass, and pilgrims and worshippers gaped at five corpses, uncorrupted and gleaming, though of parrots.

Fugitives were now a considerable populace, shying at monotony, agog for new feelings, spurts of liberty and adventure. Fetters had dropped away, bounds were shattered, the unbelievable was established for all to see. There was scant inclination to envisage a settled home here where winter would not be for ever repulsed by merriment. The body had relaxed, fatigue allowed sleep and dreams, but all was preparation. Castles could be stormed, churches ransacked, markets pillaged, before a further Garden would be reached, remote as carpets, but limitless, orgiastic, hitched to the providential, a stupendous kick into the balls of fate, the grand climacteric of 1500.

Sunlight was always unfurling from yellows to golds towards the first mountain slopes, gnats hung like veils on the languid air, leaves were sallow. Under a canopy, tawdry but upholding his eminence, Hans watched. Frau Holle the witch with shining bubs, hands gloved with silver, mumbled her spells; he looked again and saw a peeled, whispering birch leaning against the light.

He would lie for hours, his head awry with drink, lips apt to froth, too slothful, too tired to attend to his famed Little Pike, his Pork Sword, which throbbed too little but could still revive, at flesh pale or burnt, forked, haunched, slobbering in mad-bull frenzy over breasts seen through closed, drugged eyes as the cones of Broken Mountain. His own small eyes stirred, then gleamed, prying into greasy wrigglings, underworld cavities deep as sea; though bodies had become blurred, identical as leaves, he saw all possible bellyings and grovellings, feeling himself strip one girl, drop on another, joining the madcap dance. Sopping, tangled roots jutted and weakened, crammed with Garden needs and impulses.

He sighed with dazed satisfaction. His visions had born this rich harvest, tingling with summer. It was nothing that he was slovenly, over-fattened, spotty, his hair lustreless; what Master Wilhelm had called a shapeless lump of dough. He gurgled happily at a bowl of rabbit stew, rook mince, dumplings; smiled vacantly at a girl tearing a wing off a captured gull, at others burying a live cat, leaving the frantic, whimpering head exposed, then stoning it; at a boy and an old man quarrelling over a strawberry; at races for a pebble or a stick dipped in honey, women belabouring each other with spades; at a boy crying as he tried to rub away his wart.

Lulled and stupid, dangling a sunflower, kept loggy with beer, sometimes wine, he seldom piped and not always remembered stories, though sometimes, to Grete, or to no one in particular, he might begin a drooling, benighted description of a glass mountain, sky journey, a tower that turned with the sun, only to relapse into incoherence or be distracted by a crow making colour above dazzling water.

Men winked. Small, precious Hans with his dumb queenlet might soon be tempted into a tourney with a cockerel, wielding cucumber or loaf, or a bout with deep-shafted Hilde. She had once inclined towards a nunnery, incessant prayers, mouldy bread and milk, woeful chants, dry barren nights, but now allowed entrance to anyone sufficiently tooled. In New Times, one should not be too virtuous, passions need no longer be secretive as a gippy's handclasp. As God enjoineth, *Go ye forth and multiply*. Let not flesh become undernourished or overripe from neglect.

Nevertheless Hans had not wholly forfeited position. One evening a decrepit beggar, blained and filthy, was dragged in, hoarsely pleading, the words rattling in his throat like granite chips. 'Mary and the saints . . . young sirs . . . young sirs. . . .' Standing by were those champions of New Times, Heiner and

Johannes, leathery as tanners, bare but for short breeches and stolen stag-boots, both hung with knives whose glitter detracted from their slabbed cheeks and stable-boy spunkiness. They wrinkled their sensitive noses, their lordly faces scowled, in disgust fortified not by a suspicion of spies but a need to swagger.

'You bring us nothing. Such as you . . . you take, you take more. . . .'

Some girls, two Garden-naked, tittered approval: the stalwart pair had themselves much to bring, if much to take. Familiarity brought no contempt. Older people looked undecided, not very interested, and none demurred. In the blur of rowdiness, upsurge and satiety they grudged little but lacked energy for the less than urgent.

The old man, on his knees, struggled to lift an arm, but, very weak and bent, desisted, resigned himself, bowed by the weight of mere survival, with strength only for a groan. But before he could be hustled off, another voice, not powerful yet startling, intervened.

'He'll stay. He must have food.'

Angered and incredulous, the two youths saw not an armed Westphalian or exotic scholar, but Hans, unescorted, holding a thin stick, gazing up at them, his face less doltish than usual. Under the straggly flush of hair his eyes were bright and coherent. Wandering from his perch, bare save for a limp sash, he stood between the old man and his baiters, his mouth losing its now habitual pout and tightening obstinately. He was probably mindful of many old torments.

The score of onlookers, not caring to move, saw discrepancy between the youths' hesitation and the unremitting glare of their blades. They wondered at Hans's temerity, then saw a slow hope straighten the old scarecrow and felt a slight quiver in themselves and others. They felt more, at the sight of Heiner and Johannes cowed and already retreating, absorbed into the milling groups beyond. Hans remained less smiling than, so to speak, overtaken by a grin, doggish in its fealty, then vapourish and infantile.

Leaning negligently against a wagon was the Angel of the Lord, Prince in Exile, Albrecht, outstanding amongst so much flesh and soiled raggedness, glowing in delicate grey hose and white cape, unadorned yet with the smart effect of jewels. His gaze seemed anywhere but on Hans and the beggar; he was unconcerned with the graceless ruffians but had made them flee.

The village, bereft of almost all its children, and now dwarfed by the upstart township barely a league distant, morosely celebrated harvest, much of it trodden down or illicitly cut. Rites were perfunctory. Their faces rusted, they bound the dry sheaves, their red, calloused hands moving as if by themselves, their eyes thickened over the husks, so that they sometimes stumbled into each other without realizing it as though in a weird, cumbrous dance. Harvest music was lacking. The fiddler had departed. Piper? Don't mention him. No one cheerfully shouted the antique cry *Ooanswald*, or leapt over stooks, hopped round the corn-spirit fashioned from the last sheaf, decorated and sceptred with a willow switch, to preside over cropped, glistening fields, reassuring the indignant earth before joining the last ghosts of summer.

Almost furtively, the broad, awkward men stooped, bound, carried: they spat, groaned and cursed, their women behind them gleaning and refilling jugs.

That their children might have abandoned them, probably for ever, would deny them provision for old age but affected them less than the strain of their labours, though such labours were yet a refuge from harsh forebodings. Their blood spoke of retribution, perhaps gibbetings, for crimes not their own. The Tax had been paid, chimney-seat recalcitrants had been punished by rinderpest Master Wilhelm, but inexorably the Castle's grip would tighten, the nearby herd of scoundrels plunge the entire region into ruin, the innocent be rounded up with the guilty. Each day brought grim tidings. Huge, swart Swabian miners were on the way, under standards of Barbara, saint not only of miners but of guns: miners were an underground breed, terrorizing and befouling, descendants of demonic giants who had fought the gods of lost peoples.

116

Scared, bewildered, lost, even the men crowded into the crumbling, lustreless church, their virility and stubborn beliefs unavailing. With much of her blue robe rotted away, nailed to a wormy rood-screen that reminded them of a gallows, the Virgin, affronted by the meagre offerings, was deafer than usual, her eyes blanker, her white smile no more than a promise that next year's harvest would be worse.

Unresisting, they were rebuked and chastened by the priest. They sang penitential hymns, invented extravagant sins at confession, hoping that enormities would win greater forgiveness, but no child returned, the Castle lowered gaunt and menacing, and, on the windless forenoon, without warning the mountain forests shook violently, then were unnaturally still.

From Hans, daftie changeling or elfin sprite, only evil could have been expected. He should have been exterminated like his twin. But Albrecht! Yet who, after all, could trust an Albrecht? He had never been one of them, he owed them nothing, his pledge was elsewhere, his very mother a bawd who never ventured amongst them.

With considerable satisfaction the priest would survey them in a calculated silence, long enough for some women to start weeping and the men to slump further into misgivings, until, one bony hand aloft in malediction, his voice aiming inflexible hammer-blows, he intoned, not in Latin, sonorous but meaningless as a sough of the wind, but in their own dialect, his meaning inescapable: *And the Lord said unto Satan, whence comest thou? And Satan answered the Lord, From going to and fro on the earth, and walking up and down on it.*

Imagine that! Satan could be encountered at any milestone, be found at crossways or behind a wall, or walking *to and fro*. This must explain their children's dementia, the hideous temptations, the entwining of Albrecht and Hans, the beautiful and the squalid, like incest, forbidden, uncanny, though of course frequent enough.

The sky remained troubled with vain intimations of rain, preying on nerves already raw, though above the peaks it flared red gold and the stars sparkled unchanged against the white run

117

of the moon. The world itself was threadbare, awry, possibly from some Turkish calamity, a gigantic fissure in the yellow Lands of the Hun, or some monstrous sin by a great one which had rightly infuriated God.

Humble folk have few certainties. They know that God's punishments are unforeseeable but deadly: that from a subterranean river, not charted but as real as Castle and Mountain, dart supernatural particles that infect the sinner and the righteous alike, upsetting intentions, edicts, faith, revoking oaths, against which Grace, though incomprehensible, is the only defence: that a collapsing star denotes a woman's agony: that a piper's tune can wickedly deceive those hitherto sinless: that from seeds planted in Adam's mouth grew the tree from which the fatal Cross was hewn. It might be that the virtuous need know nothing more.

Despite the scalding summer, convictions abounded that Fimbul was almost due, delivered by the appalling 1500. Planets were ceasing their music, the sheep were being separated from the goats, to wailing and gnashing of teeth.

As August ended, the Garden of Delight clamoured with exhilaration crowning, and, please God, prophetic. At midnight, on the border between August and September, the first child was born, the child of hope, prince imperial, and, bunched in sacking, tiny, scarcely moving, without a squawk, laid on the Frith Stone between godfathers, Hans in simpleton gratification, Albrecht, son of the morning, quietly gracious, while the mother wept joyfully, and though the father did not appear, was known to none, a multitude embraced, sang, lurched in hackabout mirth, some confiding that the infant, wizened as a walnut, was really a Barbary monkey, deserting the Castle for fruitier times. Most, however, were swept on a gust of happiness for the child of hope, guarantee of the future. Like Hans's stories, the birth harked back to days even before Old Times which were best forgotten. For many more, it was a harvest special to the Garden. Life in its providence coloured the year in rosary sequence of festivals, carnival outbursts. Thus it must have been long ago, *at one time* under the flashing star, with the three astrologers from Sparta or Egypt, the devoted animals, the terrified, hugger-mugger king in his wicked palace, and when honest folk could expect a flounder in the pan.

Under skies now cleared, at noon blue as Mary, lemon after sunset, thoughts of rain banished probably for ever, celebrations lasted three days. In the genius of festival, mummers' frolic, existence itself was improvised, riddled with jests and surprises, rag-bag rhymes, many-tinted caps and leggings impudently contrasting patches of nakedness. Uninterested in any baby, the children, bright elves of creation, twirled in manic flights, beat shovels, stuck on barely recognizable animal masks, leap-frogged, whistling and screeching, over sweaty lovers, robbed provision dumps, cramming down forcemeat, onion curd and apples in this surge of sheer being, the tides of excess. This was a fifth season, cleansed of sin, death, judgement, brutal law, without priest or Graf. Those three days would be remembered through eternity. For so long, the merry-makers had lain on verminous earth, inside a stench apparently inescapable, had been hunted by tax officials, pardoners, conscription-mongers, monopolist millers, yet very occasionally dreamt of a golden emperor, a spire crimson and colossal, a meadow of pearls, chips of the moon. The true Empire was of feasts lit with the unearthly, as in the halls of Friendly Ones; of Green Stone radiance; and of scents, nameless, wafted from an ornate carriage, from silks and satins said to be laundered in boys' urine, or from a shining window barred against the jostling, huckstering street.

The third day was a natural summit of this exultant rainbow communion, the rave of poverty. An armless man, bacon-faced, attracting old jokes about hiding things up his sleeve, danced in Flemish clogs, a whirl of jerks, flourishes, well-managed somersaults, grimacing wildly between his own obscenities about Plough Saturday, Escape Sunday, willing heifers, squeezing pimples, Jack lost in undergrowth, and still lower quips about girls' quivering quivers. Dressed as women, bearded woodsmen acted fandangling playlets of Adam and Eve, Onan harried by an indignant ghost and a cruel stepmother, knights fighting. In the last, the ever-restless Heiner and Johannes, reeking with plum spirit, in ploughboy clumsiness tripped each other, staggered up bespattered with blood, women wild with admiration, imagining this expertly staged. Noisily greeted was 'Lake Ladoga', a Balt reciting the popular ballad about the Jew's daughter tempting a Christian lad with a poisoned apple. All joined the chorus:

> *Come in, come in, my pretty child,*
> *Come in and bar the door.*

Coped in purple-dyed sackcloth, with elongated artificial rump, waving a spade, a mock-bishop besought alms, affecting a High Folk delivery, then preached, sardonic, jeering.

'Hear ye, goatlings and sheeplings, the promise of our comrade of the blessed order of vagrants, despoiler of virgins, creator of evil, who killed his only-begotten son that ye might live as ye always have done, in shit-bound sin and pigsty filth. Live more abundantly in suffering, toadying to Father that unjust stewards be rewarded, the Mammon of unrighteousness befriended, the meek trussed for Caesar's pleasure, the Empire cleansed with refiner's bitter fire, and the rich installed for ever on the stinking necks of the poor who exist world without end, amen.'

'Amen' was roared happily, and, dropping his lordly pose, he reassured them in broad Bavarian, 'Ye are the salt of the earth.'

At once a lithe 'Syrian', stained with walnut-juice, in tasselled gown and mauve and red turban, rather casually performed miracles. Hunched over a pile of ashes, with a flutter of hands, his whispered incantation sounding like a snigger, he threw across the ground an oblong shadow, which changed to smoke, human-shaped, swaying, gesticulating, before sinking into the ashes. His hands fluttered again, at once a blotch, very visibly, covered Scarcely Seen's sun-blistered cheek, then he removed it with a bardic praise-song which nevertheless contained a caustic allusion to the long-nosed Graf's parentage. The Syrian then vanished, not into ashes but into Donk's tent, having made a man's dagger leap from its sheath.

This was a Passover night from which that old jade the moon

hid herself, perhaps disavowing the threats of vengeance on earthly masters: the Sultan would find a dart in his neck, and his Prophet's beard tied up in knots, abbots and indulgence-sellers lose their balls, though a cheer, laughing but amiable, was raised for the Emperor: now triumphant over barbarians, now pursued and defiled, poor old Fritz strapped to Fortune's Wheel might seek refuge here and be grateful to the valour of unseen but powerful Nevis.

How does such celebration end? Not with a dignified procession headed by Albrecht, not with the proclamation of a finely phased master plan, not with an exquisite prayer of thanks for salvation or superb silence. How else can it end? You already know.

Forgotten throughout the inflamed mood, the vengeful and satyric, now, as bodies tired, desires slackened, from the seething, greasy flesh, the fumes and smells, Hans, barely awake, heard cries from the salt of the earth. A story, a story. He was swiftly up, needing no cajoling but voraciously reclaiming allegiance, surrounded by elated faces, the bearded and ringleted, the branded; faces shrewd or credulous, faces like lard, like roasted boar, children's faces knowing, arguing; faces of back-street Maggies, Italian cutthroats, the bruised, ravaged and the very simple, packed within the silvered, fuggy dark. Hans could have recognized Donk in his glory, the Jackdaw, Stinger and the Ant, no longer a child but less than a woman; Big Hilde, not yet big in the belly, Scarcely Seen . . . but he saw none of them, only the dim, rippling crescent of Garden Folk, dependent on himself alone, folded in the huge night of the German Empire.

A torch was lit, held high behind him. He waited until the clamour subsided into shuffles and murmurs, then all were silent, trained on the flame-lit idol, ill-favoured, badly shaped, tufted by His Highness the Devil, the despair of God, yet who had bathed in the underground river, seen the wondrous, the miraculous, was product of lusts long prohibited yet beckoning. Some listeners had lain agonized in dungeons, been stretched for the knot, the clamp, the pick, had trembled at the Inquisitor's question, and had choked youth away under verminous thatch. These sprawled in quiet, toxic satisfaction after the long day, the long journey,

121

clasping mugs, waiting. Like the blind, this shepherd thing saw with a difference. His dribble of words could transfix them like the Syrian's passes and juggles or their sluts' promises.

Huddled nearest him the children were more familiar with what would come and would resent novelty. Dearer to them than top or hobby-horse were heroes neither real nor imaginary: the giant without a heart, the fish giving golden rings to an ungrateful hen-wife, Joachim on the Hillside, the snake woman, the kitchen-maid's fur slipper, the palace of ice. *At one time.*

Hans began his last story, husky, as from a throat thick with must, yet thrillingly distinct and confident, and at once the most hardened, the poke-eyes, tainted dry-bones and ravaged tarts, many hearing him for the first time, realized that they would hear nothing of cock-sucking Templars and circumcised Saracens, of fornication with unicorns, of bakers' daughters pouting and greedy, cuckolding the blacksmith. But they were content, solaced by drink, the flame, the comfortable hush, the languor so cooling as delirium ended. Weak and absurd, he softened them as they lay inert, knelt, stood, meshed in what a chronicler terms *raptus*, a state neither drunken nor mystic but 'appertaining to benediction', softly dreamy, in which a snatch of song, an unexpected positioning of tired words can ease the soul from the body, into madness or salvation, which are sometimes identical. Dumb Grete, crouching dimly behind the story-teller, could be an other-world wraith befitting such a deliverer. Everywhere the shadows of dwellings, wheels, stores, animals, vague and shifting, assisted this Trojan story for the healing of spirit.

'At one time,' Hans nodded in happy complicity, 'was a gate, black; tree, green; river, white. An' sheep, 'oney, jar of gold. Also' – the peaky face creased shrewdly, the voice paused, then resumed before the first stir – 'a lie, and wind. They come together for stories. The gate begins fust.'

He nodded again but only to himself, glad of intimacies with the mettlesome gate.

'A man in blue dress leaves dog to mind house. Sets out. Why? To find lost wife. Wives lose themselves, an' more.'

Men chuckled, their women shook their heads, not disputing but resigned.

'Look, 'e did, in deepest earth, blackest forest, under bridges. Fought mountains, for tracks an' traces. She was nowhere. Then stag with silver 'orn, p'r'aps she's inside it. But it shakes great 'ead, sogs off fast. 'e can't follow, too tired. Slow too. Didn't know it but treadin' the path to 'ell.'

Again he stopped, miming alarm. A voice breathed, 'Go on.' Old and young repeated it and several strained to see Half-hanged Jok, who had also trod such a path.

'Soon saw the 'ell-dog with heads, all quarrelling awful, an' the 'igh Fok an' like covered with fire. Screams like billies kept from nannies. Bog, muck deep as you think. Snakes yellow, browns, black. Sees 'orses, men atop. 'Orses only bones, slime-green. Men's faces dug away. No skin, only bone. There's a tower on 'ill, outside it are piles of dry grass, dry cowshit, brambles. Inside, the moans. Tall women stand roun' the tower, spears at ther' feet. They watch the ground. Down, down below, the snakes, the bog, the fire, the screams. Fire's climbing the 'ill. The tower's gone. Then, look, a man lying on stones, all chains. Look agen, from 'igh rocks, a snake drips poison on him. There's girl, swan-feather, holding cup over 'is eyes to catch poison until it flows over and she must go empty it an 'e howls. Our man in blue dress leaves 'er, kneeling, holding up cup. Then, farther on – is it a day, is it a week? – there's 'is wife. There she is, standing in same black clothes beside another girl, all bare, starkin'. Flames are round them but they're safe, cool, rain on leaf. Wife 'as apples, which dried-up old men want. Apples make them juicy agen. Man sees that between 'im and wife are coins, 'umped up, an' kings' crowns, gold plates, sparkin' rings.'

His head drooped, top-heavy with words but, transfigured, in solitary radiance, he was far from the gentle heads and curly fleece of his lost sheep. No one could recall a stammering, deformed imbecile, snottish, spluttering, whimpering as the stones flew and the boots descended, his eyes only tiny swellings on a cheese face. Strangers, chewing dried peas, thought of buried days, of tag played round the pump, clambering for birds' eggs, a rare kindness wrung from Father, Mother's tame bird with eyes

123

jabbed out to make it sing sweeter; first lessons – feed the hog, beware gippies, tinkers, lepers and bakers' dozens; happiness at bacon flung from a wedding feast or swiped from a cart, trembling at a knight, sinister and unfaced by his slitted helm; silence at swans on a dark-green flood dipping heads into the sun scattered like golden ducats in stories. The time of the purple giant akimbo, glowing in the night. Hans could tell of the sea where waves collapsed like weary hounds, then sprouted cornflower and daisy: he had seen gingerbread houses, painted stoves large as carriages, ladies in nothing but gems and crimson boots whose smiles split men across the middle, and a witch who could hide behind her little finger. If souls existed, they were fed by such stories, rare as baked sturgeon or Rhineland wine.

Exhortations loudened. 'Go on . . . go on.'

''issings and thunder, there really were 'orse-stinks that slew. Saw red eyes big as the mill-wheel. More gold, lying around like shit. But nobody wanted it, no one cried cheer for it. Too much smoke an' pains an' bites. The man sees kings sink into bog, 'ole towns breakin', but 'e's un'armed in 'is blue dress. Wife steps to 'im. Look, she's laughing, 'e's no flummoxin' ghost, they run out of the smoke an' fire, wanting world above. The other girl weeps but they're far away. The path's steep. At the top there's the scape-hole, the dog lies with all 'eads asleep. Now they're safe, on dew-drop grass, in the sun. But as the sun strikes 'er, she's suddenly just a bit of mist, like she's falling back, isn't she, down the 'ole, gone in grief, nothin' left. The man's alone in empty field. 'e calls, but gets 'is own voice. 'e must go back home, long long way. Many days on, sees roof, hut; 'is own dog waits, jumps up, falls dead in joy. That's what the gate told.'

From a bleary sight of the gate they felt the day at hand when Troy and the Garden, paradise and hell, would, rejoicing, hurl down all gates.

18

Autumn was about, in scattered browns and golds, moving slyly like a poacher, Castle ladies giggling about spendthrift trees emptying their purses. Harvest was over, the land, Jörd, Earth Mother, the sun's daughter, was fulfilled, though leaves remained strong, mountains darkly glistening, their peaks flaring at sundown. Only the Castle was naked and barren amid Reaper's Month flounce, and weary labourers confided that the Graf, girthed by the wicked Tax, had fled, or was dying from guilt, God's anger, having heard the pipe of that red-headed sprite lording over the rude, insurgent camp, with all the world wondering which brood of civets had fostered him.

From as far away as Holland babble drifted about Ephraiss, an ancient seer who had foretold a false Christ, sweet-tongued and perditious, sealing hands and foreheads with the sign of the fig, which Jesus so hated but which could outlast all. Amongst his followers, sinners, malefactors and splash-me-and-run Dickons, women would be equal with men, feasting in harlot revels. The patchwork Empire clattered with exchanges about the rebellion – malapert, the Archdeacon of Mainz termed it; barbaric fledgelings were growing charmed lives, two had sprouted wings and, though excommunicated, condemned by the infant Bishop-elect of Gandersheim, placed under the Ban of the Empire, they had gathered an army, with Roman breastplates, Mongoloid swords, tarnished antique shields, as though some discredited Caesar had returned, trumpeting for the downfall of Christendom. In darkened valleys and remote tyes old wives mumbled about crazed knights gathering in forests, the Swabian miners incited by a wicked Merlin. A broadsheet, printed surreptitiously, hailed the parish-pump Little Piper as the Second Coming. Fiery crosses suggested wholesale rebellion, innocent fires in meadows were stamped out by scared landlords. *Hunt* assumed unpleasant meanings.

Yet the Castle had retained its earlier mood, not quite levity but certainly lighter. Without carnival love, without christening or blessing, somewhere in its shambling depths was felt an effulgent presence, a febrility, hidden but somehow evident. If literally unseen, so was the divine. Scurrilities in garderobe and around Great Oven and amongst gatehouse bawds were livelier, with stories taller than Lentleheimer's spire.

More ladies were about in flimsier attire, dawdling by windows, gossiping in arbours, primping and singing: the shadows glimmered with damascenes and polished hair-styles. They no longer moped behind screens and walls, secluded like reluctant nuns. They were light-eyed in nimblejack pleasure, roused as if by a tournament. Pert noses lifted, soaped hands trembled prettily, in playhouse display. They told each other that the noxious children were reverting to stoat and fox, very impiously. That the Saviour, whose love of mischief should not be overlooked, transformed sinners to swine, was a very different affair. An Austrian girl, recently married to the Graf's cousin, anxious to ingratiate herself, repeated the wisdom of the Holy Father, Gregory the Great: *Cursed be he who restrained his sword from the shedding of blood*. She gasped a little, as she had at a cock-fight.

Overhearing some of this, Uncle reflected that sensible rule is almost always safeguarded not by the shedding of blood but by the telling of lies.

Yet outwardly nothing had happened. Night fires still glittered from the infamous outlaws, songs and imprecations could be heard, sickness must be rife. Yet lords and ladies apprehended a new sensation at work amongst them, even perhaps a fresh presence, discernible in the Graf's eye and gait. Once more he was moving more briskly, looking younger. He must know what others did not. The Emperor must have promised support, the Swabians have been ambushed in the mountains, and manifold curses have dispatched many to hell. Reappearing in long violet mantle, the Graf said no more than that, though no magician had revived the hound, his hawk had recovered her feathers, her little bell tinkled again. Clearly, burning crosses and nonsense about a Second Coming distressed him not at all, his following bowed at his approach, even the barbican troops gave him a grudging salute.

The Graf almost smiled, and certainly lifted a gloved hand,

but concealed his thoughts. Within himself he was even more gratified. He had a plan, not wholly or indeed chiefly his own, not yet to be disclosed even to the Fighting Commandant. He enjoyed his silence, and had always relished the old Roman noble who, in a field, when questioned about policies to be adopted towards his chief rivals, said nothing but flicked off the heads of the tallest nettles.

Undeterred by his master's preoccupation, the Fighting Commandant was stately with importance, his scabbed features, bulbous as his codpiece, grim as he enrolled yet more men, conscripted smiths and farriers, ordered women to collect dried fox-tongues, useful as poultices for arrow wounds. He dispatched messengers, he clanked up and down before the ladies and handed the Clerk bills for unavoidable expenses, and doubtless remembered Jesus's injunction, as reported by the Confessor, that we should behave as though we were to live for ever yet die tomorrow.

The Clerk, while frowning over the expenses, was content. The Tax had been collected and could be spent. Ducats, the Pope himself had remarked, are not to be sneezed at; a promulgation, if not quite a bull, and to be readily accepted. Almost more important, unaided by the Confessor, he had discovered design in the riotous troubles of Christendom, so markedly degenerating into 'Europe'.

The world sinks, but only to rise, dies in order to live, suffers to attain salvation. Avoiding the Confessor, not caring to proclaim truth to Uncle, the Clerk, who knew all that could be known about time, explained to the others that history, another word seldom used and not always understood, derived less from gardens, trees, apple and snake, but from the number three.

Ladies yawned, men turned away, but others, perforce, listened. In fresh white gown, very earnest, pleased with his own industry, indifferent to his lowly place at table, the Clerk expounded doctrine, the Confessor, by nodding at set intervals, managing to suggest that his junior was recalling what he, in his eminence, had previously taught him.

The Clerk explained a treatise, centuries old, by Joachim, Abbot of Fiore, a region otherwise obscure, by which the past was seen to outline the future and clarify the present. Like the Abbot,

127

the Clerk, as befitting a tax official, was dedicated to numbers, and disclosed Joachim's thesis that mankind had been destined to endure for eighteen centuries. For six the stern Father had reigned, ending with Charlemagne, succeeded for an identical period, by the loving Son. This period was now concluding, as all could witness, making room for the Holy Ghost, which would doubtless welcome the Second Coming but, more certainly, end with the Last Judgement, itself preceded by wars, insurrections, Fimbul famines, through which the righteous must strengthen themselves to endure, add a cubit to their stature, work for the Kingdom, for what blasphemous agitators call New Times, though in such times lay their doom, the doom shared with heretics, Turks, the wilfully ignorant, and those who seek to cast off rulers, laws, godly customs. The Holy Ghost, on such evidence, had limitations as a ruler.

Some, he continued, using words as deftly as he did numbers, were wickedly pretending that none but the perfect have the right to survive. But man, by nature, is imperfect. In these mountain lands only one man had approached it, all knew his splendid Name and indeed Honour. 'He is one of those who build the dykes and suppress the violent, who rebukes licence and heals the murrain in the soul.'

The Clerk then calculated, to no very pronounced glee from his hearers, that for three more centuries the righteous themselves must strive with the unrighteous, until, not silly pipers and treacherous renegades, but a band of monks, wise, strict and steadfast, would restore harmony by total victory and superior lives, ushering in Last Years, for the elimination of the perverse, unnatural, refractory, grievous and condign, and forfended by God.

The words rolled from his prim mouth, giving them more pleasing visions: of others' torments, their own place in the world, of the eye of Providence. Well-being was rooted and certain, deliberate as a heron; the Emperor, whatever his privations, remained Emperor, and was owed total allegiance against Devil and rebels.

That night all were convinced, not by the Clerk's exposition

128

but from the vague, wordless, the felt but unspoken yet as unmistakable as a horn sounding from distant woods, that the Graf's years of distress were at last ended, indeed rewarded, pat, as if on a mummer's cue; that the wolf's-head outburst and false shepherd were vanquished, superior lives burning away iniquitous tares. This was agreed, though no clash of arms was known, no procession had been dragged to the Horse, the crackpot messiah had not sought Judas's fate.

Lords and noble deeds would prevail, together with Holy Church on her rock, Uncle's exquisite learning, and the unseen radiance whose hypnotic blossom so enthralled the Graf, through whom the Castle would be renewed, the land restored. Repentance would avail nothing, a rebel ceases to be human, retribution was due.

19

The Garden was blighted. Overnight, frost had begun out of season, desolation stalked with a scythe, colours falling dead. The very dogs lay disconsolate, as if after a beating. A children's song lingered, unheard but remembered, twisted to new meanings as a boy known as That's Right sprawled amongst docks, coughing his last.

> *Summer slumbers, all must cease*
> *Lady Brunhild's lost her fleece*
> *for want of the golden prince.*

Toughened survivors, mauled by war and want, slouched, squatted, talked in low tones, hands tight on their weapons. They disregarded the young who, bewildered and lost, stood on feet that had forgotten dances. Faces long familiar had smudged, some were unrecognizable, withered by hopelessness. No pipe sounded and the sun, part of the wreckage, remained buried behind Broken Mountain on these days of dour cloud and a chill, searching breeze that whipped up dust, flattened the shabby grass, shook ramshackle dwellings. Pots, ladles, platters and jars were strewn everywhere, the long tables were empty, benches overturned, while the very young waited for food or wandered lost between tents, thick spokes, sheds tilted as if lamed.

Albrecht had gone, evanescent summer king, silver enchanter, slipping through a slit in the air on an evening of bluish mist under a pale gold sun.

Slow to comprehend, horrified at accepting it, most of the young at once thought that he had been abducted by the Castle, though a few girls tearfully imagined him melting like a sick star or cat-ice reflection, or stolen by jealous angels. Men, however, worn by experience, scorned such dreaming and Donk stopped the heart by uttering the unthinkable: 'He betrayed us. Was always one of *them*!'

In appalled confusion, legends were revived or invented, to account for monstrosity. A nobleman had splashed himself into some gritty cowgirl or ditch drab who bore Albrecht, whose delicate perfections were Satan's wiles to trap the unwary and mock the common lot. Again, mankind had been betrayed. Beauty had trapped red Adam, thus scourging mortals for ever.

A broken Switzer pikeman, dark-pelted, taloned, a white cut sprawling across one cheek like a displaced grin, and with snarling tongue, swore on his mighty bag of all trades that Albrecht had been a demonic son of wicked Nero, condemned to roam the world inflicting deception and malice until the return of Jesus the Judge. At this even children most loyal to him remembered that he had never allowed himself to be seen naked, and Johannes Ox-Face, stamping in anger and fear, maintained that Albrecht had kept to his tent so that none could see that he had no shadow.

The Garden had gone, leaving only wide, stifling dereliction, smells, uncertainty. People must retreat to Troy Town, but at once recalled that the mighty city had fallen, fallen. Immediately, only at first surreptitiously, many were stealing provisions, oiling wheels, nailing down boxes, attending to horse and mule, swearing that murderers lurked in the woods, Jews had poisoned wells, suicides were rising from crossways.

The Trojans were unshaped, they changed plans hourly, though some had gone by morning. Vision was distorted. The Ant, hitherto petted, sported with, enjoyed, was abruptly disliked and ridiculed, then bloodily assaulted. Girls like Big Hilde were feverish, their eyes ill. Hans, save by Grete, was avoided, for too close association with the traitor. He could be seen sprawling on the ground, stupefied by drink and other-world fancies. Fearful glances were attracted by the Castle brooding under mountain peaks and a darkening, windy sky, once again dangerous.

Rain began, slaty showers from clouds scudding over the world – were they really clouds? – recklessly hurled against mountains, churning the ground, breaking through trees, forerunning the bleakness ahead, submerging rocks and cliffs in shaggy greyness. Nights were shaken by thunder, the Devil's snore; once lightning lit the Castle, momentarily revealing a glaring mass of stupendous, heightened walls, whirling turrets, detached from the earth, about to crush all, until suddenly extinguished, leaving the world, an old woman grumbled, dark as Jewish blood.

Broken-toothed Heinrich told the Stinger that the storms meant that Albrecht lay knifed or strangled under the earth. There he lay, his stars malign, his smile neither friendly nor unfriendly, a sacrifice. Overhearing, several nodded, simultaneously knowing that this was not so. He would always be untroubled, arrows would turn aside from him, monsters retreat, lawyers succumb. Fleeting in sunshine, he vanished in rain.

Dirt was mounting, a smell like mouldy rope sunk into all reaches. Grete struggled to speak, vainly, as people groped for spoils – handcarts, tools, knives, clothes, particularly boots, A girl, foraging, lost herself in the commotions by the stockade and, rain still falling, was quickly surrounded by grinning rag-tags. Drenched and scared, she gazed wildly about her, then stood bowed in helplessness, as a fractious joke hardened into ruthlessness.

'What's the bid, brothers?'

Eyes gleamed in complicity of lust. 'Couple o' spoons. Copper jug.'

"alf my wife . . . the lesser 'alf.'

Their victim shivered, trying to shake off the rain, uncertain of their mood but knowing that there was no escape.

'Let's see her Queen of France. Wouldn't pay donkey's pizzle without that.'

'Circus talk, brother. But she needs a bung in the bung-' ole.'

''er virgin's bower.'

They were grimly determined, bearded, resentful creatures of earth and stone, not strutting peacocks flaunting hues of paradise. No Hans would appear from a story and placate them with a rose, or shame them by a sad smile. She was soon engulfed in a brawl, her assailants kicking, struggling, cursing, falling in slippery mud, pulling themselves up, lunging, fisting, starting blood.

Total disintegration was forestalled by the Castle, from where a supporter stole through the night to confide in the few still manning the stockade that Ritter von Statz, Fighting Commandant, was about to mount his attack, not with a score of worthless archers but with a full company of horse and foot. This restored some measure of purpose and cohesion. Donk, Trojan hero, had already deserted, but Pox Harry, thickset, face and beard scorched by Eastern suns, yelled for stronghearts to join him at the Frith Stone with all available weapons, and more obeyed than might have been expected. 'Hear ye. . . .' His voice was harsh but reassuring, his arms swept above them as if hurling stones, which they soon might be. Before he finished, the rain ceased, shreds of sunlight drifted across Broken Mountain.

Goaded by prospects of action, men desperately formed teams and were soon dragging wagons through sodden refuse and ashes of dunked fires for an outer defence ring, women braced themselves to tip or sharpen arrows, to rewind, reload, and told each other antique remedies: all agreed that a live dog or bird pressed against torn flesh would absorb the pain.

'They're coming.'

A hoarse voice which Hector might once have heard. Men

surged to the northern barricades and at once saw some hundred hireling footsoldiers leaving the lower coppery band of trees, with pikes and halberds, arquebuses upright like quills of some forest monster, glinting in dull air. They were led by a casqued sword-bearer, perhaps the renowned Ritter von Staltz, though he was scarcely imaginable without his horse. Over the Castle a cloud was rimmed with gold, like a phoenix feather.

No parley. On Pox Harry's order the defenders waited, keenly observing that the enemy, still insufficient to encircle their wide quadrilateral, was preparing a mass frontal assault. Taunts brayed as hands tightened on stones, slings, bows, shoddy lances, thin, dented shields. Not yet holding range, they saw grey lumps of metal and leather advancing on them with some precision, soundless, resolute until an intervening strip of marsh made them less orderly. At their back the Castle, lowered between earth and sky, its crowded battlements suggesting innumerable reserves, at the behest of old Long-Nose.

Now they were within bowshot. A long, tense moment, then Pox Harry shouted. Once only. His knockabout artillery discharged stones and arrows backed by a roar loud enough for thousands, then they leapt fence and ditch, scattering children and dogs, the girls amongst them waving knives, iron scissors, slivers of glass. Their counter-attack was not blind, most – Balts, Prussians, Scots, Rhinelanders – were bred from savage conflicts within and without the Empire, though such unbloodied cockerels as Heiner and Johannes were to the fore, headlong, raging, swiping with clubs. Each man trained himself on a single target. Each sensed rather than saw a dim, gashed form buckle, sway, dodge, gasping in pain, staggering, collapsing like a fall of soot. Manic, scenting triumph, they wavered, but only for breath, rallying at Pox Harry's command, against the odds ramming through, in the break-out.

Defeat notwithstanding, the Graf was unperturbed. He had consented to the Fighting Commandant's plea for battle reluctantly, sceptically, and was in truth not displeased by the outcome. Without benefit of advisers, impatient at others' folly, he retained his plan, his master stroke, simple and perfect, yet overwhelming in its effect and now due for fruition. It would embalm his Name, convulse rivals, fortify the imperial honour.

Down below was another night of swill-pots and song, rape and crazed dance, and by morning the place was exhausted and vulnerable, though Pox Harry, almost sober, managed to tramp the rounds, shaking prone figures awake, barbarously swearing, so that, when the trot of horses was heard, dozens came running, reinforced by more as a trumpet blared from without.

Five riders, emerging as if from the sun, armoured, all edges and shine, were lined outside the stockade, the ground still littered with arrows, gloves, shoes, an occasional corpse fly-spattered, caked in black blood. One rider held a white pennant, another nudged his horse forward, visor half-open, powerful, as though the trumpet-call still lingered and he were a Greek champion challenging Troy.

In utter stillness, half-chanted in heraldic ritual, distinct as chimes, his words were undeniably archaic, massed in bemusing splendours inherited from centuries of legal trickery and stylish knavery.

'Hearken to the considered generosity of His Excellency and Lordship the Graf. Hearken all of you. You have fought with a degree of valour. The Graf, renowned and acknowledged for his profundity and verseship of chivalric keepances, imbued in total correspondences appurtenant with everything respected and hallowed by the divine and the profane, greets the very lowest of you, saluting your worth, respecting your rights, and obeisant to the ever-presence of God and his Son. Yet he withal reminds you that, what to you have been battles, have been in all veracity but petty skirmishes. His proper troops he has not yet troubled himself to exercise, though daily their power is magnified. But his benevolence in the stipulations of favour calls a halt to the unchristian, his grace and pleasure desire no more blood, however trumpery, no further anguish. Thus and therefore, because and resulting, he wills that, forgoing just and necessary surrender, withholding the courtesies of abject submission, you select some number of yourselves under his oath of Christian love, his sworn promise of safe conduct, to address him in formal conclave in the Castle which has protected you throughout mortal generations, secure in your loyalties and fidelities. He invites these to ascend the Mountain, partake of his libation, under sealed promise, in all its veritable and extraneous worth fee-simple. . . .'

But jeers, threats, howls were scattering the high-flown promise from Baron Crinkleface, Lord Pig-whistle Nose, begetter of lies, bastard of horse-wind and adders, thief of common rights. The emissary went irresolute, his thick metal about to shrivel, his horse uneasily tossing its head. Behind, the escort strove to hold fast.

The uproar dwindled. From the magnifico declaration was conviction that the Graf had surrendered, or that there was no longer a graf, only a phantom in a castle that had lost its gilt and tang. All waited.

Fingering his sword, aloft on a cart rearing above the stockade, jerkined, thick legs bare, matted hair tumbling, Pox Harry, Hector of the dispossessed, swore again, fouling the air, apparently denouncing the stipulations of favour, urging further attack, the last breakthrough, his oaths more fearful than any castle. They clanged defiance, as, there, the stockade at his back lined with followers, his veins straining, he stood to drive the insolent herald into a wolfpit and dispatch him.

His Trojan posture, drumbeat oratory, however, were wasted. He was still high, still swearing, patchy eyes aflame, when, from below, came a sound like wind in dry grass as the armed mob was sucked apart, making way for a signal apparition, in soiled blouse, weaponless, and at once Pox Harry was irrelevant, ludicrous in his vainglory.

One king moves out, another moves in. During the din and clash of the charge and the squalling, Green Stone brilliancies of success, Hans had been fed like a tame pig by a few children at Grete's sign but was largely ignored. Now he reappeared, passing down the avenue of hushed faces to stand beneath Pox Harry's farmyard dais, his own face, latterly so fluffy, infantile and petulant, steadying into peculiar solemnity, even dedication.

His presence astounded them, Pox Harry himself blinked incredulously and seemed to forget his position, his very self, while the herald sat his restless horse, what a chronicler described as *a sensitive steed*.

Very little is plain as a Prussian, simple as a spoon or cradle-song, undisputed as the Emperor's legitimacy, and so much about Hans – or a child – demands the language of a poet or musician, though this is usually overlooked, acquired inadequately, then mistranslated. The following is only surmise. Hans, sulky at being no longer applauded, grieved and puzzled by Albrecht's disappearance, touched by a silly desire to please by imitating what he had once heard or even seen, or perhaps by some fluke of understanding, or perhaps in search of Albrecht or conforming to whatever he believed Albrecht would wish, uttered – all have agreed this – some imprecation or interdict so gross in its obscenity that it startled Pox Harry himself, so that no chronicler cared to inscribe it, each contenting himself with such a sentence as *the shepherd then affected them with a homely epithet*.

One imagines him standing by the rather sorry shanty-town defences, amongst its hard-breathing, large-eyed survivors, his back to Pox Harry, himself clambering down, now powerless and abashed, whatever the passions seething within him. Hans is peering forward as if comforting sheep, blinking hurriedly, then smiling, slowly, cautiously, yet with a self-satisfaction now covering him like fat.

Such a figure, ageless, deformed, never wholly explained, is set for ever in saga, epic, fate-tale, legend; he is dwarf, goblin, demon from unknown regions, who by appearing on time can overtake history and by some impudent wink or absurd riddle puncture the momentous.

Indisputably he outfaced war-crusted Pox Harry, once the herald's clear tones had reached him. All eagerness to surge forward and wreck the Castle, overcome mountains, reach Hungary, Asia, far Cathay evaporated at his words.

'I will talk them. Lords an' ladies. No dangers. There's tidy space for everyone.'

His voice, never loud or shrill, childish in its waywardness,

136

so often stammering, fumbling in eagerness to remember and describe, yet had Friendly Ones' authority. 'Take no 'eed,' he treasured his moment. 'You gave crown. I'm chosen. I go.'

20

October darkened the land, mountains broadened, pines were taller, denser under the low sky; mists descended, rivers tumbled in grey swirls and chokes, but the Castle remained spirited, amassing light like fortune spurred by the Graf's unusual good cheer and fortune's caprice. Most knew that Albrecht, if not visible amongst them, was within hailing distance, though with consequences difficult to calculate.

In furred, pearled cap and a robe purple as Caesar's, alone save for fleeting servitors and a flea-ridden mastiff drowsing on rushes, the Graf attended to a collation of goose in cabbage sauce, a hunk of soused pork, sweetmeats arranged on daintily tinted sugars, a jug of yellow wine. That the goose had died senile, the pork been extracted from rot, that the wine must have been watered from marsh, the very trencher lying unnoticed on a pocked leaf resembling chips of a gravestone to be left to crack the teeth of the greedy poor, left no more on his consciousness than a ghost's footprints on sawdust. He was Graf, he was father of Albrecht, his will none would dare question. His plan, *their* plan, had succeeded. Had the kitchens served him a branch, calling it venison steak, he might at worst have deemed it too lightly baked, and the reek of onion, plantain and stale cheese have actually pleased him.

Nevertheless, despite his exaltation, his profound, tearful relief, the day had begun with an untoward incident. He had chanced on a book lying on a chest, open as if for himself; an old volume, hand-scripted, the margins decorated with spiralling leaves entwined with snakes, transforming to birds, with rhinestones sunk into the soft velvet covers. The lettering was so elaborate that he could scarcely spell out the title, the far-famed Raymond Lull's *Book of the Order of Chivalrie*.

Compliment? Insult? Warning? Nothing in sublunar existence was accidental.

Chivalrie, he admitted, was well enough, the condescension of nobility, but why write about it? War verses sicken courage, the Gospels traduce the Saviour, who considered it best to write only in dust. No holder of the Golden Fleece owes aught to books. The misery passions of Isolde and Nicolette that the Gräfin had perused so assiduously died on the page more swiftly than they did in life with the sharp sword dividing their naked parts.

Irresolute, mingling curiosity with exasperation, he read what he had been intended to read, which made him wonder whether Lull had ever led a charge, responded to the clarion, raised a siege. He had probably been more craven than a tortoise and more flamboyant.

To a Knight apertaineth that he be a lover of the common weal, and the common weal be greater and more necessary than any special good.

What insolence! It justified his suspicion of books. They possessed a silence that was not inert and harmless but that of the sudden rise of a snake. All over the Empire they were mounting, fed by new and unruly universities, real plague-spots, and by feckless, myopic princes. They thickened the atmosphere by multiplying words. Mouldy scholars, discontented monks and immoral students were opening books in thousands and releasing horrors.

The Graf was chewing a goose gobbet with the same care that he did his fingernails, then swallowed wine, though barely aware of so doing. He had already locked away the book as he might a poisoned toothpick, but the reference to the common weal had revived many quiet fears. Such a phrase was an excuse for riot and disruption, and accosted him with unwholesome images: fingers in a dark porch clutching a knife, a foot without toes, insults slung like horse manure, the Gräfin's last day.

He had once imagined, or dreamt of, pacing through a hundred rooms, successively smaller and less magnificent until he finally reached a cell where waited a masked figure standing above axe and block, the door inexorably being closed, then bolted.

Squaring insignificant shoulders, he regarded the long, ponderous walls, their dusty hangings and spreading cracks, glad of their strength which yet did not repel further nauseating images. Unfinished babies floating froglike in a well, a dried, sparsely haired Turkish head with fallen eyelids, a huckster auctioning a two-headed goat. Were others plagued thus? If only the Gräfin. But Albrecht.

Certainly Albrecht. His melancholy fell away, then instantly seeped through again as he remembered a dream that recurred like a canticle in an unholy mass. Lost in a maze he was frantic to escape but the more he strove the more he was trapped, pulled towards its centre by some inevitable current, to confront something crouching, like a blurred witch in a storm. Always he saved himself by waking, shivery, damp, breathless.

Hearing footsteps, he reached for his goblet. An ingratiating face hovered, that of a scrawny, shabby sergeant from the gatehouse.

'Sir . . . at your orders, the churl's brought in. They've roped him. There wasn't need. . . .' He waited, unwilling to say more yet evidently with more to say. His master's depleted face flickered impatiently though, as always before others, the rest of him remained still.

'I'll see him. Let them untie him.'

From behind pillars and beneath thick steps that strained up into darkness the watchers saw Hans, guarded by men-at-arms, stumble towards the motionless, unblinking Graf.

An hour before, encouraged by shouts and tears, snippets of prayer and song, clutching his pipe, he had stepped from Troy, alone, to approach the iron shapes on tall horses, then trudged after them in midget valour, up to the Castle. Once within its walls, he was greeted by scullions and pot-boys with curiosity, contempt and a certain covert fellow-feeling. When he was fettered, an older man emitted a bleat, the rest laughing, slightly too loudly, for, together with their other feelings, was the wariness due to any redhead. Red was the mark of the false and perjured, of Thor and Judas. They also knew that his capture would anger the valleys smudged by rain, agitated by rebellion,

139

and that stew of iniquitous madmen, Turk-lovers, Christ-haters and the wanton.

Empurpled, his robe rigidly grooved, the cap glistening, the Graf waited. After a clatter and shuffle his chilled, pointed eyes could scrutinize the stunted, dirty-garbed, red-haired shock-head bundled before him, not kneeling but standing, barefoot, with uncouth face, gazing up at him with a smile not insolent but trusting.

The Graf's first, rather humiliating sensation was relief. He saw nothing more dangerous than features like stale bread, above wraps probably verminous and hands stained as a tanner's. He prided himself on scrupulous judiciousness. Here was no leader, no Black Thing from a hellish cavern, not even a scamp, merely a grub, jerky, negligible and apparently hungry.

Hans inspected a face frost-bitten, as lavishly beaked as the Soldan in stories; arranged as a lord should be, and almost near enough to touch. From such dropped no dung, and despair they knew not.

'Bring him a stool.'

The voice was ordinary, it was kindly. A stool was produced and, at an abrupt gesture, Hans was placed at a table, legs swinging, opposite the Graf, with a half-loaf, actually white, a trencher piled with meats, a jug of wine before him. He saw himself not high on a mountain but in an underground hall, which, if less magnificent than that of King Alexander of the Seven Skies, had some semblance to the palace of the Dark Prince, which had many walls but no doors or windows.

First timidly, then avidly, while the Graf waited and several of the household slowly collected in the outer reaches, Hans gobbled, chewed, swallowed with bumpkin lack of style, thrusting food through a muzzle rather than a human feature, so that a lady giggled disdainfully until silenced by the Graf's slow, baleful stare, which empathized that notorious Evil Eye. The wine was unknown to him, yet a reminder of Maytime berries, his long-ago crowning, the kingship by which he was called here, welcomed, despite the men's mistake at the entrance. His cheeks swelled, likewise his belly, while the Graf contemplated him as he might

140

a gargoyle, unprepossessing but not demonic, caricature of mortals not at their best. That this little wretch, rooting away like a hog, could bewitch by music, deceive by eloquence, was credible only in gatehouse parley and dishcloth jokes.

Graciously, he made another sign, Hans's jug was refilled, though his head was swirling giddily. Gradually, while nothing was said, his chokes and small belches subsided, and a pinkish glow floated through him, a promise of words which he must set free. Bright petals, silver stars. Briefly, he saw the Graf replaced by a long-faced, thunder-coloured rat, leaning on one elbow, now dipping bread into a shining pot, now drinking from a cup like a mermaid's tail.

Words came. A procession. He rubbed his mouth. A tentative smile gained strength and became confidential. 'I look down. From 'igh. From green under sky. There's a great tree down there, which only a nix-naught-nothing sees.'

The Graf's good humour was nudged by disquiet. Such a tree was a very dubious growth, like monks. This ugly scrap of being might be more wide awake than his foolish blink suggested. Yet Albrecht, in his advice, with his cool, independent care, had insisted that he was harmless, a little crazed, spinning tales out of himself which lacked substance.

'They tell me. . . .' The Graf paused, peering forward like a goose, wondering whether he was demeaning himself, curiosity being the primal sin, yet from an uncontrolled part of himself, wanting not subservience or gratitude but what could be called nothing less than affection. 'I am informed . . .' – he feigned irritation to ward off any affront to his dignity, aware of menials listening – 'that you know many tales.'

The little blue eyes, rather too pale, were animal but not quite bestial. They blinked again. A stuttering eagerness was repeated in a jerk of the hands, like stitching.

'There's deal of tales. They come. They are. They make light. Glass.' He recovered his feeling of safety, his trust.

'Where do they come from?'

Surprise dawdled on the face cakelike under the grotesque hair.

'Anywhere. Mine. Sometimes . . .' – he seemed to be allowing a precious secret – 'sometimes I like stupid, sometimes I see know-all.'

The Graf's pouched face and intentness encouraged his gabble. He looked around, saw more faces and was happy. Faces were always there, like his sheep, to listen and wonder, urge him for more. The Graf's now quivered.

'Knight. Sleeps under a tree. Is it summer? Does a golden dish 'ang above? Does. Gold scraped from the sun indeed. Four queens ride by, grey ponies. Wake knight. Give, they say, that dish to she you best love, love best.'

Unwillingly, the Graf yet found himself respond: 'And did he?'

Hans shook his head. 'Not know.' Interruption always dismayed him. He could see four queens, the blue, the white, but the knight had disappeared. Then he remembered. Love did not matter. He looked comically solemn. 'Queens were pigs. Four pigs.'

This startled the Graf. His heart tolled, over-loud. His own dream, of pigs fantastically elongated, bound into a sprawling, agitated heap, like a fat, rosy country girl naked on the bed, showed that this freckled, carroty serf, spawn of diseased mating, yet carried, or knew something of himself, a contact which might be less artless than he pretended, and reach indeed to the Gräfin by some process left undetected by the pious. This shepherd was the flap-tongued carrion sort she favoured, unbefitting her station, unbecoming to himself.

He was further displeased to see that Hans had left the table unbidden to stand under a tapestry, very faded and torn, into which, having spat noisily, he was peering with impudent familiarity. The Graf himself had never inspected it with any care, and now realized that it depicted a man, almost naked, sitting by water, a fishing-net beside him, and fingering a harp. His head, through the grime, seemed circled with leaves, and trees were bending as if to listen, forest creatures, the horned, beaked, tusked, crested, feathered, the weak and powerful alike ranged around him, arrested like the fish emerging from the pool.

A grubby thumb jabbed at the harpist.

'Comes far. Other side of mountains. Up from the river. From

142

the valley of lost things. 'e's bin wounded time, then more time. Changes one to 'nother, an' gives back life.'

Tremulously, as if in guilt, people were filling the long hall. Order was overlooked, rank forgone, the Confessor stranded amongst bath-house skivvies, the Cellarer with squalid cooks, and, amongst dusty masons and thick-hided fighters, high-born ladies, even in this dropsical light gleaming and lacy, under coned head-dresses, surveying the scene with condescension and mannered surprise. Enveloped by varlets, seamstresses and a few squirelings, Prince Narr, lord of peculiar, might be recollecting himself, distinct as a unicorn, amongst the smoking ruins of Carthage. Uncle, of course, was not with them. Rector Magnificus, up in his library, he must be seeing all and hearing much from those equivocal Venetian spectacles.

For some of them, the Graf's much-argued safe conduct allowed its recipient a particular distinction, a mild halo, which, though altogether weak, remained unusual. All acknowledged that a redhead, like a dwarf and cripple – Hans partook of all three – could often be accursed yet sometimes be blessed.

Finely aware of them, addressing them, with the Graf, in words that flowed in many colours, many shapes, though to the scornful he was merely drunk, basking too lavishly in the Graf's magnaminity. He pointed again to the tapestry.

'King o' a thousand palaces. Steals fire out of sky with bright mirror. Two wives. She 'ose beauty 'e loves. She whose ugliness 'e doesn't. Wants to love 'er but can't. Plays 'arp to 'er, she tries smile, they're both cold, 'orrible cold. Good people follow 'im as 'e walks about, wicked don't. Now, it's this. A snake, all silver, begs music king to fight a giant. King loves the people an' water, trees, clouds, 'ills. So picks up sword. Does it shine, does it strike? 'e drives away 'airy giant so snake gives 'im Green Stone. Does it flash? Sparks brighter than people ever saw. Lord or lady, sparrow or goat-boy with 'and enough for that stone will be young always and always, an' be loved an' strong. Fire in wind. So the king gives it to the wife 'e don't love, ugly, cowshit lady. She takes Stone, your 'onours, kisses it, which makes king love 'er so that she's almost dead.'

143

A sigh shook through the hall, ears strained, eyes were dilated, senses quickened, Hans now larger than had hitherto been perceived, his head fiercer, his voice stronger. Only the Graf was unaffected. He was cold. Any story of wives, fair or plain, loved or hated, smelled of sneers, mischief, even conspiracy. Stories themselves, like songs, entangled the honest like cards, gippy potions, lawyers' texts; rascally friars and Irish sing love in a greenwood while snipping off your purse. *The lily, the rose, the rose I lay.* In such was enchantment which respects neither ruler nor spirit.

As the story continued, the Castle was becalmed in a missal world of gentle animals, runic weapons, woodland heroes restoring the land, bright dew refreshing leaves and grass. Many felt strangely youthful, frets and anxieties overcome by the soul that guided them away from gross feedings, charnel-grounds, fever-beds stinking like burnt leather or a bad neighbour. Fears of rheum and blindness, plague, decrepitude, pox and unanswered prayer subsided. The robed assassin lurked no longer, the terrible bull ceased to roar beneath the earth, days were not distorted by rites badly performed, Turks were absurd. Instead, an instant of compassion, tenderness which could almost extend to the barbarian children far below, whose lost leader Albrecht might now be very near, in some secluded alcove, one of those with charmed life, a sort of magic. This shepherd fellow had powers, not showy, he would transport no one to paradise, produce no elixir, yet . . . and yet. . . .

The Graf, Prod-Nose, felt no magic and had ceased to listen, though earlier words had forced his thoughts to stop. *Valley of Lost Things.* Spoken vulgarly, with intonation very careless, they yet arrested. Could such a valley exist? A desolation heaped with the mislaid and forgotten, the discarded, the stolen. Much that reproached. Promises, lands, fortunes; wasted days, septic privacies. There they might lie until, as Uncle knew from stodgy Paracelsus, fire sweeps across the world leaving only the word of God brooding over waters.

His attention drifted back to the now breathless, obsessed voice, and at once he was bored. This was as trashy as the worst of the lost things. He bit one nail, scraped another. Also, he was ashamed of that tiny initial spurt of sympathy for the young rebel, itself not only disgusting but a betrayal of Albrecht. Some saw his yawn, like a wavelet, before the lips closed very tight. The story was finishing, the audience still entranced, diverted from Castle monotony, by this parody of courtly entertainers perched before them like a hunchbacked cobbler and mightily pleased with his own recital, diverted as they had been by the Gräfin's death and indeed by the petty intrusion of the children's revolt, so greatly superior to gossip about a lady's stomacher, a Burgundian exquisite, a dropped glove, or a faecal observation from Prince Narr.

Such stories, of pellucid kings and cowlike queens, were commonplace enough, though congenial, inherited from the sub-existence of crones and midwives, digested from the forest tribes, tusky sons of Thor who had split open Rome, forged miraculous hammers that clanged against the world, saved Charlemagne's thousand palaces. Ancestral stuff, heroic, but gradually shredded into old folk's chatter, tavern songs and children's nonsense, suspect lore and lost meanings in tune with Prince Narr's jingle,

> You cannot define
> the Rhine.

Like dreams, they enclosed obscure intimations of fate, knots seldom wholly untied. Stories of floating islands and mirages were warnings, or traps. A dimension of delusive gifts, vistas, prospects, subtle derangements of reality which made too prolonged attention to the redhead perilous, if fascinating. A story long known amongst them concerned a jealous younger son who dreamt of stabbing his elder brother who, next day, fell from his horse and impaled himself on a rock.

The story ended unexpectedly, in mid-sentence, was left inconclusive, faintly disturbing, with a prince inheriting the land which gave him no happiness, through a lady who gave him less. People looked at each other, perplexed or irritated, until, in his deadly way, the Graf spoke.

145

'Our young friend needs to retire.'

The last of the spell dissolved, murmurs resumed, most drifted away, the story-teller was but a malodorous villager with head like wool from his own sheep dyed in hellish matter and with paws rather than hands, too ordinary to be necessary. Already he was being led away.

Apprehensively, his advisers collected round the Graf, who remained at the table. He allowed them a forbidding nod. 'Suffer little children to come unto me. Well, gentlemen, I have done just that.'

The silence was that often compared to the silence which occurs whenever a student pays his debts or a goose wanders over one's grave, until, led by the Confessor, they hastened to congratulate the Graf on his piety, only Prince Narr contenting himself with a grin in very bad taste.

21

The cell was narrow, fetid, with mossy, oozing walls. Hans sat on straw in near-darkness. He was tired, too feeble, he thought, to trot a mouse. Usually darkness presented pictures, prettiness, colours: a lady in water removing her silks, another on a glass tower, Albrecht smiling, stroking a horse, saving him from flying stones and mud. Now, his thoughts were pale. He wanted his pipe but the men had taken it away.

Fatigued by the long day, the wine, his own story, he had slept a little, and now tried to relive the intoxication of the Garden, the kingdom of the moon, the rich folk so struck by his marvels, dazzled by an Emperor Earth. But he was cold now, and for the first time ever, lonely.

On the bench, above the pail, was a jar, almost emptied, of unwatered wine, very sweet yet stiff, its heavy fumes confused without soothing. Dusk must be near, hour of the wolf.

Later, tiny rustles and scuffles meant that he was alone no longer. Mice, and, through layers of gloom, he fancied a rat, reminding him of the Graf, more kindly than people thought. People had once been animals, animals could become people.

Wearing only a shirt, he fingered his Little Pike, stubbier, smaller from the cold. Desultorily he pulled it, then desisted, letting it flop aimlessly against his thigh. To dance with Little Fritz might not be permitted and, despite the dark, he felt watched, not only by mice. Beneath his skin a mouth uneasily nuzzled and gnawed.

Though he slept, all was blank. He saw nothing. Dawn was shambling behind the tiny window, the mice were silent. He missed them, and wondered how much longer he would be kept here, convinced that the Graf would not forget him. Albrecht might come.

Words lit him within. 'He done nothing, only something.' But what?

People were coming, they must be bringing food, which not all of him wanted, though he'd be glad of more wine.

The door groaned, grey light gushed in. Five leathery men entered, with straps. He looked, weakly, at their pocked, not unfriendly faces, then rose, straw dropping from him.

'Time for bye-bye, my boy, so let's get along with it.'

He did not understand. A second voice was rougher. 'Off with it. Strip.'

The custom was for an Ostler to be paid with the clothes, though this he did not know. When he was naked, the flame rose in his joy-bag, though he might be punished. The men were gazing at it, expressionless until a grizzled fellow winked, for it was now rich and full, red tip gleaming under its hood. Another muttered a word too low for him to hear, though it pleased them and he smiled, ingratiating and uncertain.

The air was cold, they were in a hurry, they thrust his hands behind him, tied them though without hurting, then, more loosely, his feet. A third carried a cloth gag, for once a small girl had wished to assist the jailer but, in her terror, had accidentally bitten him. The gag, however, was not now used. Hans waited until the youngest man, like a hunter, beardless, scrubbed rosy and clean, hoisted him on to his shoulders, and they tramped

147

through twisted, clammy passages that soon led into a cobbled yard, entirely enclosed by high, blank walls.

The gallows, almost central, was not the Horse but the smaller one, above a midden, always used for children and dwarfs, jocularly called 'Father', even by the victims.

Hans examined it. Three tall sticks, very stained, damp, perhaps tearful, for trees could weep. The bit of sky was nothing. They weren't allowing him more wine.

His Little Pike has shrivelled miserably in this cold and the loss made him abject. They should have done this to him in the night when his soul was larger. Yet a small soul escapes more quickly and he should be grateful.

The men, though unwilling to agitate him, saw without compunction his spotty face pucker as though for weeping. His distress, however, was not fear, and he managed to beg them to untie his legs. After death you ran to a fisherman, following your soul like a star, to get it back. He would need his legs.

They did so, exchanging more winks, and pleased to add to the pleasure of those secretly looking down at them from all levels of the Castle. A trussed bird squawks more but dances less.

Thousands of rot-souls in our Holy Empire are hanged yearly but few survive to boast of the experience. Half-hanged Jok would describe the road to hell but never the painful means of reaching it. Theo of Malthausen had done so, for his execution had been halted, thanks to a drunken and inexperienced hangman, a badly adjusted cord, God's favour, of course, and the merciful intervention of a papal legate. For a pot of beer he would regurgitate recollections of a mass of red, splintering lights, a white fury of bone, thumping pressures on the spine, the blood boiling and throbbing, the gut fiery, the oar of a river in flood, then, in agonized slowness, a sun cracking, black lines criss-crossing. That slowness was the worst, a dancing-bear clumsiness in a nightmare. Theo would end by comparing his ordeal to a dish of wild cabbage, bad eggs, nettle soused in sour wine and gulped by an impotent lecher seeking a cure.

A number of kitchen-hands and soldiery gathered in the yard; the spectacle was familiar enough but they could still enjoy the redhead's prancing antics, his frantic kicks and struggles. A girl said that he was learning to swim, and joined in the laughs.

The body, no longer quivering, was left, jerked up and forlorn; would be left on the rope for three days, a precaution, Master Wilhelm insisted, against spiteful haunting. The rope itself was his own perquisite, for it could ensure health and banish danger. Around the corpse, people saw the air lose weight and colour, and said that the flesh was sucking in both. At night, looking down, they could see in valleys and across the plain bone-fires flaring, purging the noxious, and in rich apartments, dim oubliettes, fever-ridden huts, wooden daubs of infernal sufferings were waved, to ward off Black Things, and, amongst the superstitious, some slightly disfigured themselves – cutting off a piece of beard, removing a false curl, piercing a finger – to avert the Evil Eye.

The Confessor hastened about the Castle reassuring those rabbit-hearts for whom the killing, if not important, had nevertheless been . . . what should one say? They evoked no desire to say anything, but all found reasons to avoid the Graf, and delayed facing each other until the Confessor provided them with what sounded like absolution, or, the Cellarer imprudently murmured, an excuse.

'All the Fathers, onwards from the Blessed Martin of Tours, have taught that promises made to a rebel, a heretic, a blasphemer not only lack validity but, if fulfilled, are actually injurious to the true course of the world. We are instructed, nay, we are taught, *Judge Not*. This is well said, judiciously expressed, for judgement impairs justice. To forgive evil is to be condemned. It is meet that impediments to the divine be removed.'

So ample were von der Goltz's resources, so fluent his opinion, his *considered* opinion, some thought his dogmatic insights, that little further needed to be discussed, and nothing was discussed.

By the third day the small, limp carcase was arousing considerable gaiety amongst the High Folk, noticeably the ladies, one of whom, ostentatiously covering her nose with an English woven handkerchief, suggested decorating it with ribbons and holly, though the Fighting Commandant advised against doing

149

so, for he had noticed a growing number of vagabonds, for-esters and pilgrims at the gatehouse awaiting scraps from last night's suppers, and though they too were inclined to laugh, such laughter was dissimilar to the ladies', denoting not amusement at a well-deserved death but pity, even support. Common people hold that laughter assists the soul in its flight, lamentations obstruct it. They also think that God mysteriously cherishes the hanged.

'I did not,' the Graf announced to the Clerk, 'allow torture.' He was pleased that he had had the last word, without reflecting that the last word is not always final.

22

The gold of Friendly Ones inevitably turns black. At the end of the long week, Troy, the Garden, the Camp, what you will, reeked of illness, dereliction, mire from departing wagons, after a Castle horseman had ridden round the perimeter contemptuously within range, parading a head, still with some red hairs, fixed on a short staff.

For some, the failure of the sun, the fall of the Castle at the sound of trumpets or a sky-blown command from Nevis could not have astounded them more, but all capriccio imaginings were at once ashen, firefly spirits were quashed by sight of that raw head. Here was a plague village or one of those cities of the dead known to gippies, oppressed by the hush between sodomites chained breast to breast, then drowned. Hans's death itself shocked very few, and there was little anger at the Graf who had done no more than behave like all grafs, perfidiously and pitilessly. A Bavarian, who had strangled his harridan wife 'in the hills', suggested that in slicing off the head the Graf had been merciful, for the soul had thus escaped more easily than if the body had been left strangled. That's why the rich claim to be beheaded. The Bavarian, pulling his short, coarse beard, continued with an air of sagacity, 'Though he probably felt pain, he didn't suffer.' People nodded, someone laughed, the spindle-shanked Graf wasn't too bad, though his men were wicked, and a dumpling was more desirable than a Hans. Those who now remained were feeling neither anger nor panic, but nerveless, in a void. Old and young drooped in mute ranks, wishing to be alone but not daring to.

A number prayed, relapsing into Old Times, and, mourning Hans no more than they would a fading dream, they knew that they faced the lash, outlawry or death. Old Times were providential, toilsome and hungry but predictable, without heights or depths. Dreams and stories had exhausted them. No dumpling, rich and glistening, would fall from the sky.

The severed head had eventually been slung at them, falling into a puddle, alarming a couple of dogs. The face was yellowish, like curd, with sagging eyelids, a black tongue protruding like a slug, through lips swollen, cracked and as if bilberry-stained above a neck ringed with dry scarlet. The hair had been largely pulled off, revealing a bony skull, somewhat chipped.

No hand cared to touch it, it could have been Tartar, leprous, devilish. They stood regarding it, unable to disperse until Grete retrieved it and walked away alone, holding it tight against her, to some distant place to do what had to be done.

In small, bent clusters the children sat hoping to be unobserved, hungry, but afraid of joining those scavenging, rounding up dray-horses, nailing up boxes, cording bales. The Ant was ill, gasping, probably dying. Scarcely Seen was seen no more. The child with two logs had thrown them away and sat under a broken beam, sightlessly fumbling with a stone. A cold breeze swept from the dark mountains and grey, solid sky. Flies crawled everywhere, drunk from sores and cuts, the rotting fruit and meat too rotten even for the famished.

In New Times each day is a year in miniature, with seasons and festivals, but perpetual winter now fell, with no spring crowning, harvest, divine birth. One might brood, if at all, not on some cowskin story-teller, easily discarded, but on Albrecht, for charm, high stepping, and beauty have prerogatives immune to manorial rulings, Castle edicts, imperial prescriptions, even to what a high gentleman in green spectacles calls *a pragmatic sanction*. Strangeness, the magical, which without warning troubles the

151

waters. Hans had been but Albrecht's serf, bound to his silken will, a batch of rages and sniggers. His stories were idle, his Green Stone a fraud. Seeking protection from the Castle he had betrayed everyone.

Albrecht was already neither cursed nor praised, had become unreal, like an actor starting off tears or cackles at will, yet, his part completed, the barn door closed, ceasing to exist, with only a ghostly half-light as a memorial to wonder.

Big-girthed Broken-tooth Heinrich was saying that Jesus, when young, had blinded another child for trampling his mud dykes. Sweet Jesus himself! Hearing this, some women were convinced that Albrecht was Jesus's favourite brother, the one who betrayed him.

Throughout, the atmosphere was deranged, distorted further by October mists and early, sullen dusk. A sheep had been seen in the outgrowth, unnaturally large, wandering lost and, someone maintained, attempting to speak. Many saw it collapsing on frosty grass, staggering up in lopsided convulsions, then attempting a weird dance in an irregular circle, feet uncontrolled, out of step with each other, children, dazed with hunger, hoarsely confiding that the apparition was Hans who, a man said afterwards, had lied his way into their hearts. At night, from moon-drenched slopes sounded hollow keenings, howls, cries from unidentifiable birds, and once, across the field where Hans had kept his flock, there straggled a procession of wolves, their pendulous lips long as Frau Holle's green teeth.

Such visions were of course the customary dues to dead heroes, though the sottish story-teller had never been much of a hero, not one of those who stand in the sky with folded hands and silver wings. Children, generations ahead, would learn of him strangling snakes in infancy, curing a leper, after conflict forced to choose between flight and self-sacrifice, and, with his pipe, taming wolves, causing a pair of vast shoes to dance, and a besotted girl to drown amongst wild flowers. The most famed German poet wrote verses of him piping down painted leopards and unicorns from a ducal standard, to frolic together.

Scarcely eighty now remained, undefended, preparing escape

before the Graf struck. Plans must be determined, feuds settled, stores divided. Children, all privileges lost, hovered about them wailing for food, seeking protection, most of them striving to recollect their lost homes, the dour mother and morose father. A Heiner, a Johannes, a Heinrich, having claimed much and too loudly, loped about impotent and disregarded.

The year itself was rotting; storm followed storm, women putting out scythes to lame the screeching gale-maidens as they flew past, tents and shacks tottering, falling, dogs howling amongst broken poles and discarded stakes. Spring cravings, festival rites were as though the earth had dreamt, awaking to this barren manginess.

Daily the population dwindled. Ill-tempered mercenaries had polished their weapons and marched out, soon followed by the better-spoken fugitives from Ulm and Trentingben, a motley of hedge-croppers, vagrants, students and their trulls accompanying them, the pack-asses and carts filling the miry roads.

The children stayed with the last survivors, whimpering as they were driven from stewpots and fires. None gainsaid their fathers' right to kill them if they slunk back to beseech mercy. At night they heard in the wind the cries of other children, long dead.

Finally the Fighting Commandant gave orders, grandly peremptory: 'Destroy everything, set fire to the rest.' His eyes cats and dogs, a lady sniggered. He need scarcely have bothered. His men rode in some glee, found the defences unmanned. They charged in a powerful curve, smiting and lashing, and flames were soon spreading, dim shapes fleeing through smoke or kneeling with arms outspread. In blue and black fumes the assailants were beaked and abnormal on gigantic horses, their hands misshapen in massive gloves. Hoofs pounded, the fires crackled, the weapons crushed and cut, purging accursed ground, wounding, stunning, though the killings were not numerous and almost all children were spared. Rulers need those over whom to rule, empty air pays no taxes.

23

News arrived, irregularly, like gasps of a librarian pandering to the temptations of curiosity. The Margrave of Greiser had died, he who bathed twice a year in a barrel of vension stew, afterwards distributing it to the poor, whom he usually advised to eat less and feel better. At Trier a crow had been arraigned for theft and, found guilty, was burnt, in a cage not of wicker but metal, to prolong the jollity. The University of Prague had sent the Emperor a gryphon's claw, to cure blindness, but His Majesty, whose sight was excellent, had lost it.

There is a valley very deep and broad, one side exceeding terrible, with raging fire, the other no less unbearable by dint of constant hail and icy snow drifting and blowing everywhere. Both sides are crammed with souls tossed from one to the other by fury of the blizzard. Together with the deadly cold is terrifying heat.

This held an uncomfortable reminder of another valley, that of Lost Things.

Dejected by success, the Graf, while the Fighting Commandant recounted his victory to the women, left duties to his council, and was reduced to reading such matter. He sighed, pushing the manuscript farther away, the work of an Englishman, Bede, who, like all his countrymen, respected princes less than God advised.

He had confessed his thoughts about the hanging to – who else? – the Confessor, who assured him that a seven days' fast would assuage any misgivings. For five days now he had consumed little, obeying wholly in spirit and largely in body. This was not sensually gratifying or piously encouraging. Lack of meat slackens temptation but without enlarging any love of contemplating beatitudes.

He had been trying to contemplate not beatitudes but purgatory, which the Confessor had mentioned with unseemly emphasis, unbefitting his station. Hitherto he had been indifferent to purgatory, though he must now admit that it might be concerned with him, despite having purchased several centuries' exemption from Brother Helmut, itinerant indulgence master, with clever eyes stuck in a boiled face; a transaction to be concealed from Uncle, who opined such precautions to be magic of a quality very suspect.

Purgatory, a death beyond death, the Confessor had said with authority, was sited off the far coast of Ireland. Where else? There might be drifting the Gräfin, less immaculate than the foolish were claiming, thin and bloodless, her face wrung with an unpleasant question. Had she been present when the shepherd boy chattered and munched, she might have treated him as an equal, and – his spirit groaned – there had been that queer instant: he himself had felt a mysterious and absurd need to embrace and confide in the uncouth, dirty urchin.

Against such thoughts the Castle was no protection: they ambushed from beyond the air, like feckless music and shrewd strangers.

He could remember no days of good cheer; hunting, feasting, praise, joyous lust, only, not precisely a ghost, if a ghost can be precise, but a presence: puny limbs, graceless face, a neck nastily crooked.

There was more, none of it cheerful, save proximity to Albrecht. The Emperor had lately defeated the Hungarians and held triumph on the Danube. 'We Germans,' he proclaimed, 'once mastered the whole world and will do so again, more than ever before.' He had condescended to express displeasure at the wicked behaviour under Broken Mountain, but had dispatched no praise, no reward, to his most loyal and devoted liegeman who had restored honour to the German nobility and chivalric orders. Rebels were Black Things, dark fires, two-legged wolves; a graf, as exterminator, should be acclaimed as liberator, received into the Golden Fleece. That stinking children's camp had ripped open surfaces and revealed perils threatening the Empire worse than any Hungarian or Turk. He had ensured that all was now quiet: landless clans were scattered, the plain was scorched wreckage, rancid scraps of flesh being pecked under a manikin sun. Master Wilhelm reported that the diabolic children had slunk back to their parents, stunted folk crouching in shame, who had belaboured them ferociously, leaving two dead and others maimed. No one could jib at that, certainly not reproach the Castle. Boys were back in fields, woods, stables, girls were lumping dough, baking, washing with customary foul rhymes against demons, which do no great harm to anyone, not even demons.

All this, high praise due to a Graf, yet the Emperor blatantly refused to acknowledge it. Far worse, indeed. 'A word given even to a madman,' His Majesty had pronounced, within hearing of the most exalted, 'is nevertheless a word.' Overnight a lampoon was regaling the imperial court, comparing himself, the Graf, to the three vilest men of all, Brutus, Cassius, Judas, lying the deepest in hell, lost souls fathered by the Devil.

Here, in his slightly leaking apartment, he was full of pity, pity for himself. The cold, dingy atmosphere added to his twinges of alarm, akin to his horror of touching feathers, his disgust of cobwebs. Walls, stove, table, his very maps were dulled, as though he were caged, so to speak, under a dry sea where cargoes had fallen, split and lay about at random.

Master Wilhelm had also, and over-casually, mentioned that a white stag had been seen bounding in the mountains, dangling a golden pipe from its horn and calling in human tones. Libel of some malcontent drunk on that mendacious mountebank, Ovid.

Only Albrecht could comfort him, not with his words, which were usually few and unwilling, or real companionship, but with his finely refulgent appearance. By some fluke of lineage or divine grace he could dispense effects more thrilling than the best of wines. But, before he could properly show himself and partake in the Castle day, he had been overcome by sickness, or had feigned so. However, he was said to be recovering and might soon come. Until he did so, the Graf would be unable to repel memories, incited by Hans, of his own childhood. Father's strictness and fondness for detail, Grandfather's extravagant whims and clamorous celebrations of campaigns now seen to have been mainly illusionary. Both had scourged him, often, Grandfather savagely, for nothing very much, afterwards caressing him, soothing him with gifts; Father, methodically, as if fulfilling a sealed obligation. Grandfather had terrified him while gaining his admiration; Father he had loved though not liked. Both men had enforced on him the oath to the Name, to the lands, though they, not himself, had lost so many of them, through battle, mortgages, legal webs, the magic of phrases: farms, mill and river rights, headlands, fishponds, villages, counties.

Reliving that meal with the shepherd, he saw much that then he had not; a guard's spear badly held, a jug out of line, a tapestry ill-balanced. The subsequent hanging, as Albrecht had put it, a sacrifice for the general good, had been followed by the Confessor's absolution, which should have removed the nag of uncertainty, pain, even a measure of Christian guilt, absurd but spiteful as old men wishing each other long life. He could not, however, efface the ignoble child, feral dribbler and sniveller on the rope, agonized into hideous antics. Had it been correct, had he known how to, he would have mourned, with a degree of ceremony.

Surely the Emperor had misjudged, been erroneously or maliciously informed; please God he, the Graf, carried no blame. You don't judge a nobleman by the state of his chimney. Rulers have always to act, if possible act well, but mistakes, faults, even crimes are praiseworthy beside idleness or retreat. Jesus himself, one knew from the Confessor, nay, from the Gospels, had not been consistently admirable, had been apt to curse the innocent, condemn the ignorant and heal the worthless. Even by transforming water to wine, doubtless an amusing performance, he had swindled the vintners.

Mother Church had her own deviousness, her ecclesiastical slipperiness. Invited to explain the defeat of godly crusaders by the ungodly, priests had only to reply that the godly lacked sufficient godliness. As for pains and penalties, none had protested at Minden when the archdeacon burnt Alice-Where-Art-Thou? for decorating a tree for *Allfather*, though, had she done so for 'Father-of-All', she would have been rewarded.

By forswearing a lewd, unnatural, no-account piper, securing his followers from travail and immorality, one should be awarded gratitude unstinted. Instead, in the valleys, some monkish ranter with a soul like dirty snow was arraigning him as murderous Antichrist, probably to be thereby honoured by the Emperor.

The Graf did regret that so many had heard him pledge Hans's security, he who had lifelong upheld the sanctity of all oaths, promises, guarantees, those dykes against mountainous seas.

Rising, he shuffled between the naked, lugubrious walls, damp as if sweating from something insufferable, then, knowing himself unobserved, gave a small, cautious hop, without knowing why. Really, however the Emperor might disparage him, his offence, if offence it were, was trivial. Until a few years ago Frisians had regularly killed children to avert ill-fortune. Injustices occurred daily. Uncle had mentioned, as though it were a witticism not polite but acceptable, that at the court of Holland-Bavaria several low-born citizens had died in a brawl; the assailants, of higher rank, had had to pay a fine, not only to the Duke, which was just, but, more controversially, to the victims' families and, moreover, to finance a thousand penitential masses before undertaking a pilgrimage. A brutal sentence which even Grandfather would have deplored, though perhaps noting a useful precedent.

Pondering whether to withdraw into a map, the Graf scrutinized a crack in the wall, heard a glum drip, regular as a heartbeat, and, disapproving of such imperfections, sniffed at a pot of basil. The silence and heaviness of gaunt stone forced him up again, he crossed to the door and stood irresolute in near-darkness above twisting steps, hesitating between above and below, wary of sly women and those grinning rascals who chalked long-nosed faces on walls.

Wondering where next to proceed, he indulged in what he considered serious thought. He considered himself as transcending both Old and New times, and now, once again, reflected on the sublimity of lordship. In Rome, Dijon and Aix rulers had flaunted jewelled capes, resplendent coronets, overlording Christendom. Sultans and padishahs trailed nations like stars in a black net hung from the top of the firmament. Those ducal hogs in Burgundy maintained grip by a constant display of riches and colour, a reminder that his own treasury was empty. The wren, most abject of birds, yet could be seen in a golden crown, and was said to be kin to that overpraised bardic nuisance, Arthur. The very shadow of Caesar manipulated people like yeast. The great rulers were immemorial spectacles of Honour. Even the Gräfin had known of Henry of Trastamara, crushed at Najera by the astute Black Prince, not from lack of valour but because he had, in knightly courtesy, abandoned an over-advantageous position before the battle. Even in infidel Egypt Mamelukes had shown true chivalry by refusing to renounce the long-sanctified sword and use firearms against the Turk, preferring death to disgrace.

Woefully, he, Graf of Grafs, while sharing such Honour, had lacked opportunities to display it, and was accused of besmirching it by revoking that safe conduct. A journeyman ruler, he oversaw, he gave orders: rents were yielded, harvests gathered, rebels and the docile alike bent the knee when he uttered a few quiet words. Men very much worse were canonized for very much less.

Still above the darkened steps, one hand on the wall, the Graf was dismayed by recollection of Uncle speaking of some ancient kings, powerful before Rome herself, and who were obsessed by numbers, as though in uncanny guilt. They calculated that they would enjoy sixty centuries of prosperity, then sixty of decline. Gradually they lost hope, convinced of their approaching doom, counting the years. They began to lose battles with upstart Rome, question their gods, surrender to astrologers. When a brazen trumpet shrilled from the sky, they knew that their cycle was finished.

Sensible people need know no more of numbers than that the world was four, controlled by the life-giving Trinity, which made seven, unbreakable and irrefutable.

So still in public, he now twitched violently, then his neck felt swollen and he choked as if grasped by relentless hands, nauseated as though from an uprush of feathers. Even ghosts have ghosts. In a vile jumble he saw the Gräfin's last minutes, Conradin's head bleeding in dust, Hans swinging, not quite dead while soldiers laughed and drabs clapped.

Yet he quickly steadied, rebuking his failure of nerve, wondering whether, deep down, he had joined the Tuscan kings.

159

He strove to escape those dire visions of death, like a youth poised to ram his trull and attempting to distract himself with thoughts of fountains, pinnacles, trees, to prolong his pleasure by withholding it.

He could not, however, shed despondency. Repeatedly he served his people but his Name attracted no blessings, no babies were brought to him for benediction and, much as he disliked babies, he resented their absence, and now Hans's maladroit behaviour would make him reviled as a Herod, slayer of children, as he already knew from scullion whispers, seditious pamphlets, disgusting woodcuts. His heritage had been sullied. Grandfather had once saluted a woman, who almost immediately bore twins. He had fought battles, or at least read so in chronicles, his prayers had averted famine and subdued plague, but no nectarine princess besought his favour. His labours had earned him no nickname, in hatred or affection: he was not Blue Cheek or Wry-Neck, not even Long Nose, not the Handsome, the Virile, the All-loving, the Great, but merely *Him*. A university doctor had once named him 'Ash Brother', which he had thought a flattering reference to a god, until the Clerk, needlessly pedantic, interpreted it as 'nonentity'.

His feet at last regained strength, he turned from the steps and their steep gloom, pushed a door, and entered more a recess than a room, bare save for a stool and an empty brazier, though of course scrupulously cleansed of cobweb and mould.

He shivered, attempting to soothe his fears. Did the power of music consist in forcing singers to concentrate and not let loose their hidden evils? To test this, he recalled a song the Gräfin had enjoyed, but, attempting to sing it, merely started to croak.

Impatiently, he groped for ways of escape. He must transform liability to credit: even the most ignoble magician could transform a broken pledge into an expression of glory.

Grabbing the stool with unnecessary effort he sat, shrouded in sullen light, a trapped fugitive, flinching from the blows of his own heart, a wanderer pursued by glaring forebears, an illusionary wife, a hanged child and the Emperor's sentence. *A word is nevertheless a word*. His Majesty's wisdom would entrance Europe for ever, crushing all extenuations, what the vulgar termed excuses. That he had saved the imperial throne was already dismissed as negligible.

Thoughts swarmed with undiminished licence, though they provided some relief. He snatched at one as he might at a brilliant butterfly. He too could tell stories, in his turn dispense wisdom to Emperor Frederick, outbidding any foolish Hans.

A Marquis Paramount of Higher Nevers had undergone a sermon from a crazed Franciscan, Brother Richard, and then summoned serfs and villeins and, to flutes and trumpets, granted them freedom, revoking all bonds, forgoing all rights, cancelling taxes. All had wept with delight, praising God, the Virgin, all saints within hearing, before rushing to seize field strips, claim their neighbour's pasturage, plunder the woods and divide the commons. Two summers later they regathered, many of them bruised, wounded, limping. They invaded the château, imploring the Marquis to restore their servitude and save them from the unending bloodshed of complete liberty. He was offended. Ceasing to farm, he was now raising sheep, thereby freeing not only the villagers but himself, for sheep required no surly labourers who grudged labouring. Nevertheless he listened with courtesy, smiled sympathetically, and in stately language supplied by some Jew or Lombard, in daintily regulated phrases, refused. Infuriated, they rushed upon him, his lady, his children, slaughtering all, wrecking the château. They then sat down, bemoaning their lot. Fields were devastated, animals had gone, new vendettas would destroy themselves. Finally, in contrition, they swore fealty to a statue of the headless Marquis.

The Graf sought refuge in his own sapience. Such follies would have occurred here had he meekly surrendered the Tax, feasted the rebels, dispatched the ill-bred shepherd to the Emperor with a recommendation that he should be given command of an army or licence to preach in a cathedral.

The Graf looked down from a narrow aperture at a courtyard where, despite his wishes, weeds had cracked the paving. But he scarcely noticed. The future . . . a word he seldom considered and never uttered, much to his credit, for the further men stumbled from the Crucifixion the dimmer it became.

He considered the difficulties of these New Times. There was, or had been Niklaus Cusanus, lowly though a cardinal, a learned busybody who delved into the pratings of abominable Mahomet, preferring some of them to the words of Christ. May Cusanus be damned, as he probably was. He taught that evil and error derived not from sin but mere ignorance, whereas, the Confessor tirelessly reiterated, Jesus in his mercy had constantly berated the ignorant, and would never have loved that horrid little piper stuffed with heathen memories and now wormy.

So the Graf told himself, yet without confidence, for he had a secret acknowledged to no one, barely to himself. By some freak of instinct, the Devil's gibe, Hans, unlovely and silly, had tempted him into a region incomprehensible and thus dangerous. Mahomet and Cusanus had done less.

He had dreamt of himself in rags, begging at hovels, but in words unknown to the peasants so that he was mocked and driven away. Only a naked, red-headed child attempted to hand him a crust, though he, and all of them, were out of reach, however strenuously he struggled towards him. He had woken denied every pleasure of dreams; girls stripping, golden ducats lying beneath the pillow, finer still, the floating isle from which had stepped a dazzling being, neither clothed nor naked, neither boy nor girl, yet unmistakably Albrecht.

The unpleasant thought lingered that the Gräfin would have respected Hans as she did Albrecht. The three, on separate levels, understood queer details of words, rhyme, colour. *The thorn-loving goldfinch on the Virgin's finger*. Hans had unravelled meaning from that threadbare tapestry, had seen the four distorted pigs.

The Graf wandered farther, back to a childhood day, almost forgotten save in other, and distorting, dreams. He had stolen from the Castle into mountain woods, timidly venturing into realms unknown save in nurses' tales, with mossy caves, eyes and claws glinting from leaves, the stir and crackle of invisible presences. Framed between pines a stag's head was suddenly

162

stark, instantly gone, yet leaving a faint imprint on the air. A high, lichened boulder must once have been human. Baffling marks lay on pine-needled ground, beetles crawled, a white and scarlet toadstool made a midget, perfect canopy. Birds called, aware of what he could not see. Colours were distinct as never before and meant no more than themselves – blue was not Mary but blue: plumage and leaf, root and mud, blackberry and pool were distinct and entire. Insects hummed like the nerves of the earth. As the sun declined, pines resembled monks, they showed faces, they whispered, not understandable but telling. Colour, shape, movement threatened, tempted, cajoled. He stripped and ran naked in spendthrift freedom. Through branches he saw one far-away peak smudged by cloud, another sun-drenched, aglow with what in her meanderings the Gräfin had called beauty.

Hitherto he had always feared trees as monstrous and untamed overgrowths, but for those few hours they had been welcoming with gifts, rewarding, as horizons were to be for his wife. Amongst them, Father's schemes and defeats, the routine of advisers, messengers, priests and troopers were as naught. Some old teacher had bid man learn from the ants and here, in summer hum, he enjoyed responses from insect, bird and plant he could feel though not fully identify, and indeed had never done so, save as the passionate joys of release, fleeting, but a breakaway from Castle mess, coarse boasts of raids, women, treacheries. No stag would jeer at his nose, no raven urge his duty to the Name.

He had been breathless for what he could not see, for what would not occur, but in such breathlessness was extraordinary power. The exhilaration had so astounded him that its irresponsibility afterwards appeared shameful and he thrust it away as deep as he could, though fragments might echo during solitary rides, until colours once again became blank, as if at a funeral, and silence no more than a sterile gap between guards' footfalls, bells, random clamour. On that one day, under huge brown shadows and triumphant greens and blacks – he had never realized that each colour could be so prodigally nuanced – silence itself had shape and depth.

Today, the future, time. Prince Narr played with a conceit, 'a time, times, half a time'. Fool and clown, he might yet have fore-bodings about New Times in which a graf, despite virtue, valour and public spirit, might become one with knights, grotesques in a crumbling manuscript. Indeed, if the Clerk's accounts could be trusted, the Castle would collapse into the maw of the Fuggerie, those skinny-eyed Augsburg usurers, juggling with figures to bemuse the honest and courageous. 'Bankers,' Uncle said, smiling too tolerantly, 'teach money how to live.'

The Graf recovered, as, in his stubborn way, he always did. The future had a solution. Albrecht. In that beloved word was a silversmith of nature, almost transparent, who had risked all in sending messages from that infamous camp, revealing its weakness and delusions, advising the adroit safe conduct, thereby showing allegiance and Honour.

Striding through the Castle, expressionless, but acknowledging respectful bows and salutations, the Graf allowed himself to uncage to the Confessor the suspicion of a smile. Once more he had surmounted a crisis, wrested triumph from setback. He would formally adopt Albrecht as Heir, send couriers speeding towards the Imperial Chancellery and Heraldic College. Begotten in an idle hour in a pigsty outhouse, Albrecht was a Ludwig-in-Luck who had drunk elixir, like a star sustained by himself alone. He would further enlustre Castle and Name. He made sense of those moonstruck songs in which flowers change to virgins, trees bow, doors open without hands. An Albrecht should either be drowned at birth or acknowledged as a son of God with an abstruse and hidden name. It was as though some third person had, to put it decorously, had a hand in his birth. Thus, whatever he did, he would be praised, whether he murdered nephews in wood or tower, burnt a saint, supped with a statue, sauntered through circles of fire to win a beloved.

Briefly, he thought of Albrecht's mother. Banished from his presence, she had troubled him no more. She might still be corrupting men like a river-fay, inveigling them beneath the wave, or transforming herself not to a swan or hedge-blossom but to spiked poison-fruit.

Progressing through the Castle, it might be said stalking, the

Graf concealed his contempt for all those demonstrating obeisance, knowing that such as they were always more grateful to those who persecute them than to whoever rescues them; who toil in the vineyard, distribute the harvest, strengthen frontiers, stop up rebellion as they might a badger's sett, bend their backs to support the Empire, leaving silken dances and gallantries to others.

He reached the vaulted hall furnished with a throne raised on a small platform. Seated, he communed, he held sway, self-belief now reviving, now ebbing, like the eye of a dying pigeon. This made him wonder whether a ruler possesses two souls; one had perhaps urged that brief intimacy with Hans, the other a need to destroy him.

The century was crumbling while lobster cardinals bestrode naked pages and the Empire quailed beneath the lightning-riven cloud-mass of the Turks. Christendom too might be rushing towards chaos, a charger tormented by hornets. Redemption might come through the clean and sharp and flashing: a miraculous drive against the East, a messiah gleaming like a chalice above storms.

Yet again he was on his feet, involuntarily, inevitably, crossing to the West Tower.

Against all orders, someone had entered the Gräfin's room, tilted the mirror, unbolted chests of books and paintings. Someone. Then, rhyming with his thoughts, a step sounded from outside and misgivings vanished like snow.

Albrecht had come. At long last. The Graf felt tearful, then very strong.

24

The Castle was lit, watched from valleys as if it were a comet, celebrating the Graf's signal dispersal of rebels and Albrecht's adoption as Heir, Albrecht being greeted with ceremonious courtesy rather than acclamation.

Long boards were crowded. In draughts, the candle flames made the feasters look unfinished, even half-eaten like the loaves and nut-cakelets scattered between them.

The Graf, bare-headed, face grey as his hair, neither eating nor drinking, sat at a small table above the rest, his dress sombre, disdaining the jewels and brocades, polished Münster leather and ermine flaunted beneath. His sole companion was Albrecht, his rich violet robe, long, scented hair and fresh skin doing no service to his father's scarecrow physique and lack of colour. Uncle had not considered the festivities appropriate for him to join them. He had attended no such occasion since agreeing to help entertain a collection of ecclesiastics making for some council. Few were sufficiently sober when, very pleasantly, he had addressed them on the 'Exercises of the Soul in Moral Complaint' and, though he had refuted Augustine, praised Pelagius, reappraised Aristotle and quoted, very aptly, the learned Hildegard of Bingen, he himself admitted that the evening had not, in his own words, rollicked.

Tonight, however, Prince Narr had contrived performances excelling even Uncle's. A scarlet-sleeved Levantine had culled flowers from the air and tossed them to the rafters. They fell as balls of cloth, which he tore to scraps, which at once flew away squawking. A Milanese singer had moaned and trilled about lost loves and deserted gardens, a juggler played with eggs, very messily, a dancer mimed the whirl of the sun and the quiet traipse of the moon and, a concession to the Fighting Commandant and the ladies, two sweaty, bare-breasted breaknecks had wrestled in the square between tables, slamming themselves into idiocy. The Master Cook had been rowdily cheered for parading a boar's head cooked in goat's milk, speckled with candied apricots and dried plums, the dripping fat giving it a wide, atrocious grin. Mouths indiscriminately fell upon charcoaled fowls and quails, pastried lamb chunks and cinnamoned goose, bowls of parsleyed herring, cod smoked in oleander and rosemary, dace in egg, brawn soused in unidentifiable wine. The high-born rejoiced in the minced and stewed, the mashed and roast, the boiled and baked, the basted and buttered, the spiced and sprinkled and the over-peppered. Gulped from blue, seldom-used Florentine goblets, almost vases, with slender, twisted, double-edged stems, wine glittered above trenchers of cheese, dark Prussian, pale Dutch.

166

To honour the Graf before winter storms closed the passes, several notables had arrived: a battle-scorched burgrave, several fragile marquises complaining of cold, a dukeling, primed to sniff out territorial prospects. In furs, gold medallions, silver chains, at a special table almost level with Graf and Heir, they incessantly toasted each other, mouths seeming to open more often than they closed, though once the Burgrave muttered about 'darkened wives', at which a marquis, his thin, ridged face blank as a common shield, indeed itself a shield, nevertheless implied that society strained itself to survive only for purposes of revenge.

Uproarious Castle paladins were accepting dues earned by their prowess, headed by, like an Argonaut, the Fighting Commandant, veritable tusker, who had galloped into history. Prince Narr, with no place on bench or stool, moved between the dribbling mouths and thrusting hands, pausing to drop a pun, riddle, witticism or spiteful rejoinder. In steepled hat of green and white coils, he was abnormally tall, for his trailing gown of pleated taffeta and long sleeves concealed stilts so that he paced capriciously in and out of the lights, heronesque, supernatural, an illusion enhanced by features blanched with paste, eyes ringed with black, a pink, artificial beak rivalling, perhaps parodying, the Graf's not in gaudiness but length. His yellow Hollander ruff suggested a plate supporting some unknown fruit. He was sufficiently adept to eat copiously without appearing to devour anything. As always he spoke not to individuals but as though to a group, some of it invisible, often as if refuting a question that none had asked. From his height, his freedom of movement, he displayed awareness not of the Graf and Albrecht, the illustrious visitors and the victorious Commandant, only of himself and his unique excursions in former times. Halting to dip a salute to swaying ladies, raise a sparkling hand to an emblazoned lord splashed with too much liquor, Prince Narr chatted, murmured, half sang; his words were spray, sparkling, falling, vanishing, while ridiculing the faces, rashed, mottled, sweating far beneath him. His joke about the witch's bushy broomstick shocked and delighted the ladies and turned the Cellarer scarlet. As the din swelled and clattered, bottles swung, goblets lifted to retrievers of valour, honour, nobility, he overheard a compliment aimed at the Graf, comparing his feast to the miraculous feeding of the five thousand. Before the Confessor could pronounce absolute truth, Prince Narr's tongue deftly flickered, voices hushed, mostly with reluctance yet withal transported by the vestigial mystery of fooling.

Prince Narr moved his arms, the sleeves suggesting huge wings flapping under his curved, extended beak. The wide ruff glimmered, the voice unexpectedly human, if not wholly masculine.

'I can say much about those five thousand. I did not count them but the number is accurate enough. I was certainly far from alone.' When he smiled, the face under the paint was wrinkled and seamy as a map, his carmine lips pouted in feigned disapproval. 'That afternoon! The heat! The buzz! The smells! The sheer nastiness! Pharisees clucking. We all had to bring our own food. Whole families. Dried bread, very dry. Dried figs. Dirty wineskins. The usual manner, accompanied by many undesirable manners. But some families, very mean, very poor or very clever, hadn't brought sufficient. Now, the Lord's miracle was genuine, if far-fetched. It was not in feeding the lot but in persuading all those Jews to sit together in peace, without argument, and share their food with others, contenting themselves with little. There was no hair-splitting, there were no abstruse texts long as an ostrich's neck, a salamander's tongue or a drunkard's belch. A miracle none could dispute, and I, my respected friends, never have.'

He carelessly removed his nose for another, dark red and shorter. His tone also changed, from sincerely frivolous to mock-sententious. His shadow, thrown over the celebrants, was vast and dramatic.

'Jesus's words almost always had a double meaning. One meaning he concealed from those oafs the disciples – all save John, of course. Even the parables, most of them stale, worried and bemused them. The privy meaning he reserved for initiates: young, quick-witted, attractive. He himself was unattractive in all but his voice, and he said very amusing things, often said little else, but, if you understand, without joking. He was also something of a prosecutor, could certainly crush the authorities whenever he wished.'

He was elaborately reminiscent, making sure that his words, though soft, reached the Graf and the guests, themselves now speechless.

'The situation is curious. Love flourishes on the unseen, goes putrid on the bed. Though circling round each other like cocks, loving each other to idolatry, Jesus and God never actually met. They didn't need to. Whereas Helen, I remember, couldn't stand more than a night of any youth, however pretty. You will all remember not only this, and the withering in your own beds, but the words of thrice-holy Augustine.'

The Confessor began an assent, then hurriedly desisted. No one else stirred, Prince Narr's eyes widened, dilated within their black rings, and he sighed, disappointed. 'Great August wasn't speaking of curdled cheese when he said that yearning deepens the heart.'

The victory feast resumed, in underworld hubbub of brief quarrels, sudden threats, erratic dances, spurts of song, and still the Graf sat silent, secure with Albrecht, with the distinction of his guests whom he had earlier received with gifts of some lavishness. The colours below flared, ebbed into glimmering pools, revived, reaching into the darkened rafters.

The Confessor, inadequately inspired, was having to listen to the Clerk, though he would have preferred to be with the grand visitors. His eyes remained bright, his cramped cheeks cracked into smiles, but he knew that the younger man coveted his place and privileges. Both were attempting to maintain decorum, despite the ever-rising clamour.

'From the doctors of Salerno' – the Clerk's thin voice managed to penetrate the laughs, grunts, hiccoughs, foul sallies and clumsy insinuations thrust towards ladies –' we have the unquestionable prescription for corporeal . . . bodily,' he amended, as if doubting his superior's understanding. 'Yes, for bodily health.'

While the Confessor lifted his glass for more wine, as though unaware that he did so, the Clerk declared with a severity at odds with his barely completed face, tallowy, pocked, and his hesitant stance:

'Doctor Quiet, Doctor Merriment, Doctor Diet.'

Two of these doctors were emphatically absent, the third already too obtrusive, and the Confessor, who disliked discords and noise, somewhat nervously dropped a morsel of capon, then frowned as he might at an erroneous quotation from a Gospel. Others, overhearing, glanced up at the Graf whose lack of gluttony was exemplary, and though his merriment was never evident, he was owed many chuckles at his jest played upon Hans the Mad Boy.

Confessor von der Goltz was looking to his own dignity, avoiding the sight of a sweating, brawn-faced feudatory scuffling at a lady's waist while he fed her with the impure and indecent usages of language.

'We might,' the high-minded Confessor said, determined to keep ascendancy, 'consider the blessed Francis. Prey to mortality like the best of us, he was dying, but still bespoke apology to his body. "Dear Brother Donkey, forgive me for treating you so badly." An example for all of us.'

An example that would not be followed throughout this hectic night.

The Burgrave, at the exalted table, was noticing the Castle's shabby appurtenances, lack of dignity, signs of disrepair. The Graf's face, lean and sunken under ragged hair, was at the turn between premature decay and actual old age, with the texture of a marsh-woman's legs after rain. He was also reputed to have the Evil Eye and the Burgrave hastily looked away at the Heir, from whom at his accession changes here might be expected. He and the Graf in their silence resembled chess players, each unwilling to make the first move, and aware, in different ways, that all comes to whoever is insufficiently vulgar to hasten, grab or implore riches, lands, an embrace.

The Burgrave, pleased with his astuteness, reflected that, in this changing age, the Emperor must reduce all petty rulers to chessmen, on boards of his own making.

*

Enlarged by so many treatises, dialogues, compendiums, dissertations, Uncle's brain must have swollen beyond natural limits. He drank the sweets of copious learning, and here, in his library, he had through many years grazed contentedly on his preoccupations. He had been pondering not on rebellions and compliments, but on a sagacious French viscount who had ordered a baby to be deafened so that he would never hear words. The Viscount, and also Uncle, was curious to know the result. Without words, to what would the mind revert or ascend? Perhaps it would achieve no more than a madhouse of sensation; violent smells, instinctive terrors and greed, nuances unbelievably subtle, colours unknown to others? The Viscount's logic, however, proved imperfect, for the child's wordlessness allowed him no more than babble, so that, though he became a gallant warrior who was literally to lose his head at Agincourt, he had never been able to reveal the rich, Eden-like intoxication of a mind pure and unoppressed by language mossed by too much tradition.

Uncle enjoyed toying with words. He had been reading Aiden of Leyden's thesis on the English word *Dog*. This being *God* reversed, the implications, unnoticed by the barbarous islanders, practical but lazy, incapable of logic and indifferent to philosophy, were innumerable. Was the *G* in one identical with that in the other? Presumably not, Aiden inferred, for, awed by its divine associations, the letter might shrink itself into another – *S*, for instance, very unfortunately. Delicious nonsense, Uncle concluded.

Words, he mused, could mean both more or less than themselves, must be snared in their constant movement: each was susceptible to the past, was shadowed by the future. Their identities posed the most profound of all human debates, save of course Pilate's *What Is Truth*? though the hapless Roman might have been joking, more probably bored. Through words, man, or rather, a few men and, recently, a number of women, struggled to project themselves beyond the superficial covering of years, vows, statues, fortresses, fears, commonplace personality. The lure of distance. Beliefs and dogmas were tribute to the inadequacy or misuse of words, in which symbols were mistaken for facts. A

171

minor probability, originally ridiculed, degenerates into absurdity and is revered. Gustav Kreckting had misread an alchemic text, thereby changing his betrothed to salt, thus inviting, and indeed receiving, complaints.

At this moment, however, Uncle's entertainment had been disturbed by an intruder.

The Graf, having further complimented his noble guests, promising them a hunt on the morrow, had pleaded fatigue and withdrawn from the feast with its mounting din. Albrecht had accompanied him, the Graf had hoped for a talk, but almost at once, with a deft, considered nod, the youth had left him and, disappointed, shying from his own company, the older man climbed the turret to Uncle.

Like Uncle himself, the circular room was thickly scented with aloe, ambergris, Limoges attar, and doubtless much else, suggesting exotic growths, deserts lit by mirages, proscribed temples in luxuriant groves. The concentration of so many thousands of words in such sugary space must rob the air of health. Letters, the Graf had learnt from a friar, himself a writer, had been invented by a demon cutting them on a tree, to worry men with desires unbecoming their station. So much reading, if not worrying Uncle, had certainly increased his corpulence.

Swathed in elaborate folds, a sharply wrought, cat-faced amulet hanging from his neck, genial though detached, Uncle surveyed the Graf with customary banter of eye and tone. A tall stove decorated with heraldic birds and foliage exuded a warmth unknown in other reaches of the Castle. Several oil-lamps gave gentle, unwavering light. Books and manuscripts rose from floor to ceiling, enclosing the two men with parchment and paper and linen, jewelled leather and pargeted cloth.

Writings from Alexandria and Thebes, from Cairo, Paris, Cordoba, Oxford, from Rhodes and Athens, Ctesiphon, Rome, Byzantium, Ravenna, from Mopsueta and Toledo, Baghdad, Jerusalem, Tyana, Carthage, Aberdeen and surely the Tower of Babel. Here were the orthodox and heretical, gnostic and pagan, devout and sceptical. Arabs who conceived God as Light, Greeks who identified the soul as a bean, Dutch pamphleteers agitated by the proximity of

1500. Uncle enjoyed the ludicrous, and the high world of statecraft, administration, and the prolonged organization of military defeat showed little else.

From far beneath sounded shouts, choruses, the occasional crash.

Uncle had laid aside the green spectacles, their colour would not have magnified his nephew's beauty. Smooth as alabaster, his own roseate features pooled into a smile, not humorous and without very obvious goodwill, but as though he had remembered with ironic pleasure a pope observing that the myth of Christ had served well not only the papal court but quite possibly mankind also.

None of Uncle's cerebral appreciations interested his visitor at this or any other hour. At the tread on the steps, Uncle had quietly laid aside other appreciations which the Graf might have appreciated better, a pack of Persian illustrations of young male and female bodies, delicately athletic, neatly allusive. Now, the Graf sat upright on an uncomfortable, high-backed chair, and Uncle reclined, or rather lolled, on a green and gold divan, opulently cushioned, which complemented his blue and yellow satin robe and wide scarf embroidered with kingfishers and water-lilies. Each had wine beside him, Uncle requiring it more. To enjoy the company of his feudal superior was akin to gaining sight of Jesus's foreskin, difficult but not wholly impossible, for that shrivelled treasure had been looted by some Turk, sold in the market and had, they said, passed to the Precentor of St Lambert's, Münster, who had twice unsuccessfully besought the Fuggers for a mortgage on it. The great bankers had most courteously pleaded that the relic, undeniably precious, unquestionably unique, rightly belonged to God, who might legally reclaim it for whatever purposes.

The Graf needed to talk, while knowing that talk with Uncle led nowhere, save deeper into confusions he wished to escape. In this place, as in the Gräfin's apartment, he lost authority, should he give an order it would fall indistinct as a leaf upon snow. All was oblique, concealed, thus mocking: the multitudinous crescents of books probably included not one map, that rampart against the fluid, the transitory.

'The world,' Uncle resumed, in his customary manner, 'is a solid mass of pure illusion.' His grey-blue gaze was placidly content, suggesting that, for all save himself, life was a liability, though towards others he could feel very considerable sympathy. His perfumed hands made an inconsequent movement and he smiled in deprecation of a remark so very platitudinous. With the Graf considering the complexity of everything, Uncle added, 'Existence is simple as a shin-bone, which does, of course, vitally support weight.'

'But the Devil? There must be something . . .'

'There is very little. God may have discovered some flaw in himself, cast it out, decided not to eliminate it, and allowed it to go its way, perhaps as a joke, an expression of the divine nature.'

'But why?'

Uncle's patient forbearance was ample as the divine nature, in which it doubtless partook. He sipped his wine.

'God must have been bored, inhibited by his own perfection. He sought the delights of caprice, the tests of challenge. Without the Devil there could be no motion, no history. Simply two mindless and idle creatures under a tree in empty sunlight. Light without illumination, for which darkness is required. Messiahs come from the dark, to save us from excessive torpor, and show us that the lilies of the field achieve more than the hypocritical and legalistic. The Fall was thus in truth the Ascent, with our forebears at last given something to do. To put pearls in the sow's ear, delineate the trials of Ulysses, build Rome, perhaps even walk on waves without too much boasting. That paradise, that aberration which we have heard call Garden of Delight, is the narcotic fancy of Eastern lazybones, and of our own not-much-goods.' He glanced complacently at a segment of books, many coloured in the unwavering glow. 'Heaven of course can be reached. Salvation by diligence and insight. Perhaps the Devil helps this by ill-intentioned gifts of accident and chance, which some prefer to call Grace. The Devil can also bear the blame for God's mistakes. Like any creator, God experiments, and some results are woeful. We have only to look at people. Conceivably, he sometimes fails to understand his own works, cannot control them, may have to demolish some, may remember others too late.'

Uncle's smile was reminiscent. 'I suppose you should remember that the Saviour especially commended the unrighteous.'

This did not commend itself to the Graf. The atmosphere, so late at night, cloyed and sickly, was yet as full of edges as a lawyer's handshake. Uncle's conversation, so fluent and masterful, suggested too many directions simultaneously, speaking of seeing music, touching words, consuming light.

He must ever remember that, while no lily of the field, he alone was ruler, helping to straighten the Empire's crooked paths. Could he but discover the wondrous sword of Attila, or Wotan's ash-spear which cut down those born of wicked blood. One heard that the spear which pierced Jesus had yet to be found. He himself was a messiah, restocking forests, resowing fields, mending dykes, overcoming revolt, validating the Tax, rearing and reconciling Albrecht, more glistening, more perfect than himself. From the Gräfin's wiles and plaints he had rescued not only Albrecht but the land. In expunging her relics, her very name, he rounded himself off, discarding imperfection like God vomiting the Devil.

He too swallowed wine, felt better, and thought of Uncle but as a hired adviser, overfed and underemployed, like Adam and any dreamer in a Garden of Delight. Yet, through a lattice of the unspoken and unspeakable glinted one inescapable doubt, which Uncle's dexterity with words could surely disperse.

As though mentioning in afterthought an insignificant clause in a charter unworthy of lengthy perusal, he murmured: 'I had forgotten. There is, there was . . . an excrescence, vile as a tanner, untouchable, talkative as a sparrow . . . a dwarf, they called him Little Piper.' The Graf was gratified by his own flow of words. 'Very ugly. A wanton trouble-maker and fomenter of evil, a leper amongst the blind. He got himself hanged. Just retribution, as all say. No mistake, verily no injustice. Of course not. Yet . . .' – his lips at once dried, he reached again for the wine – 'I am not quite at rest. He was boggy, defiled, a torment to any good spirit. Yet I cannot wholly forget him. What does this mean?'

'Mean?' Uncle's purring face, incredulous, shut into a repertory of creases, then regained the blandness of a duck's egg. 'It means nothing at all, unless you care to give it a significance it scarcely merits. To forget it will free you of unnecessary stress and enable you to reach, shall I say, a stage nearer salvation.'

At the Graf's nod, more of relief than a recognition of full enlightenment or salvation, Uncle lifted a hand like a tutor benevolent and well paid. 'Your little scoundrel died well enough, so I understand. He might have done well to remember a proverb known throughout sensible Italy: *The strongest on earth are the Pope, the Emperor, and the good loser.*

The Graf, knowing himself in no way a loser, momentarily suspected some derogation, but no, Uncle, ever courteous while somewhat unfeeling, could only have meant Hans, though the thought of him at one with Pope and Emperor was unsatisfactory. Nevertheless he felt himself absolved, and his relief was such that he did not hear the next remarks, though sensing that the revels beneath seemed diminishing, so that he envisaged his honoured guests stepping heavily, unsteadily, over long avenues of the drunken and insensate. When he regained normality he again heard Uncle.

'Did not the Prophet of, as they call it, the infidels, though he denounced poets, speak in terms not unpoetic? *God will not reproach you for vain words, but will certainly do so for what you store up in your heart.* He also said, and we do well to remember it in our stronghold here, *Thou seest the mountains and deem them well established, but in truth they are as fleeting as clouds.*

This was less reassuring. The mountains, though badly designed, had always been a sure defence of the Castle.

'We learn,' Uncle was almost flattering, 'we advance. Formerly, a warrior like yourself, when wounded, could be healed only by the rust of the weapon that had injured him, moistened of course by the saliva of adders. Our own apothecaries know better. There is a time for everything and now is the time to share wisdom as we do this wine, eternally fragrant though it is not. I am not one of those who believe that the blind see farther than most. My books tell me otherwise.'

With an expression of mature understanding, he selected a

volume freshly printed, ashine with affluent superiority. 'An Emperor of Rome wrote this, pure wisdom dispensed from a position so often grievously improvident, imprudent and imbecilic.' His large, clean lips quivered as if at a private joke. 'Yes. He wrote this': *See how brief and nugatory is man's estate – yesterday a speck in the womb, tomorrow a mummy or ashes. So for the time you are given, a mere hair's breadth, live by reason, and part with it as cheerfully as the ripe olive falls, praising the season that produced it and the tree that gave it fruition.*

Uncle himself was showing no inclination to drop into oblivion while praising the sources of it, but the Graf's thoughts were flapping elsewhere. He did understand that he had a chance of renewal, like the sunlight leaping up the dark mountain on that childhood day almost forgotten but eventually retrieved. This, and the earlier disparagement of the blind, made him almost smile in rebellious freedom. Suppose Uncle himself went blind, smitten by a divine hand he had thought the invention of servants, and was thus unable to read, so that these thousands of pages encircling him would evaporate, leaving him with nothing, like that archduke goaded into madness by his daughters, left howling on a storm-bound plain, consigned to the Valley of Lost Things.

But at once his thoughts rebounded from Uncle with an effect of pain. A ruler's sin, even some trifling error, can infuriate God and blight the earth by jolting the heavens. A last effort of conscience accosted him, like an impertinence from Prince Narr.

'Yet the death of that child.'

He could not continue, but Uncle's rejoinder was soothing as a psalm.

'God protects his own. You should berate yourself only over matters of importance. These are fewer than many imagine but nevertheless can be said to exist. Deaths are not one of them, certainly not a shepherd's. Why waste your acknowledged good sense on what is ultimately unknowable? Thomas Aquinas solved your anxieties for you when he taught that amongst the divine miracles are articles of faith which God made incomprehensible so that faith in them might be rendered more worthy and, as you might say, more faithful.'

The Graf did not say this but once again was relieved beyond comprehension. He had faith, he had certainly matters of import-ance to consider, he had Albrecht.

Uncle's chuckle was soft as a wink, as though at a witticism tuned so precisely, so artfully, that even the most milky disposition would find no offence.

25

Winter spirits can steal your soul, cast it across some black tarn to be seized by a mysterious white hand, or remain wispily hovering above water so that you may drown attempting to retrieve it.

Earth and sky merged in common harshness, fields were empty, little stirred save rags over a deathbed, or the Devil, trailing tattered souls and ragamuffin dupes, walking freely and tarnishing all he saw. Up here we call him Neken, bane of the north.

In German universities the knowing repeated unpleasant details of Adam of Bremen's foreknowledge of the darkling end of the world. For the humbler, summer with its unnatural outburst from children and, some maintained, animals, had foretold Fimbul, and old tongues clacked about the giant wolf swallowing sun and moon, a head, scaled and monstrous, lifting from ocean, and golden apples falling from Lady Orsel's hands, forever lost so that earth and its glories will age fatally.

Roads were clogged by mud and fallen trees, Broken Mountain was invisible, and in mist the Castle seemed protected by a dragon's breath. Surreptitiously, Forlorn Fires were lit by those who thought themselves cursed. Several children, not wholly cured of summer's lunacy, muttered 'Nevis', no longer remem-bering what this had been but pursued by dream-fragments of extraordinary pleasures now lost, as unicorns are lost, in the twirls of immeasurable longings. Nevis was bound in the magic of Cathay, Trebizond, cities of porcelain and silk.

*

The world froze, pines were now frilled with iced snow, though the sun shone on a hard blue sky, glacial mountains sparkled and, within the Castle, the glitter reached the depths of the Gräfin's mirror, with ice and glass held fast.

Before it sat a youth who had never been youthful and would never appear old. He enjoyed what he saw, the face of New Times, pale, reflective, with glinting eyes, sharp mouth, pointed chin. The doublet, scarlet and pleated, contrasted with the pallid skin. Frozen splinters of light fixed behind the trim head suggested a shadowless aura. He examined himself with an impassivity at one with the still air, icy slopes, snow-dappled trees and cold sun. For an instant he smiled at the conceit that he had stepped from one of the Gräfin's lost paintings, in which a slender, melancholy student pondered responsibilities and revenge under towering battlements.

Albrecht, if seldom melancholy and never happy, was always content. He smiled at himself, coolly friendly. The memory of the Gräfin interrupted his ruminations. He had appreciated her flesh; her spirit had luminosity foreign to the Castle, though her fancies were too unpredictable, her reserves too reserved and irritating. In southern lands she might have had influence, possessing insight and silliness in equal measure, together with that insubstantial allure which the sensible do well to avoid, for therein lies madness.

Her death, chiming with his own initial plans, had been convenient for all. He thought, not of a stepmother and foolish wife quietly starved or stabbed, but of a girl lying in water, girdled with sacrificial flowers, puffy with death, sinking into the forgettable. Did she seek vengeance? No great matter.

Some Fleming would come in spring to paint his portrait. He must be slightly smiling, more sardonic than amiable, and with some negligence holding a skull. The Gräfin would have sat nervously clutching a rose, as though it were too heavy, and imagining perfection.

He could spend the morning thus entranced by his reflection, and had almost done so. The future too was warming. New Times, new chances. Throughout the Empire, ageing men were imprisoned in obsolete patterns and rejoicing because of it, like goblin Hans capering in his own stories, thereby demonstrating that listeners are susceptible to nonsense and prefer magic to reason. The New Man rejects magic, drowns old lore, cuts degenerate tales adrift, and, austere, resolute, soars beyond the caprice of mood and sensation.

The Graf, of course, deserved some respect for withstanding certain bleats about the sanctity of promises, his willingness to accept the necessity to discard stale beliefs. The hoary and mildewed might mutter in safe corners about betrayal, but Hans's rapid extinction had caused no earthquake, no convulsions of planets, but merely settled a minor emergency. That parody of Troy, the animal children and brigade of brigands, at first an intriguing interlude, had rapidly become unsavoury, then nauseating, no masterpiece of simplicity but a prolonged farce.

The Graf had obeyed instructions but, like almost all here, was old and tired, and would go no farther. Their stuffy Castle was only crumbling layers of poor light, unpaid debts, barren, etiolated women and mothlike buffoons. Uncle, of course, might yet have uses, perhaps replacing that skinful of tedium, Prince Narr.

The Graf was one of those boors who are always correct and never right. Uncle had genius without talent, though from him one learnt a word entirely new: *Modern*. It meant 'I am', and let in fresh air, a bracing gust of assurance. Empires collapse through loss of faith, not in dogmas which pretend that words, masquerading as providence, fate, design, can supplant nature, but faith in useful facts and opportunities. *Modern* covered situations unique, or slowly reviving.

Popes and emperors were mistaken in considering statecraft difficult, whereas it was nothing more than the ability to see matters naked, stripped of poetic and outmoded principles. Numbers, saddled with occult absurdities, were being rubbed clean: 1500 was significant only in refraining from being 1499. In Italy and France rulers, hard as *Felsenbein*, and understanding this, were enforcing their monopoly of cannon and power-mill, centralizing their authority more rigorously than Rome, exchanging castles for palaces, mints, harbours. They could see that Turks have their usages, like sewage, like Hans, for their challenge could excuse taxation and conscription, also enlarge the brain, though too late for the Graf.

After their last quarrel he had told his father, 'I know *what* you are, I do not know *who* you are', paralysing the old fellow by making him strive to comprehend.

Those freak-show prophets, impoverished conjurers, bandit knights, unlucky alchemists, faithless friars, residue of dried-up seas, had intoned *He will come*, none realizing that, in guise of New Times, he was already amongst them, whip in hand.

Albrecht again reflected on the children's revolt. It had yielded him rather more than a transient pastime. Like God, a nobleman should delve into human dross and submit to a season of discomfort, folly, delusion, the better, so to speak, to hone the corners of the round world.

Though one might always remain in the same dwelling, in unchanging disposition, steps could be chosen, up or down, to different rooms, more subtle atmospheres, more pleasing occasions. Rooms with trapdoors, bars, hooks, manacles, rooms with soft couches, lutes, where girls waited and tables glittered with fruits and wines, rooms where orders were given, missives were received from great ones, and bearded figures bowed like those dolls whose antics, jerked by strings, were mistaken for magic.

No other in this shabby do-nothing province would compete with his energy, drawn from knowledge that no one was born with a soul; unusual talent was needed to create, complete and sustain it. He would be needed, for some hooligan extravagance might already be brewing, to cleave Empire and papacy, and in which the futile episode of Troy would be wholly submerged. Struggle would always outwit harmony: to provide history, even the Trinity must be in perpetual conflict with itself, like the three heads of the dog of hell yapping at each other.

Fractured by fierce winter lights the mirror was attempting to grin. Finally Albrecht left it, slowly approaching the door.

I am. Heaven treasure my graces.

181

Afterword

Epic collects around a name, which, like a statue, is both more and less than the original bearer. It deteriorates to legend, can stabilize as myth or sink into slogan. A nineteenth-century historian traced 'Nevis' to a corruption of *Nero*, who, in some regions, as late as 1500, was thought to be still alive, preparing a descent on the Empire. In widely scattered traditions Hans was remembered as a frog-prince. The children's revolt was sometimes confused with the Children's Crusade, three centuries earlier.

A story must have an end, though the best do not.

The two extant screen treatments of this story, one French, consistently brutal, the other, German, suffused with uneven magic, a Green Stone glimmer around ravaged innocence, share identical endings, from a dubious but not quite discredited source, embellished by a salon quip from George Bernard Shaw.

Several other films were planned, but aborted. Two Hollywood scripts, like all others, centred on Albrecht, the first for a silent movie starring Rudolph Valentino, who died prematurely; the second was to feature Franchot Tone as Albrecht, Basil Rathbone as the Graf, Charles Laughton as Uncle, though the Second World War prevented it. Hans, insufficiently real or presentable, never warranted a major role. One of history's oddities, he was half remembered for a cause not his own: he had no causes, could never have followed Abraham Lincoln or Winston Churchill; his stories would have disobliged John Updike and bored Somerset Maugham; he would have crept away from Sedgemoor or Culloden and been remembered for what he was not.

The ending? Probably a hack's invention, though perhaps a smallish girl had really stood beneath the Waude Oak, where no name could be uttered, and, still dumb, she was not tempted to do so. The sky was a handful of pale-blue flakes between leafless twigs. Frosty grass had whispered under her feet. A blood-red sun was fixed above the mountains.

182

She had escaped from late afternoon stone-picking on Misery Mount, for which she would be whipped by Father's woman. She shivered but stood resolute, in thin coat and leggings facing the grooved, ivied mass. Her face, pitted, already worn, beneath a soiled cap, had adult sternness.

The great tree, world centre, was memorial to spring: the dances and rhymes, the chaplets of daisy and may, the scuffles behind bushes, the crowning, all that had been stolen by the man in the Castle who wore fur, whose great boots hid cloven feet, and who rode starkly alone on the mountains.

Out here, alone, despite her deafness, she too knew a story, silently repeating it. Listen.

At one time lived an archer lad with an arrow that never missed its mark, also a fiddle. You heard its tunes and at once were compelled to dance, dance over heath and meadow and, unless it ceased, into heaven or hell. One day the lad shot a rook which dropped into a quickset hedge. A beggar saw the bird, which would nicely fill his pot, so reached into the thorns, deep into them, to take it. But there, the lad started playing his fiddle, the beggar had to dance, tearing his cloak, his hands, on the hedge until, in despair, he flung out his purse and, stooping to grab it, the archer stopped playing and his victim escaped, leaving the rook behind.

Somewhere, Grete knew, drifting through the wide world, was the magic tune which, once heard, makes hunger, thrashings, taxes and hangings vanish into a hole. Hans had once heard, and never lost it. His pipings, attempting to trace it, almost succeeding, never quite failing, were silver and green, spreading like these branches to fill the air. She never heard anything, yet she too knew the tune, like the story, existed, like the Green Stone, which you did not need eyes to know when it appeared.

Albrecht, with his lily body and jewelled eyes, was, everyone knew, possessed by Satan, with his bag of teeth, though Hans had loved him as the Lord had loved Judas. Now he sat in the Castle and wore *raiment*.

The sun burned, a cloud became fire and fell apart, releasing dusk.

She was a clod on the immense, soundless plain, the awesome mountains dimming like the Castle. The place was forbidding: on a calm summer day the Oak would suddenly quiver, the leaves opening like a woman calling her children. Still close to the tree, she felt enchained, scarcely able to move, yet, risking her soul, managed to pull from her girdle a small knife. Frowning, almost wizened, tight-lipped, she dug into the grey bark, laboriously cutting a design intricate in its very clumsiness.

Finishing in near-darkness, she waited, holding her breath, but, though a bird darted, the tree remained motionless.

In after years, that carved pattern induced academics to dispute about mazes, symbols, secret cults; peasants quarrelled, concocting several unwholesome words, though opinions gradually agreed, identifying it as an emblem of religious dissent which, gathering murderous pace after 1500, substantially reduced the population of the Holy Roman Empire.

DATE DUE
